THE
ELEMENTAL'S
GUARDIAN

THE ELEMENTALS TRILOGY
BOOK ONE

S.W. RAINE

The Elemental's Guardian has been rated Moderate+ for:

- Significant substance use
- Some profanity
- Moderate violence
- Brief mention of overdose

For more information on MBR ratings, visit:
https://mybookcave.com/mybookratings

To Judy, who knows my writing and style

almost better than I do.

CHAPTER 1
Ferenc

Ferenc felt most at home in the sky.

He couldn't remember exactly when his taste for flight started, but that love—that longing—for gliding through the air had always been there, deep inside of him.

The money wasn't his favorite part about being a freelance test pilot. While it definitely helped, the sensation of sheer bliss mattered most. Flying was like pulling a fast one over Mother Nature herself and getting away with it—to a certain point. Gravity was a cruel mistress.

Ferenc focused on the blanket of black clouds ahead. He'd successfully completed test plans through storms in the past, but this one didn't sit right with him. He had an excellent and natural feel for any aircraft he flew and could sense exactly how they behaved. While jets were easy to handle in most conditions, flying too fast in heavy turbulence sometimes caused structural damage—something Ferenc sensed this aircraft already had.

Lightning flashed inside the dark, dense clouds. Ferenc checked his radars and flipped a few switches before descending into the summer storm to finish the test plan.

A familiar British voice sounded through the headphones of his flight helmet: "Stick to the perimeter, Jazz-Nine-Two. Bring her home."

"Roger." His voice had been called "folksy" on occasion; he'd sometimes been told it held an infectious calm.

But a frown soon made its way to his face. There it was again, that barely detectable oscillation through the frame despite the

1

buffeting turbulence. The jet was built to withstand battle damage, but that wobble made the skin beneath his flight suit prickle. He'd need to record it in his report.

As he slowed to maneuvering speed, a bright light illuminated his surroundings. He flinched back as something slammed into the front of the jet, rolled up the nose from the momentum, and came to a stop at the canopy. Ferenc froze as he stared into an equally surprised pair of emerald eyes.

All the training in the world could never have prepared him for a moment like this. It wasn't an everyday occurrence for people to fall from the sky, especially when the radars showed there was nothing around him for miles. Usually very level-headed, his brain simply couldn't compute the sight of this woman, soaked platinum-blonde hair whipping wildly about her, watching him with bulging eyes.

How she miraculously hadn't splattered like a bug against a windshield was beyond him. His head tilted, his mouth opening—to say what, he had no idea—but a shift in the aircraft pulled his attention back to the larger issue at hand: while distracted by the sudden appearance of the woman, he'd forgotten what he was about to do and had lost control in the turbulence.

He'd have to worry about the woman later—if he didn't regain control soon, they'd both be in trouble. He reasoned that if she hadn't died on impact, she would manage a bit longer. Muscles tense, he slowed his speed as the jet jerked about, his skin going cold as the blood instantly drained from his face and body when the woman slipped from the aircraft.

As she fell, a large bolt of lightning struck down, briefly illuminating her form . . . and then she disappeared.

"Shit!"

"Jazz-Nine-Two? Report."

His heart racing, Ferenc tried to chase what he had witnessed from his mind in favor of his current situation. A loud clatter helped hone his focus.

"Jazz?"

"Lost control in air pocket." His undisturbed voice did not once betray the jackhammering of his heart or his concern with the loud rattling. "Maneuvering speed failing."

"Copy, Jazz-Nine-Two. Climb and maintain one five thousand."

Before he could reply, the aircraft gave a judder, and

2

one of the tail stabilizers tore off, causing the jet to spin out of control through the air. Clenching his jaw, Ferenc pressed a few buttons and flipped some levers, but every time he attempted to slow down to regain control, the aircraft rolled. The only way to straighten it was by increasing his airspeed, which was what had gotten him into this predicament to begin with.

"Unable."

Another flash of lightning evoked fresh images of the woman, and Ferenc desperately tried to blink them away, but quickly found himself drowning. For the first time in forever, he couldn't think straight; he couldn't focus in the most critical of moments.

"All right, Jazz-Nine-Two, amend altitude and report."

"Unable, I'm in a spin." Despite being thankful for the British woman pulling him back to reality, it didn't matter what new direction she gave him; all chances of recovering and safely landing were no longer viable. He needed to eject. "Just lost a stabilizer. Bail out! Bail out! Bail out!"

Those last words tasted bitter. He was the best at what he did. He took on the dangerous jobs nobody else wanted for that exact reason. And never once had he needed to eject . . . until now.

He mentally ran through every item on his standard ejection checklist as he positioned his body in the seat—helmet against the headrest, feet in the stirrups, legs against the braces, and elbows inboard—before grabbing the handle above his head and yanking down the face curtain.

The canopy propelled away, and the downpour quickly soaked him as the seat thrust him out of the jet within half a second. The exertion of nearly three thousand pounds of force on his body was excruciating, and it knocked the wind out of him. Now he understood firsthand why pilots could only have three ejections in their entire career. Thankfully, it was over in the blink of an eye.

There was a split second of weightlessness—his favorite part of being in the sky—after the seat fell away before the butterflies fluttered and squirmed inside his stomach as he fell through the swirling clouds. Thunder angrily roared around him with a deafening pitch.

Ferenc tilted his head back to assess the situation and found some of the suspension lines from his harness caught up over the top of the chute from the chaos of the ejection.

Despite his clear mind, his heart still pounded, threatening to escape his chest. With a few deep, controlled breaths, he tugged on the lines to find the one that got snagged to yank it free. Unfortunately, it was impossible to figure out as pockets of the orange parachute sail billowed wildly, obstructing his view.

He reached for a small compartment in his flight suit and pulled out a hooked knife. With it gripped in his gloved hand, he brought it to the line he thought was problematic and cut it.

Nothing happened.

Before he tried another line, one of them snapped on its own from the force of the updrafts and downdrafts, then another. Ferenc's stomach dropped, sudden dread rising as he began falling faster.

He was going to die.

The constant light show brought the blonde woman back to the front of his mind. He could still vividly picture the look of shock on her face.

A loud snap pulled him from the flashbacks as a third line broke. His breath caught in his throat as the parachute fully domed out, untangled, slowing his fall.

He broke through the storm clouds and quickly calculated his altitude before attempting to judge where he would touch down. Each potential landing zone within the large Floridian wildlife and conservation areas in his line of travel rapidly passed by. Because of the storm, he was moving horizontally much faster than vertically.

Not wanting to touch down in any body of water, he juggled with the parachute risers, preparing for his landing, and growled when a powerful gust of wind jerked him back.

One of the rigging lines snapped, and Ferenc braced for impact with the ground, but another stormy blow lifted him back up like a rag doll. With a little more string pulling, he finally landed, falling along one side of his body as they trained him to do, maximizing the number of impact surfaces.

A cry escaped him as sharp and sudden pain seared through his left shoulder upon contact before he tore across the ground, dragged by the wind through his still-billowing parachute. He reached for the harness to disconnect as swiftly as possible, but his left arm wouldn't cooperate—the pain in his shoulder was so severe, he almost blacked out.

4

With the hooked knife still clutched in his other hand, he cut a few more lines, tumbling, rolling, and finally skidding to a halt. Ferenc lay there, tangled in the soaked parachute sail, dizzy and disoriented. The blade easily jabbed through the nylon as he thrust the knife upward and dragged it across the smooth material, peeling away the fabric and exposing himself to the torrential rain.

Another flash of lightning jerked his mind back to the woman while the present yanked him toward the paralyzing sensation threatening to overcome his body. His heartbeat thrashed through his ears louder than the thunder, and he wheezed against the suffocating tightness in his chest.

He discarded the knife in favor of tearing off his mask and helmet, and he gulped the air—almost choking on the downpour—before sitting upright. With his injured arm cradled against his body, his free hand grasped the side of his head. Suddenly hyperaware of the musty stench of worms and flooded dirt, he tried to regain control of the panic and hysteria that finally settled in after being levelheaded for so long despite everything.

Ferenc was still alive; now it was only a matter of surviving until someone found and rescued him.

5

CHAPTER 2
Olivia

O livia didn't know who she was looking for, but she was confident she'd found them.

Lightning exploded onto the stormy beach coast as she stumbled forward, her balance lost. She fell to her hands and knees with a wince.

A jet, of all possible things in the world, had run her over.

A jet.

In the sky.

"Get up, get up, get up . . ."

Her mind reeled, but she willed herself—with a mutter through gritted teeth—to stand back up. She had to make sure nobody had seen her.

With her fingers tightly curled in the wet gray sand, she gulped down the throbbing ache in her entire body before pushing herself back to her feet, struggling to stand straight on wobbly legs. She wiped her sand-caked hands over her soaked black leggings before pushing the bangs plastered against her forehead from her eyes. Relief washed over her as she exhaled; there were no onlookers or gawkers along the deserted beach.

A tingle buzzed through her fingers as she inhaled deeply, her eyes trailing to the faint glow of static electricity inside her hands. As she slowly breathed out, the current ran up her arms and throughout her body, stimulating her bruises and sore muscles, speeding up the recovery process.

The pain could've been much worse. Thankfully, she'd been controlling the air around herself enough to not get caught in the laminar flow and propelled over the aircraft after hitting the jet's canopy.

As Olivia healed, all she could think of was the poor pilot who was definitely in the wrong place at the wrong time as far as she was concerned—yet, at the same time, exactly where they needed to be.

It was a strange thing, waking up one morning with the random thought of needing to find the elementals and their guardians. She'd dismissed it as fiction—a lingering dream—but as she'd gone about her day, the idea was no longer a suggestive whisper in her mind but a strong, evocative prodding beyond muscle and matter, reaching down to her spiritual core.

She hadn't been able to see the pilot's face behind their mask and visor, but the shift in the air—that split second before the storm's power kicked in—indicated the pilot was in control of a lot more than just the aircraft.

The inexplicable gut sensation she'd been following across state lines—that tug like an invisible blip of her internal radar—grew fervid, and in that exact moment, she knew she'd finally found who she'd spent so long searching for . . . only to lose them again when she'd slipped and had been forced to summon the lightning once more.

The glow vanished once it reached her neck, her body instantly feeling better. A couple more sessions, and she'd be good as new.

Her gaze flicked skyward amid the downpour. How she was supposed to find the pilot again was beyond her. She didn't know who they were, where they were headed, or where they were from. She'd been *so* close—the closest she'd been in weeks—to getting answers, only to have them slip from her grip in an instant.

Any attempt at locating the elementals and their guardians was like trying to find a needle in a haystack—after all, her search had started in sunny California, and the tug led her to Florida like a dandelion in the wind—but without ever knowing what type of needle she was looking for. In order to find the pilot again, she'd need to do some research.

She turned her attention toward the beach town nearby. It looked like she'd be staying a while.

The storm had passed by the time she walked up to the public library. Olivia cast furtive glances around the perimeter, her stomach in knots. Thankfully, nobody waited around outside.

7

She found an empty corner away from traffic and any potential onlookers. Her eyes fluttered closed as steam evaporated from her soaked clothing and hair until she was fully dry.

She loved that trick—heating the surrounding air. It came in handy, especially when lightning travel involved a lot more rain than she was used to. But she always had to be careful to not be seen; her abilities weren't what one considered *normal.*

Hell, even *she* didn't believe what she could do. Just like the ridiculousness of feeling the need to search for elementals and guardians, one day, she suddenly knew how to do things with air. At first, she'd ignored it. But just like that invisible lure prompting her search, her newfound abilities buzzed through her core, alerting her of their presence, and begged to be released. She didn't know what awoke the abilities within from their dormant state, but they were raring and ready to go.

With one last hurried look around her, she entered the building.

A mixture of hushed voices, rustling paper, mouse clicks, and printers whirring greeted her, as well as the beaming smile of the man with deep-brown skin—sporting an impressive Lincoln beard—behind the desk. Olivia couldn't help but smile back from the joy radiating off him as she pulled up to the counter.

"Hi, I'm from out of town and need to use a computer . . ."

"Of course!" he replied as he reached for the mouse. "Let's get you set up with a visitor's pass."

Olivia pulled out her ID from a tiny pocket hidden against the waistband of her leggings and handed it to him. With everything sorted out, she made her way to one of the empty cubbies, sliding onto the plastic chair before starting her internet search.

One of her hands reached up to rub at the nape of her neck absentmindedly. There were over two hundred airports and fixed-base operators in Florida alone, which made finding one single person a pain in the neck—both literally and figuratively. Sure, it was easier than when she aimlessly roamed the whole of the continental United States, but Florida was still pretty big . . . if the jet even came from the state at all.

The pads of her fingers quietly tapped on the smooth surface of the desk as her thoughts traveled back to the aircraft. Jets were usually military, so maybe that would narrow it down.

8

Her search revealed a total of six Air Force bases in Florida, including one nearby. Perfect. She'd make that her starting point for snooping around and go from there. With a few clicks of the mouse, a map of the area appeared out of the humming printer next to the cubbies, which she grabbed and folded up before placing it in her tiny pocket.

The sky was clear, a beautiful shade of blue when Olivia stepped out of the library, but she thought she might drown from the humidity. She skirted along the brick building, flanked by a vast parking lot on three of its sides, and hoped the tiny spot barely shaded by trees between establishments would offer enough cover for nobody to see her—and more importantly, where nobody would notice her abilities. Lightning travel was going to be a little trickier now that people ventured out after the storm.

With a squint up at nothing in particular, she concentrated on creating condensation by cooling a tiny
area of the sky to its dew point. If she could form even the smallest of clouds, she'd be able to summon the lightning.

Despite the number of times she'd done it, it still amazed her how she'd woken up one morning with the actual ability to perform something natural without objects—no jars, no ice cubes, no classroom. Her ability to control air unaided was something straight out of her favorite movies. It made no sense, but it worked. A lot of it had still required trial and error, but some results—like traveling via lightning—had been purely accidental . . . and convenient.

Soon, a thin fog produced before slowly growing thicker and darker. Olivia continued to focus on that spot, zeroing in on the imbalance between the cloud and the ground. She needed that electrical discharge—that spark.

And then it happened.

Satisfied with her attempt, her heart pounding against her rib cage from the effort, Olivia cast another furtive glance around for onlookers. A twinge of remorse built up inside her at the anticipated disturbance the next step would cause, but she couldn't dwell on it. She needed to hurry.

With a deep inhale, she summoned a lightning bolt from her tiny cloud. With a deafening crack through the air, she disappeared.

CHAPTER 3
Ferenc

It hadn't taken long for the authorities to arrive on the scene of his crash. As they'd loaded him into the ambulance, Ferenc learned a concerned citizen had reported the jet crash, and a good Samaritan called the police upon spotting his troubled descent.

He'd survived. It was more than he could say for the poor girl, however. He'd tried explaining it to the paramedics—and again to the investigating officers once at the hospital—but they'd all dismissed it as a panic-induced psychotic episode. Ferenc knew better, however.

At least . . . he hoped he did.

He staggered toward the front door, wincing at the effort of reaching for his pocketed keys with his good hand. Without the aid of the porch light, he struggled to find the correct one and tried a few before finally succeeding.

He groped for the light switch with one hand as he shut the door behind him with the other, and he gritted his teeth as his body threatened to give in before finding it. With a grimace, he leaned against the cool wall and shut his eyes, despite the repetitive images and sounds from his accident flooding his mind.

A whimper came from nearby, and his eyes shot open as his attention darted toward the outline of a beast in the darkness. He then released a heavy sigh.

"I'm sorry, Max."

He hadn't foreseen spending all afternoon and evening at the hospital, and he especially hadn't expected his stay to creep into the night. During that time, feeding and letting the golden retriever out hadn't even crossed his mind.

Another whine occurred, then a bark, which forced Ferenc to push his aching body away from the only thing
holding him up. His legs trembled as he practically crawled up the stairs toward the kitchen and sliding door to let the dog out onto the deck and into the fenced-off backyard.

The overpowering and bitter scent of sterile antiseptic—omnipresent inside the hospital—lingered. Ferenc staggered out of the kitchen and into the small bathroom connected to his bedroom, squinting as his eyes adjusted to the sudden brightness.

He shuffled toward the sink, resting his good hand down on the marble countertop, and held himself as steady as his aching body would allow. He found the butterfly closure on the wound above his brow through the mirror. How he'd managed to cut his face while wearing a helmet and visor was beyond him, no matter how hard he tried to remember.

His attention trailed down to the black immobilizer and sling holding his left arm still. Unlike the gash on his forehead, he knew *exactly* how the clavicle fracture had happened. His body gave an uncomfortable twitch, and he shut his eyes against the flashback of landing on his shoulder. The doctors had prescribed him some painkillers and told him to do initial treatment with ice, but all Ferenc wanted was a hot shower.

The simple act of undressing left him as exhausted as if he'd worked out for an hour. The tempered glass rapidly fogged up as he allowed the water to rain over his head and frame, and he held himself up with his good arm as memories of lightning striking the woman flashed fresh in his mind. He couldn't comprehend where she'd come from. It made no sense, and he hated that he couldn't figure it out.

Easily the most traumatic experience he'd ever witnessed, and he didn't even know if it had been real.

After his shower, he dragged his feet back to the sliding door to let Max in, then used the wall as leverage to descend the stairs to fill Max's food and water dish. But rather than painstakingly climb the stairs once more to get to his bedroom, he instead shuffled his way to the living room, where he collapsed onto the couch, promptly falling asleep.

Plagued with vivid nightmares all night long, Ferenc awoke to blinding sunlight flooding through the roof windows. The severe aching of his muscles and sharp, stabbing pain of his fracture alerted him to his painkillers having long since worn off.

Each movement produced a hiss from his lips as he pulled himself up from the woven throw atop the ivory-colored couch. The golden retriever paced by the sliding door, its nails clipping and clopping on the ceramic floor.

"I'm coming, Max."

He stiffly climbed the stairs and entered his bedroom, slipping on nothing but a pair of blue jeans before shambling his way into the bright kitchen and past the prancing retriever toward the sliding door.

Max darted out into the backyard, and Ferenc stepped over to the freezer after sliding the door shut, grabbing the first cold object he saw: a bag of frozen peas. He gently placed it against his collarbone before heavily dropping into the nearest wooden chair. His eyes clamped shut, and his breath caught in his throat from the discomfort and sensitivity to the cold.

Now that he was awake, images from the previous day returned, weaving past the pain and inundating his mind. He sat slouched for a while, head against the slat backing of the chair, until a muffled trill came from somewhere in the house.

His eyes shot open, and he struggled to stand when he heard it a second time. He hobbled back to the bathroom, where he rummaged through the pile of discarded clothes by the shower for his cell phone and involuntarily groaned at the number before answering. He was in no mood for this inevitable argument.

"Hello . . ." His moan was as despairing and miserable as he felt.

"Ferenc!" He couldn't tell if the woman's voice on the other end contained shock, relief, anger, or a mixture of all three. "I just heard the news!"

"Oh?" He racked his brain. She couldn't have possibly been talking about the events of the previous day; the military would've kept that information private.

"About the crash!"

His frown at her words only lasted a second, as it uncomfortably pulled at the bandage above his brow. Ferenc adjusted the peas against his shoulder, acutely aware of the frozen numbness. "Where did you hear about that?"

"It doesn't matter where I heard it," she dismissed. "It doesn't change the fact that your recklessness finally caught up to—"

"What do you want, Amy?" he cut in. He didn't get irritated often; maybe pain and lack of sleep were the reasons behind his sudden short temper. "I'm going to hang up if you just called to accuse me."

His head began throbbing like he was being hit with a hammer. He bit back a cry of pain when he tried placing the phone between his shoulder and ear, out of habit, to dig for his pills. With a quick tap on the screen, he placed the phone on speaker and set it on the counter before rummaging for the pills again.

"I called to check up on you and remind you about court on Monday. You didn't forget, did you?"

He couldn't possibly forget. Since their split, she'd dragged him into the most ridiculous of claims, only possible from having been whispered to her by her lawyer. More often than not, he'd had to look up what he was being summoned for, and each summons was a stretch of the imagination by far.

"No," he replied with a sigh. He turned on the bathroom faucet, filled the resin tumbler, and swallowed a large pill in one gulp. "I don't understand; we were never married. I let you take whatever you wanted, and you took everything but the house and the dog. What do you want now? Child support for Max?"

"That's not funny. We still have unresolved issues, and you know it. And don't think a broken bone will get you out of it."

Ferenc twitched. While not the type to evade his obligations, he just wished she'd tell him which issues were unresolved instead of constantly being surprised by the Moyon Firm's logo in the mail each time he thought they were finished.

It was her laughter that'd initially drawn his attention to her a few years back. An amusing jingle of mirth and merriment that'd broken his train of thoughts as he strolled along the beach one evening. He'd wagered a curious peek and found her with her head tossed back at something someone from her group had said. It was such an addictive laugh that he'd found himself smiling even long after he'd passed them along the shore.

As the last rays had given way below the horizon, that laughter had continuously chimed through him as he'd returned to make his way back home. Even as her lively "Oh no!" interrupted that laughter as she'd chased a runaway volleyball before it got as far as the shore.

He'd pinned the ball beneath his foot when it had rolled his way, and he'd picked it up by the time she'd reached him, her deep-brown curls threatening to escape the bun atop her head. His heart fluttered at the grateful smile that'd graced her lips as he handed her the ball, and she brushed the loose curls away from her eyes before accepting it back.

Their fingers had barely touched, but that spark that'd buzzed through his hand was enough to let him know that he'd formed an instant crush on her as if he were a teenager again, and she'd told him she'd felt the same way when they'd finally hooked up a few months later.

She'd never been so rude and cold when they were together, or even after they'd originally split. It wasn't until the last few months that she'd really gotten mean about it. He couldn't figure out what'd caused such a change.

"Goodbye, Amy. I'll see you on Monday."

"Don't you hang up on me!" she yelled, before Ferenc pressed the red button. Silence followed.

He scanned his reflection in the mirror, trailing over the numerous blue-and-purple bruises forming over his body. He removed the peas and inspected his swollen fracture closer when a bark came from the other side of the glass panel. Before he could react further, his phone rang again. Ferenc tossed the bag of peas into the bathroom sink and snatched the phone from the counter, answering it while peeking past the bathroom door frame.

"I said goodbye . . ." His voice wavered from the shooting pain as he lifted a finger to show Max that he'd be a minute—not that the retriever actually understood.

"Goodbye is usually something you say when a conversation is finished, is it not? I don't recall us even starting one yet."

The woman's British accent on the other end of the line caught him off guard, and he pulled the cell away from his ear to look at the caller ID. It was a restricted number.

"Mister Janos? Are you there?"

He brought the device back to his ear. "Yes, sorry. Good morning, Tech Sergeant."

"I'm calling to check up on you."

14

"Battered and bruised with a fractured collarbone," he admitted. The pain intensified long enough to matter, and he winced. "How much do I owe you for the damage?"

"Nothing at all. We retrieved your notes about the issues. They were present long before the storm, therefore no fault of the pilot."

"Good to know."

"You're alive, and that's all that matters."

"Yeah . . ." he mused out loud as another unwanted flash appeared at the forefront of his mind.

He was alive. Not everyone had fared so well.

"Are you well, Mister Janos? Do you need me to call an ambulance for you?"

"No." He inhaled and exhaled deeply before continuing, "No, I'm good. Thank you."

"If there's anything I can do, please don't hesitate to ask."

The wheels in his head turned, recalling his conversation with Amy just moments prior. "Hey, yeah," Ferenc started, licking his dried lips, trying to figure out the best way to ask without delving into what wasn't part of his contract—or what wasn't his business. "I was just wondering: what's your process of report? Would the accident warrant going public?"

There was a pause on the other end before she finally replied. "Our process is . . . complicated, but no, this wouldn't warrant us going public. Do you have cause for us to?"

It was curious how the military hadn't gone public with the accident, yet Amy had somehow found out.

"No, I was just wondering if I should expect a call from my insurance agent or not," he lied.

"Have your agent call us if there is a problem."

"I will."

"Please rest and recuperate well, Mister Janos."

"Thank you."

He hung up without saying goodbye, rummaging through his memories of Amy's friends or colleagues that might've been military or married to someone who was, when another bark startled him. He returned to the glass door and opened it.

"Sorry, Max."

After giving Max food and water, he wrestled with donning the rest of his clothes, then adjusted his stabilizer and sling. With the peas back in the freezer, he grabbed his necessities from the same

15

pile of discarded clothes in the bathroom and slipped them into his pockets. Ferenc made his way to the front door, slid on his penny loafers, and exited the house. He desperately needed open air to clear his mind.

CHAPTER 4
Ferenc

Everything was hot, humid, and bright under the Florida sun; the previous day's storm was a distant memory to all but Ferenc.

He ambled down the street, desperately wishing for his painkiller to kick in a little quicker as he forced himself to focus on the taste of salt in the air, the ashy smell of the hot pavement, and the chugging of car engines and their squealing brakes. Everything and anything but the lightning, the accident, or the throbbing and stiffness of his body.

His free hand reached into his breast pocket, retrieving his lighter and slim case of cigarettes. He plucked one and placed it to his lips, tucking the rest of them in the fold of his sling so that he could light the one he pulled out. He took a few puffs, then a long, well-deserved drag before shoving both items back into his pocket.

It took longer than usual, but he eventually arrived at a small tan-colored building on the corner of the two busiest streets in the city. The Little Cottage Café, a quaint little diner, lived up to its name on the inside, with its wood-planked walls, rustic decor, and patrons that all seemed well acquainted with one another.

As much as he appreciated the cozy interior, Ferenc preferred to sit beneath the striped awning outside on the terrace where he enjoyed sipping coffee, eating cheesecake—though their scones were to die for—and being the first to fill out the crossword puzzle in the diner's only copy of the local newspaper.

A bell chimed above his head as he opened the door, and the overpowering fragrances of brewed coffee, fried bacon, and grilled onions immediately fought for his attention. Some weekend

17

regulars turned and waved, their eyes bulging and darting to his sling, while the curious beachy tourists failed at pretending to avert their gaze.

Danny gave a nod and a sympathetic smile before whipping his head back to get his wispy black bangs out of his eyes. "Hey, Ferenc. You all right?" he greeted as he adjusted his sleek-framed glasses.

Betty peeked through the pass, her short gray curls smashed beneath a thick black hairnet. Her smile, both warm and motherly, quickly vanished. "*Ferenc*?! Oh, dear, just look at you!" Her portly form waddled out to meet him, drawing even more inquisitive glances from the patrons. "What happened?"

"Just a minor accident," Ferenc admitted. "I'm fine."

"That doesn't look very minor to me!" She inspected his sling and brace, then the cut on his brow.

"He said he was fine, Betty," grumbled Wilfred as he followed, metal griddle spatula in his thin hand.

"But just look at him, Wilfred!"

"He's fine," Wilfred grumbled, rubbing his balding head as he returned to the kitchen. "Right?" He double-checked by looking over his shoulder, his gray eyebrows high upon his wrinkled forehead.

"I'm fine." Ferenc chuckled, but the slight wince that occurred afterward didn't seem to convince Betty.

"Oh, you poor, poor dear." She gently ushered him to the side door. "Come, let's set you up outside. Danny, have Daisy bring his usual."

"Yes, ma'am," the scrawny man behind the counter replied.

Ferenc followed Betty out the door. The terrace was just as hopping on the weekend as the inside of the diner. In the awning's shade, a single varnished wooden table stood free of patrons but filled with dirty dishes. Betty grabbed a few of them, apologizing as he sat in the rickety matching chair, but he politely waved her off with his free hand. There was no need to apologize for a business being busy.

"Lexi!" she called.

"Already on it," came a sultry voice.

While Betty walked away with some dishes, Lexi approached from another table while pushing a cart filled with neatly stacked tableware, a striped hand towel draped over her shoulder.

"Hey, handsome."

"Hi, beautiful."

Long, thick eyelashes batted around her smoky makeup as she feigned a blush before her coy ruby-red smile shifted. Bottom lip protruding, she now wore an exaggerated pout. "What happened?"

She grabbed a damp rag from her cart and suggestively leaned forward as she wiped down Ferenc's table, her long dark waves cascading over her other shoulder despite being tied up. Though they'd always flirted—she was gorgeous—it'd never been serious. He wasn't the type to so outwardly and blatantly show he was interested, and she'd divulged being too focused on her studies of becoming a psychiatrist to have any time for anyone. He respected that.

"Broken collarbone," he explained.

"Oh, Ferenc, I'm so sorry!" She edged closer to him as she grabbed the hand towel from her shoulder, drying the freshly cleaned table. "I can't possibly imagine what you went through!"

"All part of the job," he replied, his gaze trailing a black curl of hair down past the shoulder of her white blouse to the unfastened top button and soft-looking skin peeking past.

He imagined the curvy mounds liberated from their confines, and he welcomed the distraction from everything that'd been occupying his mind since his eyes met a pair of green ones thousands of feet in the sky. But his thoughts quickly dissipated with the clearing of a throat behind him. Lexi stood straight, rolling her eyes with a clearly irritated sigh.

"Give the man some breathing room. Jesus," came Daisy's exasperated tone as she placed a slice of cheesecake drizzled in strawberry syrup in front of him.

"I was cleaning his table," Lexi said innocently before giving Ferenc a sultry smile. "All clean. See you later, handsome." She cast a quick glare in Daisy's direction before spinning around and walking off with her cart of jingling dishes, her backside swaying.

"Why do you let her get away with doing that?" Daisy set down his plain cup of black coffee.

Ferenc pulled his gaze away from Lexi to the brunette and smirked. "Doing what?"

She sternly narrowed her eyes as she shoved the daily newspaper in front of his face, and Ferenc lightly chuckled in response.

"Thank you," he said, taking the paper.

"So. Broken collarbone, huh? Did you try to stop Max from chasing a squirrel or something?"

He purposely ignored her question, the smirk still playing on his lips. "Isn't it your break time?"

"Fuck, yes."

She heaved a sigh of relief before diving into the breast pocket of Ferenc's shirt, where she retrieved the lighter and slim silver case, stealing a cigarette from it. With an amused smile, he picked up the fork and cut into the moist cake.

"You know I'm keeping track, right? I'm going to start charging tax," he said before taking a bite.

"Put it on my tab," she replied, setting the case and lighter on the table before taking a seat across from him.

Ferenc's shoulders shook as he suppressed his laughter through his bite before swallowing. He then unfolded the newspaper, flipped through to the crossword puzzle—then paused, surprise coursing through him. Not only had someone gotten to the crossword puzzle before him, but their messy handwriting was like two chickens fighting over their own chicken scratch, almost as if a child had filled it out.

When he looked up to ask Daisy, he caught a glimpse of familiar platinum-blonde hair out of the corner of his
eye. His attention darted toward a figure striding along on the other side of the street, and he blinked. *Was that . . .?*

"Ferenc?" Daisy asked.

He released a shaken breath as the memory of the woman flashed to the forefront of his mind.

No. She hadn't survived. It wasn't possible. There was no way.

He continued to gawk at the pedestrian, panic bubbling inside of him as each car going down the busy street temporarily hid her from view. He had to be imagining her.

But when the vehicles passed and she was still there, walking down the street, that theory held up less and less.

The table before him jerked as he went to jump up, the coffee inside the cream-colored cup spilling over from the force. Daisy yelped, startled, as he hunched forward, muttering a few colorful curse words before he fell back into the chair, gripping his knee.

Daisy grabbed napkins from the navy-blue apron about her waist, quickly cleaning the spill. "Ferenc? What's going on?"

20

He looked back across the road, but whatever—or whoever—he saw was now gone.

No.

No, no, no.

His eyes darted from one end of the street to the next, past tourists and shoppers already weighed down by bags filled with merchandise before noon. When he caught sight of her hair again, he fumbled to his feet and fished for his wallet in his back pocket, blindly pulling out some money while keeping his eyes on the blonde woman, who then turned down a side street. An empty feeling in the pit of his stomach befell him, and he dropped a few dollar bills onto the table before hurrying off, leaving Daisy protesting behind him.

"Where are you—Ferenc! Your total's only seven fifty!"

"Keep the change!" he called back to her as he darted off across the street.

He ignored the angry, blaring horns as he dodged the weekend traffic, but the squeal of tires froze him in his tracks, and his tunnel vision dissipated just as a forest-green hatchback came to a screeching halt inches away from his legs.

"Sorry!" he stuttered, arm outstretched defensively as the thick-bearded driver rolled down his window to shout in a foreign language. Disoriented, Ferenc turned back to where he last saw the woman, but she was gone. "Sorry," he said again as a heaviness set over him, and he gave the hood of the car a few apologetic pats before slinking away to the other side of the street.

He trotted along the sidewalk, past a few pedestrians—some eyeing him up and giving him a wide berth—and peered down every alley he passed, but there was nothing. Nobody. He rushed at full speed toward the next intersection, hoping to meet up with her, but he came up just as empty. Much like how she'd vanished from the sky without a trace, Ferenc once again had no proof the woman ever existed.

CHAPTER 5
Ferenc

He couldn't have imagined her; she *had* to be real. The incident in the sky had been traumatizing, sure, but not enough to cause hallucinations.

Ferenc's eyes fluttered shut as he attempted to get his breathing back under control, but his chest only grew tighter, making it more difficult while already out of breath. He remembered this sensation all too well, and it wasn't because of his smoking habit—he'd had his first ever panic attack after his accident, and now it was happening again.

He focused on counting: inhaling for four seconds, holding for seven, then releasing for eight. This should've helped calm him down, but aside from the growing fire in his lungs, images of the woman slipping off his plane pushed past the forced calm to star front and center in his mind.

His free hand rose and gripped at his chest so tightly, he was convinced he'd dug a hole through shirt and skin. It was like being trapped in an airless bubble. He hunched over as his world spun, unsure which way was up or down, and his legs gave out from beneath him, knees hitting the pavement.

"Hey, Mister."

The voice was distant, muffled, as if it were under water. He opened his eyes but couldn't make out where it was coming from. He saw nothing—not even the ground or the sky.

"Mister!"

The voice slowly dragged him out of the thick tar that was his panic attack. Something touched his good shoulder—a hand, maybe—and an uncomfortable current coursed through his entire body, like his nerves were linking back together after the sudden disconnect. Then whatever touched him began shaking him. The visions and flashbacks in his mind slowly dissipated, bringing him back to a breathable, air-filled reality.

"Mister!"

The voice belonged to a woman—perhaps it belonged to the blonde. The pavement beneath Ferenc's knees slowly came into focus, and he could finally distinguish up from down. His head snapped up to focus on the form kneeling in front of him.

"Whoa!" she gasped, snatching her hand away as if she'd been burned. "Mister, are you okay?"

As he stared into a pair of dark-blue eyes, his stomach clenched; the young woman before him was not the one he'd been searching for.

She glanced over her shoulder—not as one would while asking for help from the nearest passerby, but as if she was assessing all her options for a quick escape. Strands of her thin black hair, pulled haphazardly in a ponytail, whipped from her sudden movement as her attention fell back on him.

"Do you need an ambulance?" she asked.

His racing heart slowed some; the panic of the moment dissipated before reality came crashing down painfully on his body. His collarbone reminded him just how broken it was, and he forced himself to look away from the gaunt woman as he searched for the elusive blonde, who was nowhere to be found. Maybe he really *had* imagined her.

He focused back on the dark-haired woman, who continued to cast fearful glances over her shoulder like she was ready to dart away at any moment. His gaze traveled to a smudge of dirt on her cheek. For a moment, he debated on whether she was real or if he was imagining her—and everything else as well.

"No," he finally replied. "No, thank you."

A feeble smile made its way to his lips as he stood on wobbly legs. As if his muscles weren't sore and stiff enough, a sharp, throbbing pain coming from one of his knees added to the mix.

She stood as well, no taller than his chest, and emitted a sudden squeak as she took a step back, looking past him.

Ferenc stiffly half-turned. Nothing seemed immediately out of the ordinary: a few pedestrians, a few cars . . . A black sedan with tinted windows crawled down the next intersection, but he couldn't see that as the source of her terror.

"Look, I gotta run, but . . . I just wanted to make sure you were okay. Whatever you were doing down there didn't look too good."

"I'm fine now," he replied, turning back to her. "Thank you," he added after clearing his throat, stuffing down his embarrassment.

She inclined her head as she shoved her hands into the pockets of her gray zip-up sweater. There was no goodbye—she simply spun around and departed.

She turned a corner, and he could see her no more. Ferenc peeked down the next intersection again, but there still didn't seem to be anything out of the ordinary. The creeping sedan was no longer there, and nothing jumped out as threatening. He ran his fingers through his hair as a wave of exhaustion washed over him. He just wanted to go home, where he'd be more comfortable and less prone to hallucinate.

Or so he hoped.

As he shambled home, his thoughts drifted not to the blonde woman, but to the apprehensive and scared one that'd helped him.

He reached into his breast pocket for his cigarettes but paused in his steps—the pocket was empty. His hand shot down to the pockets of his jeans, where he found his keys and cell phone. When his hand traveled to his backside, he found his wallet missing as well.

His mind unraveled, rewinding to the last time he remembered having it, which proved to be a difficult task.

"Shit."

Ferenc groaned, racking his brain. Daisy had stolen a cigarette and had set everything down atop the table. He couldn't remember picking them back up, so they were probably still at the diner.

It was impossible for her to have taken his wallet, however; he'd been sitting on it. Maybe he'd left it on the table when he paid for his coffee and cake. He hoped he'd paid for his food . . . everything after the cigarettes was kind of hazy, but if anything, the café would keep his things for the next time he stopped by.

Maybe he'd return in the evening. For the time being, all Ferenc wanted was to rest at home.

When he arrived, he grabbed a handful of envelopes and fliers from the mailbox, gently stuffing them between his sling and ribs before unlocking the door. Max waited by the entrance, tail wagging with a stuffed mallard by its paws that'd long since lost its squeaker.

He ruffled Max's fur, then dragged himself up the stairs, shuffling through his mail. Bills, credit card applications, more junk mail . . . Ferenc gave a grimace of disgust at the sight of the letter addressed to him by Amy's attorney. He carelessly tossed everything on the table and plucked a half-empty pack of cigarettes and a spare lighter from a glass bowl on the corner of the kitchen counter.

"Come on, Max. Let's go outside."

Ferenc opened the sliding door and stepped onto the braided rug, followed closely by Max, who trotted around the perimeter, sniffing along the privacy fence before choosing a pleasant spot in the sun in the middle of the yard. Max turned in place three times, then lay down with an exhausted huff.

Ferenc could definitely relate as he slowly dropped himself into a wicker chair with a long exhale. He lit a cigarette and leaned back, shutting his eyes. His collarbone ached as if being tightly squeezed, and he gritted his teeth in discomfort.

It was probably time to ice his fracture again. He couldn't even remember how long it'd been since he last took his painkillers, but he hoped he could take another soon. He unfastened his stabilizer and pulled his throbbing arm out of the sling, performing his elbow exercises to prevent stiffness—which had already set in.

His mind was not kind, rarely allowing for a reprieve in flashbacks as he flexed and extended his arm as best he could, occasionally rubbing at the joint. But the flashbacks of his accident eventually shifted to chasing the ghost of the blonde woman—and his panic attack.

His breathing shuddered. He'd now had two fits of anxiety in as many days. If it wasn't for the scrawny, black-haired woman . . .

Ferenc paused in his actions, staring out at nothing in particular, wondering what she'd been so afraid of as she'd constantly looked over her shoulder. His thoughts shifted back to the slow-driving black car. Perhaps she was being followed.

The more he tried to make sense of it, the stronger the wave of exhaustion became. Putting out the butt of his cigarette in the glass ashtray atop the wicker table, he stood and turned to the sliding door.

"Come on, Max," he called, and the retriever followed with a yawn.

25

S.W. Raine

After downing another pill and using the peas as a makeshift ice pack again, he soon drifted off for a much-needed nap.

CHAPTER 6
Ferenc

The night sky threatened to swallow the sunset hues of pinks and oranges as Ferenc returned to the diner. Though it was darker and not nearly as busy after supper as it was during the day, he still preferred a spot outside on the terrace.

Aside from Wilfred—whom Ferenc long since wondered if the man ever took a day off in his aging life—the weekend morning crew had gone home for the day. Harry, replacing Danny in the evening, waved while wiping down his glasses, and Ferenc tipped his head in greeting.

"Ferenc! Twice in one day!" Wilfred called out from the kitchen. "We must be doing something right."

Ferenc chuckled and approached the counter by the large warming window. "I'll have my usual, but only if you tell me my smokes, lighter, and wallet are here . . ."

"Cigarettes and lighter, yes," Wilfred replied, "and a rather hefty tip that Daisy wouldn't accept. But no wallet."

Dread instantly built up in the pit of his stomach. While relieved that he'd paid for his food, he couldn't, for the life of him, remember what he'd done with the wallet afterward.

Wilfred disappeared to the back and returned with Ferenc's items and a small plastic sandwich bag containing his change—over forty dollars' worth. "I can call Daisy, if you want."

"Nah, I'll ask her tomorrow, but thank you." He shoved the money in his pocket, then added, "I'll have my regular, I guess."

"She'll be here," Wilfred confirmed. "Go have a seat. We'll bring it right out."

27

Ferenc thanked him and stepped out onto the terrace. The tables were empty at that time of the evening, so he chose the same seat he'd been sitting in earlier and grabbed a cigarette from the case—which was missing two more, as far as he could tell. With a long drag, he watched the few cars drive by before directing his gaze to where he'd last seen the blonde woman prior to rushing after her. Deep down, he hoped he'd spot her again to prove to himself he wasn't crazy.

Commotion came from inside, pulling him away from his current thoughts. A male employee had raised his voice, but Ferenc couldn't tell if it was in excitement or alarm, so he shifted in his seat to look.

The side door swung open, and a tiny figure darted out, chased by Harry.

"Get out!" he said, his voice a higher pitch than usual.

"I worked today!" the figure replied, spinning around to confront him.

"They said you were begging for yesterday's bread just this morning!" he countered, his voice trembling. "Now shoo!"

Even with the blanket of darkness setting in over the remnants of the colorful canvas in the sky, his face glowed beet red. Ferenc wasn't sure if he should be more concerned about the man's blood pressure or the scene he was causing in public.

"Geez, Mister." She huffed. "Money is money."

Ferenc straightened at the usage of the term "mister," a flash of the petite woman from earlier—with the same form-fitting blue jeans and gray hoodie—appearing in his mind. She'd pulled him from the depths of his panic attack, shaking him until he'd returned to reality.

She'd been skittish—constantly looking over her shoulder—but he'd figured the slow-driving vehicle had something to do with it. Now, he wondered if maybe she'd swiped his wallet and was instead looking for a quick escape before he found out. She'd stuffed her hands in the hoodie pockets before darting off, after all. The more it ran about his mind, the more it dawned on him that the loss of his wallet could've only occurred then.

When she turned around and their eyes met, his suspicions were confirmed: she froze and stuffed her hands in the deep pockets of her hoodie, hastily averting her gaze as she rushed to leave.

Ferenc was quick, though. He snapped his free hand out and hooked her by the elbow, pulling her toward him. She squeaked, and her body tensed as she gasped. In one swift motion, he kicked out the chair next to him and pushed her down into it. She fell into the seat with a forced exhale, a harried, wild look about her face as her mouth fell slightly open. He bit down on a cry from the wave of agony to his clavicle, thankful for the sling and stabilizer, else the strain would've been on a whole other level.

"I said scram!"

"I got her, Harry," Ferenc replied as calmly as he could, trying his best to catch his breath and hide the tremble of pain in his voice. "She's with me."

"What's going on out here?" Wilfred stepped outside with a plate of strawberry-drizzled cheesecake and a mug of black coffee—decaf, of course. It was too late for caffeine.

"It's the homeless girl," Harry confirmed.

"It's okay," Ferenc reassured once more. "I've got her covered. She's a friend."

"Friend, huh?" Wilfred eyed the girl suspiciously as he placed Ferenc's food and drink on the table. "I won't question it," he said as he pulled away.

"I trust you, but you best watch out for her," Harry grumbled. "She's a thief."

"I've got her covered," Ferenc repeated. "And while she's here, can we get her some cake and coffee too, please?"

Harry huffed, adjusting his glasses before walking back inside.

Wilfred's attention fell to Ferenc's hand still hooked into the crook of her arm. With a nod, he eventually walked away. When both men were fully back inside, he focused back on the girl. She was nothing but bones beneath the worn-out material. Finally, he snaked his shaking hand away, extending it out, palm up.

"My wallet, please."

The young woman blinked, confused. "What are you talking about?"

There was a brief moment of uncertainty toiling inside of him. Maybe he was wrong about her having stolen his wallet. After all, he had no proof . . . but the doubt lasted only a half second. "My wallet," Ferenc repeated, confident once more. There was no other explanation for the way she'd acted when she'd noticed him just now. "You have it. I'd like it back, please."

29

The fear, confusion, and surprise in her features slowly dissipated the more he stared her down, determined and relentless. Eventually, a frown formed, wrinkling the space between her thick brows.

She huffed, reaching into one of the deep pockets, and pulled out a brown leather wallet. She shoved it in his hand and looked away, dropping her chin to her chest and pulling her arms in, hugging herself.

He didn't scold her. He simply continued to watch her, his palm still open, the wallet still sitting there.

She brought a hand up to her mouth and began chewing on her fingernails. Her gaze flicked over to him before returning in a double take. "What?" she muttered quietly, looking everywhere but at him. "It's all there . . . minus maybe a hundred bucks. But all your cards are still there."

Ferenc finally closed his hand about the wallet, sliding it in his back pocket where it belonged, and gave her a soft, sympathetic smile. "I believe you," he finally said, and she stared back incredulously.

Wilfred brought out another slice of cheesecake and a coffee, placing it before her on the table. Ferenc grabbed his fork and sliced it through the tip of the cake as the owner hovered by the table.

Ferenc knew Wilfred was silently trying to grab his attention, but he'd have none of it. He knew what he was doing; he didn't need the staff's constant warnings.

Once Wilfred returned inside, Ferenc breathed a little easier, but when he looked back at the homeless woman, she appeared ready to run. He had to say something, and quickly.

CHAPTER 7
Ferenc

"What's your name?" Ferenc asked after swallowing his bite.
"Dormouse."

She spoke so softly, he almost missed it. And even then, he wasn't sure he heard her correctly because he could've sworn she just gave him a rodent's name.

Dormouse avoided eye contact, constantly looking over her shoulder just as she had when she'd helped him earlier. But she no longer had his wallet . . . so she must've been anxious about something else entirely.

"You should try the cheesecake," he offered, changing the subject. "It's the best in the county."

She looked down at her food, carefully licking her lips in anticipation. With one more glance over her shoulder, she then picked up the fork, dipped the tip of the prongs into the strawberry syrup, and brought the utensil to her mouth. Her eyes fluttered shut in delight as the faintest of moans escaped her. She opened them again and cut into the sweet and tangy cake with the side of the fork, practically swallowing the next few bites whole.

It must've been some time since she'd had good food. She probably didn't even have a place to sleep.

"So, Dormouse, was it?" he eventually said, looking at his food but watching her from the corner of his eye. She flinched and shrank down some, which only proved he'd heard right. "Is that your last name? A nickname? Or . . .?"

Her expression darkened, and he instantly regretted his choice of words. He hadn't meant to insult her. He was just horrible when

31

it came to chitchatting, preferring to conserve his energy and avoid being drained by engagement with the world. But there was something about her that piqued his interest and made him want to try his hand at it.

"Look, it's my name, okay?" She huffed and crossed her arms, slouching in the chair like a teenager would before peeking back over her shoulder. "It's better than being called a street rat."

He set down his fork and picked up his paper napkin, wiping at his lips before he spoke again. "I'm sorry. I didn't mean to offend."

"You didn't." Her face contorted with a collision of emotions. "I just don't like my real name."

"Dormouse is a wonderful name," he said with a gentle smile. "Very unique. I'm Ferenc." He lifted his hand, extending it toward her to shake hers, but she recoiled. "It's a pleasure to meet you," he added softly—cautiously—to make her more comfortable. Something terrible must've happened for her to be this skittish.

She did not reciprocate the handshake. Eventually, she acknowledged him with an ever so faint nod before bringing her fingers back up to nibble on her fingernails.

Her wordless action was satisfying enough. He pulled his hand back and returned to the last of his cheesecake. Dormouse reexamined her plate, fingering the remaining syrup and silently sucking it off her fingertips.

"Told you it was good," he said.

"Yeah," she agreed with another silent mumble.

Her tense posture softened, and he was glad for it. "Can I walk you to wherever you're staying?" he offered.

Her brows furrowed as her eyes shot up, then she glowered. "Why are you being so nice to me?"

Ferenc blinked, taken aback. That was not the reaction he'd expected. Her defensiveness over his natural kindness confused him. "Why wouldn't I?"

"Look, I gave you back your stupid wallet." Her forehead smoothed out, and the soft patio light in the newly settled dark sky caught the watery shine in her eyes as she fought back tears. "What more do you want from me?"

He watched her for a long time in silence. She'd had it hard; he could tell. He chose his words carefully. "I don't expect anything from you," he started softly. "I'm just enjoying the company."

32

Despite forcing her into the chair, he wasn't holding her there against her will. He was simply sitting, enjoying some food, and talking. He wasn't trying to come off as creepy or desperate.

He was never good with small talk; even Amy could attest to that. She would've found all of this ridiculous. He briefly wondered if it was what eventually drove her away to begin with. But then again, surely, she would've told him if that were the case.

Dormouse might've muttered something, bringing him back to the moment at hand, but between the city sounds of chatter, various genres of music, vehicle motors, and her fingers in the way, anything that might've escaped her was lost.

He inhaled deeply through his nose before breaking the awkward silence between them. "Besides." He took a long sip of his coffee before speaking again. "I wanted to thank you for helping me earlier, when I . . ." He trailed off, waving his hand about his head as he referred to his panic attack.

"Yeah," she said, cocking her head to the side. "What was up with that?"

Ferenc chuckled at her choice of words. It was interesting how her entire demeanor changed now that the spotlight was off her. He was somewhat the same way. "I have no idea. I thought . . ."

Truthfully, he thought he saw the very woman he watched get struck by lightning in the air. But he couldn't tell her that; she'd never believe him.

"I saw . . ."

He paused, observing the curiosity shining in her eyes and the concern in her pursed lips. He'd fully captivated her.

It'd been a while since he could fascinate anyone like that. That spark with Amy had died out long ago. And the worst thing was that he really hadn't said much. He continued to watch Dormouse. The smudge of dirt he'd seen on her pallid cheek earlier was gone. And despite being nothing but skin and bones, he found her pretty.

She grew shy again, her gaze darting everywhere but at him. He cleared his throat, pretending to be captivated by a tiny chip in the handle of his coffee cup as he refocused on what he'd been talking about.

"Well, whatever it was that I saw, it wasn't normal. The doctors and the police dismissed it as stress and trauma."

"You *did* look pretty stressed."

It was Ferenc's turn to feel uneasy as he combed his fingers through his hair, his vision turning unfocused. Of *course* she didn't believe him.

"Do you think you're crazy?" she then asked.

His attention darted to her, where she examined him much in the same way he'd been observing her not that long ago. He pondered her words for a moment.

He prided himself on being knowledgeable but was completely stumped when it came down to whether or not he knew what he saw. More often than not, he was firm in his belief of having hallucinated the whole thing. But there was a tiny drop of doubt buried deep within him. That drop expanded into a puddle, and on occasion, it flooded his entire being with such force, he changed his mind.

He opened his mouth to reply, but no words broke free. His jaw clamped shut as the memory of lightning striking the woman came to the front of his mind. He'd imagined that too.

No.

He chased the thoughts and images away. "No," he finally replied, reaching for his smokes. "It was definitely real."

"What happened?" Dormouse asked as Ferenc lit a cigarette and took a drag. "With your shoulder, I mean."

"Work accident." He politely blew the smoke away from her.

"What do you do?"

He had her undivided attention again, and he had to admit to himself that he actually enjoyed it. His lips pulled into a soft smile. "I'm a freelance pilot."

"What does a freelance pilot do?"

He was certain he didn't fit the proper definition of an actual freelance pilot. He was one of a kind and willingly did the jobs nobody else wanted. There was usually a good reason as to why nobody wanted them. "I do whatever is needed: data collecting, transportation, testing . . . Some of those jobs have even taken me all over the world. Russia, Madagascar, Greece, Brazil . . . among many other places."

He was more than happy to reminisce about his travels. Taking on jobs that allowed him to visit other countries was one of his favorite things to do—not just for the beautiful scenery, but because he was free in the air for hours at a time.

"You really enjoy it, don't you?"

34

Her voice brought him back to reality. She was sitting up, leaning forward, elbows on the table . . . and actually smiling. In spite of himself, he found that he was just as enthralled with her.

"I do." *Enjoy* was an understatement. "What about you? What do you enjoy?"

Dormouse's lips slowly flattened into a line, and she pulled back, sinking into the seat once more. She vacantly looked at the ground next to her and shrugged.

She'd seemed so relaxed, so *comfortable* before he put the spotlight back onto her. It was a pity she didn't like it; it was hard to get to know her otherwise.

Ferenc powered through the awkward silence, quickly finishing his cigarette and coffee, thankful for each passing second she didn't run off.

"Well," he finally said, extinguishing the butt in the ashtray and stuffing everything back in his pockets, "thank you for the company." He stood, stretching his still-sore muscles. "Are you sure I can't walk you somewhere?"

She shook her head, tensing back up and peering over her shoulder again. He followed her gaze but saw nothing out of the ordinary that would make her so anxious. He wished he could help, but without knowing what the problem was, he couldn't do much. And asking outright was insensitive, not to mention it would probably send her running off with the limelight back on her.

"I hope to see you again, Dormouse. I come here quite often if you need anything."

She quietly brought her fingernails back to her teeth. There might have been a goodbye in there somewhere too, but with her fingers in the way, all sound was lost in translation. And with that, she darted away, disappearing around the café.

It took a while for him to finally look away. Dormouse was so shy, so uneasy . . . She'd made progress during their conversation, but something had spooked her. With one final examination up and down the increasingly sleepy street, he then headed inside to pay for their food and drinks.

"Everything good?" Harry asked as he took the money.

"Yeah. I think I need to reapply some ice—"

"I mean about the girl," Harry said.

Ferenc blinked. There was nothing wrong with Dormouse. So she'd stolen his wallet. He couldn't blame her; she was homeless—

or so they claimed. She'd returned his wallet and promised every-thing was mostly still there, and he'd believed her. He did a quick check while the wallet was there in his hands, and sure enough, nothing important was missing.

"You know," he said, running his free hand through his hair, "you should cut her some slack."

Harry cast him a sideways glance before handing him his change. Ferenc thanked him, then waved to Wilfred in the kitchen before walking out.

He'd been all set to go home, but a black vehicle crawled down the street, much like the one he'd seen earlier in the day. He tried to catch a glimpse of the driver, but the mixture of the cover of night, tinted windows, and the gleam from the streetlights made it impos-sible.

Now, all he wanted to do was go over everything that'd been said and everything that'd happened. Something was definitely off since the storm. And so, he ambled down the illuminated streets, heading for a spot where he could think in peace.

CHAPTER 8
Olivia

S nooping around an Air Force base wasn't as easy as the movies
made it out to be. Unfortunately, Olivia was no spy. Despite her
air-centric abilities, there wasn't much she could do without getting
caught.

And she couldn't afford to risk that. Not when she desperately
had to find the pilot. There was something deep inside of her, an
inexplicable need—stronger than the deepest sense of longing she'd
ever felt before—that demanded she find the pilot, as if it were a
matter of life or death.

The waves lapped noisily at the shoreline as her toes dug into
the cool, wet sand with each step. She carried one black flat in each
hand as she followed along the bank, past the few beachgoers still
present.

She'd been unable to do anything around the first Air Force
base, and when she'd tried a second one, the strange tug deep inside
pulled her back to the beach.

But now she was lost. Confused. That baffling draw that'd led
her from California to Florida pulsed stronger than ever, more intense than it had in a long while—except for that moment right before being run over by a jet, obviously. Unfortunately, the city by the
beach still had thousands of people living in it, and she was blindly
trying to find one person.

That wresting sensation seared itself into her entire being. The
guardian or elemental was here—of that, she had no doubt. She
hoped, now more than ever, that she'd be able to recognize them as
she scanned each beachgoer's face, illuminated only by their red- or

orange-colored flashlights, to glimpse the mysterious pilot, but she recognized no one. She couldn't have anyway, even it had been bright out—the pilot had worn a mask and visor. But deep down, she hoped . . . and that desire matched both her passion and drive in intensity.

Olivia's pace matched the gentle ebb and flow of the receding tide as she made her way along the edge of the water, her focus intent. There was still nothing as she approached a rockier section of beach.

She cringed as the sharp surfaces of rocks, shells, and other washed-up debris dug into her bare feet, making walking slightly more difficult, then turned to face the water—knuckles upon her hips, flats spread outward like little flippers—deep in thought.

The lure within scorched fervently despite no recognizable souls around, and she couldn't figure out why. It persistently seared to the point she almost found it hard to breathe. She allowed the refreshing waves to lap at her feet, and, by extension, cool off the fire deep inside. Oh, how she wished she knew where the guardian or the elemental was.

"Excuse me . . ."

Her entire body stiffened at the man's sudden voice behind her, despite its folksiness. She could've sworn her heart stopped beating for a second as well, and she chastised herself for allowing him to sneak up on her.

As soon as a hand touched her shoulder, that inner sensation yanked violently, screaming at her like a metal detector upon finding a hidden treasure.

She spun around as fast as she could, and an unfamiliar series of images immediately unveiled in her mind's eye upon seeing the blond man before her: a gloomy battleground of nothing but desolate rocks and stone, volcanoes erupting in the distance, and lightning flashing in the sickly green skies above as entire armies warred with giant creatures she'd never seen before.

Her heart raced as she tried to figure out where she was and what was going on. She took a step back, and the sword and shield she didn't know she was holding clattered to the ground. She caught sight of the shiny chrome-colored bracers around her arms, then brought her hands to the smooth breastplate she wore—so lightweight, she could've sworn she wasn't wearing armor at all.

An explosion occurred nearby; a burning boulder thrown by a gigantic monster made of molten lava shattered before it reached her, thanks to the very same blond man she'd just seen along the beach, though now he was clad in similar lightweight armor as hers.

"Protect the elemental!"

He yelled the words, but in the illusion, they sounded muddled, like Olivia was underwater while he spoke them. He darted forward, sending shock waves toward an oncoming enemy.

She turned her head to get a good look at the elemental in question, but the hallucination faded until she was back on the beach staring at the blond man . . . whose eyes were wide in shock as he took a step backward, his hand pulled back as if a snake had bitten him.

"You're real!" he said with a gasp.

Her vision clouded over, her mind trying to drag the phantasm back. She didn't understand what had just happened and wondered if he'd seen it too. But his words didn't match the images in her mind, and so she blinked back her confusion, focusing instead on what he'd said.

Of course she was real. And apparently, so was he: a guardian, in the flesh, if she was to trust that apparition.

Her attention briefly fell to the injured man's sling, and she suddenly understood. "Ah, the pilot," she said. Everything had happened so fast, she almost missed it; of course he might've been injured from the loss of control in the storm.

"You!" he tried again, gaping. "I saw you . . ."

"You did," she confirmed. He was clearly having a hard time processing that information.

"But how?" He took another step back, vigorously shaking his head. "You—"

"Actually," she interrupted, "*You*. You were the one that ran *me* over with your jet."

"I don't understand."

His free hand rose to rub at his forehead before it combed through his hair, flustered like he'd seen a ghost. And she couldn't blame him; she'd called the lightning after slipping off the jet. She'd had no choice. And from his reactions, he didn't believe what he'd seen. Olivia forced a sympathetic smile to reassure him, but it was short-lived and fake.

She felt horrible about it. She knew what it was like to be in disbelief over her own abilities and had swiftly become aware of no longer being *normal*, of being a freak of nature—quite literally. The general population always reacted poorly to things they didn't understand, things they couldn't explain.

But what she, herself, didn't understand was why he seemed so traumatized by her abilities if he was the same guardian in the strange vision she'd had.

She needed to sit down, and she figured he did too. She had some explaining to do—he clearly had lots of questions—but she had her own inquiries. Olivia did a quick scan and spotted a large piece of driftwood sitting snugly by some bushes. Perfect. She motioned with her head for him to follow.

"Come," she said calmly. "Let's sit down, and I'll explain."

CHAPTER 9
Olivia

Olivia didn't know where to begin. She didn't know whether to start by telling him about waking from a crazy dream—about searching for the elementals and their guardians—and how withdrawn from friends and family she'd become as it'd consumed her day in and day out until she'd left home, or maybe about the tug she'd followed all the way from California and how it'd pulled hardest when he'd run her over with his jet. Maybe she'd start by telling him she knew who he was, not because she'd seen him, but because she'd *felt* it.

The pilot had followed her to the driftwood, but he refused to join her for a seat on the large log. He simply stood in front of her, his uninjured hand on his hip as if waiting for that explanation she'd promised. Frankly, he deserved it. If only she knew where to start. Somewhere that wouldn't instantly freak him out more than he already was. She swallowed hard.

"My name is Olivia Gillies," she started, breaking the ice.

"Ferenc Janos," he introduced in turn, that folksiness ever present.

"Interesting name. It sounds . . ."

"It's Hungarian in origin."

"Well, Ferenc, it's nice to meet you under . . . *different* circumstances."

She chuckled to lighten the mood, but he didn't seem to share in the humor. In fact, he didn't even smile. With the evening having given way to night, she couldn't tell if he was even listening to her or deep in thought.

41

She cleared her throat and tried again. "What I'm about to tell you might sound a little crazy, but it's all real. As real as you seeing me get struck by lightning."

Ferenc's form stiffened from her comment.

Good. So he *was* paying attention.

"I was going to start from the beginning, but I think I owe you an explanation for . . ." She followed the outline of his sling with her eyes. "Well, an explanation for what you saw before . . . that." Olivia pointed her chin toward his arm.

With her throat as dry as the desert, her anxiety skyrocketed over the possibility of him not believing her. She rubbed her sweaty palms down her leggings, worried about scaring him off or worse—him turning aggressive in his fear, as some people were naturally prone to do. Her stomach fluttered with each made-up scenario, making her feel nauseated. She hated it.

"What you saw wasn't me getting struck . . . it was me using the lightning to travel."

There. She'd said it.

"Come again?"

His words—his tone—meant he didn't believe her, and she swallowed the lump in her throat once again. It was bigger this time. Her heart threatened to thump out of her ribcage, and her breath trembled as she exhaled. "It's exactly what it sounds like. I can—I can summon lightning and travel with it."

The pull was so strong, he *had* to be a guardian, but he acted as if this information was foreign. Surely, he'd had the same visions as she had. She needed him to believe her, and fast.

"I can manipulate air, I can—I can ride through storms, I . . . It's not magic or witchcraft, it's an actual ability."

He tilted his head forward, and Olivia caught the very skeptical expression through the moonlight. His eyes narrowed, and his lips pressed into a fine line, which set off the alarms that he wasn't buying it. She needed to somehow spell it out without sounding like she was pulling it straight from the likes of the movies she loved watching.

"How else can you explain my appearance out of thin air, thousands of feet up in the clouds?" she blurted out. Her cheeks flushed in both frustration and embarrassment. Telling him was a mistake, and she'd never allow herself to live it down.

But Ferenc's mouth fell open slightly as his breath hitched from her words. She might as well get on with it; she was already making a fool of herself.

"I was searching for somebody," Olivia quickly continued. "Actually, I was searching for a few people: some elementals and their guardians. And you came through the storm as I was traveling. Lightning is unpredictable and fast. I couldn't shift the lightning's path, so my only option was to land on your jet. And I knew I'd found who I was looking for because I felt it. You can control the air too. But I think I might've distracted you, and you lost control, and I slipped. So, I summoned another lightning bolt to transport me to safety." She only took the time for one breath before continuing to vomit out words that made her sound more and more like she belonged in an insane asylum. "But I found you, and that's all that matters because you're a guardian."

Ferenc scrunched his face, and his hand shot up, palm out, to halt her. "Okay, stop."

She gulped down the remaining words in her throat as he shut his eyes and pinched the bridge of his nose. He *had* to believe her. "It's difficult to take in, I know, but—"

"Let me get this straight," he interrupted, trailing his hand from the bridge of his nose down to his jaw, where he rubbed at the scruff on his face. "You think *explaining* that you were searching for somebody, deciding to ride the lightning to find them, and getting caught in my path would make me think you're crazy."

Olivia gave a slow nod as her heart raced. That was usually how it worked—at least in her experience.

"But you summoned a lightning bolt—*where I could clearly see you*—rather than plummet to your death, thus making me think *I* was the one who was crazy."

Her eyes widened at his words, and her cheeks flushed in embarrassment—thankfully hidden by the night—as she shuffled her bare feet through the gritty sand. She'd been trying to keep her abilities a secret from everyone, but he was right: the thought hadn't even crossed her mind that he might've been going through similar fears surrounding the incident.

"Jesus, I thought you'd died," he scolded. "I was convinced there was nothing left of you, that you were nothing but ashes. And seeing you appear out of thin air—how did you even survive that, by the way?" he suddenly asked as he carved his fingers through his hair,

43

held it back for a moment, then finally released. "At the speed I was going, how did it not kill you?"

"All part of the air manipulation," came her weakened reply.

He stared at her. Olivia could practically see the gears in his head turning, and she was almost afraid of what would come out of his mouth next. His hand trailed to the back of his neck, where he rubbed it for a moment.

"I watched you get struck by lightning—which was pretty traumatizing, might I add." Olivia's shoulders curled forward as she shut her eyes. She felt horrible about it and just wanted to disappear. "I thought you'd died," he repeated, "but then I spotted you casually walking down the street earlier as if nothing had ever happened."

Her eyes snapped open, and her mind raced with possibilities as to why she hadn't felt him nearby as strongly as she currently did if he'd physically seen her.

"So when I saw you again, just now, I . . ."

"I'm sorry," she said in defeat, barely any louder than the waves along the shoreline.

Each passing second from Ferenc's ever-growing silence seemed more eternal than the flow of the beach's infinite grains of sand through an hourglass. And with every one of those endless seconds, the weight of his reticence was so overwhelming, she almost gasped when he finally spoke. "You said you were searching for me."

So relieved by the release of the invisible weight, her brain and tongue stumbled to give an appropriate response. "Yes."

He nodded, but his lips pressed thin once more before he finally spoke again. "I don't even know if I'm angry over the fact that you *left me* to save yourself after finding me—"

"I have no idea if I would've been able to bring you through the lightning with me," she cut off defensively. "Despite everything, I'm still new to all of this. It could've killed you. Who knows?"

"And the crash wouldn't have?" he shot back, irritation finally peeling away the friendly tones in his voice.

Olivia squirmed at his words. He blamed her, and rightfully so. But she licked her dry lips, choosing her next words carefully because all she *wanted* to do was shout that he was *clearly* still alive.

"No, it wouldn't have killed you," she replied. Ferenc frowned, and she quickly continued before he could argue another fact. "I told you: you were controlling the air. You have enough control that, sure, you were hurt," she added, pointing to his brow and collar-bone, "but not killed."

There he was, staring again, going over who-knew-what in his mind. He seemed to be a very fact-over-fiction kind of guy, and she knew this all sounded completely out of left field, but she didn't want to lose the chance that he might believe her, however faint the possibility.

"Do you ever get that sensation, when you're flying, that you're free? Like nothing around you even exists?" He gave a slow nod, so she continued. "You feel that way because that's who you are; that's *what* you are. You didn't die because you have control, and you know how to handle it. You know a few of the air's secrets and can manipulate it to your advantage. You may not know it, but you do."

Olivia didn't even know if what she said was true anymore. She was going out on a limb, and hell, the reach was pretty far. But she had to bring him to her side, to make him believe and understand. Unfortunately, his expression grew dark as his eyes narrowed, and her sense of disquiet returned at the possibility that she'd pushed instead of pulled, that she'd lost him entirely.

"I didn't *die* because I kept calm the entire time, regardless of my knowledge of aircrafts and how to properly pilot them," he retorted.

"That may be so, but I bet you're better than the rest because of your abilities to control the air around you."

Ferenc's hand dropped limp to his side. "Clearly, I'm not who you think I am."

Dread settled in the pit of Olivia's stomach. No. She couldn't be wrong. That pull was going haywire with him next to her. And there was no other explanation for that mystifying vision. She'd just have to convince him the only other way she knew how: she'd have to show him proof. And she hoped that proof might—or would—trigger *something* within him.

"Wait!" She lifted both hands up in front of her as if she were holding an invisible box. "Here."

"What are you doing?"

"Giving you proof. Just . . . place your hand in between mine. Tell me what you feel." Ferenc cocked his head, skeptical, and she added, "Please humor me. I won't bite; you're not my type." She had no interest in anyone—romantically or intimately, stranger or friend—but it elicited a faint twitch at the corner of his mouth,

45

barely distinguishable in the moonlight, like he almost wanted to smile or laugh. Relief flooded through her when he finally lifted his hand and slowly pushed it until it was between both of hers. He waited for a moment, then wiggled his fingers.

"Nothing's happening."

A knowing smile crept to her lips. "Exactly. Now . . ."

Her gaze dropped to the space between her hands. Her fingers twitched slightly as she focused on warming the air. Once satisfied with the temperature, she looked back at Ferenc.

"All right, now tell me what you feel."

He raised an eyebrow, giving her a look like it was some sort of trick he wasn't willing to fall for a second time. He then muttered something about nonsense. "I can feel the heat radiating from your hands, but other than that, nothing."

Well, he was definitely the cold, hard facts kind of guy. "Body heat, huh? Is that what your factual mind came up with?" She smirked. "All right, hold on."

Again, Olivia's attention dropped to her hands. Her fingers twitched faintly, much the same as the first time, but then her hands quivered as if she was shivering from being cold. She intended on cooling the air between her hands, but her concentration—her determination—was so strong that she created fog in that invisible box. She'd never been one to do things halfway, anyway.

Ferenc's mouth slackened as he stared in disbelief. If the fog wasn't proof enough of her ability to manipulate air, then the chill—so cold that tiny snowflakes began to form between her hands—definitely was.

He eased his hand back and lifted it to his face as he blinked, incredulous. He inspected the condensation from the mixture of his own body heat and the warm Florida air beneath the moonlight before shoving his hand back into that space between her hands.

Olivia released her control of the air, pulling her hands away as if dropping the invisible box, and swiftly clasped her warm hands around his frigid one as the snow crystals dissipated from the return of the regular temperature. She released him with a grin.

"That, sir, was called air manipulation."

Ferenc's look of shock subsided, but the skepticism returned as he cast her a sidelong glance.

"All right, I don't know how you did it, but I'll admit it was impressive."

"You can do it too," she confirmed. "It's like . . . the most basic thing."

He watched her for a long moment. She could tell that he still didn't fully believe her, even after witnessing that. But she'd run with it. It was a start.

Ferenc finally lowered himself onto the other side of the log. He pulled a slim case from his breast pocket and retrieved a cigarette. Olivia wrinkled her nose some. After taking a few puffs—and politely blowing the smoke away from her—he finally spoke. "So. Now that your search is over and you've found me, what's next?"

Her heart sank. She'd never really stopped to consider what would happen after she found an elemental or a guardian. She had no clue if something magical was supposed to happen, or if they were supposed to have all the answers to her questions, like explaining the tug and why it'd pulled her on this crazy quest that made no sense. Her little display didn't seem to trigger anything guardian-like in him.

"I don't know," she admitted, briefly looking back at the water and twinkling stars reflecting off the surface.

"You don't know?"

"No." Olivia's hair danced along her mid back from the movement of her head. "I didn't even know I was looking for you, specifically, until I found you."

"Then how did you know I was the one you were looking for?"

"I told you; I felt it. You were controlling the air, whether you want to believe that part or not. But as to how I got here all the way from California—"

"*California?!*" he repeated, incredulous.

"Yeah. I woke up one morning with a—a deep *urge* to find elementals and their guardians. I thought it was a dream at first, but the urge grew. It was like a—a tug. It pulled, and eventually, I just . . . followed." She brought her hand up and pointed to her chest, in the spot right above her heart. "It's a feeling. A feeling that I just knew. And I have no idea why."

The soul-crushing weight of Ferenc's silence returned before he finally spoke again. "What if you're wrong?"

Though his silence didn't last nearly the eternity it had the last time, his eventual question bore a whole different kind of weight—one she was painfully aware of:

47

what if she *was* wrong? That was the million-dollar question. Something should've happened by now if he really was a guardian.

"You know," Olivia started, as Ferenc finished his cigarette and extinguished it in the sand under his foot, "I never saw your face. Up there. When you ran me over. So even after summoning the lightning, I still didn't know who I was looking for until not too long ago, when you touched my shoulder and I turned around. I saw something . . . weird."

"Like what?"

He watched her with great focus, genuinely curious, but she didn't know if he was serious or not. After all, he'd barely believed her about the air manipulation, and she'd practically made it snow in eighty-degree weather. She contemplated for a moment, then dropped her chin to her chest. "You wouldn't believe me."

"I probably wouldn't," he admitted, "but sometimes, when you think you're crazy, it turns out you're wrong."

Her attention flicked back to him. He was right, in a way; he'd said that he thought her dead, and yet there she was, flesh and bone, sitting next to him. "I saw . . . *you*. But not as you are now. You had weapons. Armor. You were telling me to protect the elemental."

"You keep using that word. I don't even know what an elemental is."

Truthfully, she hadn't known either. She hadn't ever heard the word until that dream.

"It's a concept coined by some Swiss physician named Paracelcus in the sixteenth century, corresponding to the four elements of antiquity: earth, fire, air, and water. Apparently, elementals are beings who are half spirit and half person."

"So, they're stories and myths."

It wasn't a question; it was a statement. Olivia parted her lips, but she couldn't figure out how to defend what she still didn't fully know or understand.

"Well, it couldn't have been me," he then dismissed. "I don't own any armor or weapons."

"I know what I saw," Olivia replied, flustered. She couldn't be certain the man in the vision had been Ferenc all along, but she also knew what she felt.

Her eyes fluttered shut, and she tuned into that sensation, the tug that screamed at her that he was the one.

Sure enough, it was there, loud and clear. But he didn't appear to realize he was a guardian, so it seemed she was stuck until she found an elemental. Maybe they'd have the answers she sought.

"I need to find the elementals."

"What would you be looking for?" he asked, his voice quieter than it had been. "Or *who*?"

According to her research, elementals were sylphs, gnomes, salamanders, and undines. Whether she was looking for actual mythical beings or human representatives was another matter entirely. "I don't know."

She fished deep inside for that feeling, but with Ferenc right next to her, she couldn't work out if it even pulled her in another direction or not.

Olivia opened her eyes. Ferenc remained quiet—no doubt lost in his thoughts as he stared at the twinkling lights above. If only she knew what was going through his mind.

She pulled herself up off the log, slipping her bare feet into her flats that'd been set down nearby. "I want to give you some time to process this," she started. "You know what you saw, and I confirmed it. We can meet back here tomorrow night, and you can ask me anything—any question that might've popped up between now and then. I can't guarantee I'll have an answer, but I can certainly try."

"Can I ask one right now?"

"Shoot."

Ferenc picked up his extinguished butt before he stood as well and turned to face her. For the first time, she took notice of his height and build: a full head over her—and Olivia was tall—lean, and toned. No different from how she'd seen him in her hallucination.

"What will you do if I don't come back?"

Olivia's stomach dropped. After everything she'd said and done . . . She needed answers for why she was drawn to him. She needed to know what to do next. He couldn't just leave her hanging like that. Her core grew hot with frustration at her muddied and panicked thoughts before her chest tightened and her eyes stung with the onset of tears.

She took a calming breath, which shuddered as she exhaled. Guardian or not, she couldn't expect him to follow along on her journey. She had to do this herself.

49

With a heaved sigh, she stomped off without answering, her flats partially sinking into the sand, which seeped into the sides with each step, the smooth yet gritty texture uncomfortable against the soles of her feet. Her hands had formed into fists, but she relaxed them and slowed down as her vision blurred, angry at herself for being vulnerable. As she wiped her tears, she took a few more deep breaths before continuing on.

She'd return. Ferenc was one of the guardians she'd been searching for, after all. And if he didn't meet her at the beach, then she'd follow that pull just as she'd always done.

CHAPTER 10
Ferenc

He didn't want to believe it, but he couldn't deny the fact that she'd created actual snow crystals between her hands in the warm Florida heat.

Ferenc returned to the road to head home, his thoughts thundering louder than the waves along the shore; he not only considered everything Olivia had said, but especially what she'd *done*.

None of it made sense. But then again, nothing had ever since she appeared from out of nowhere in the sky. It was impossible for the impact with the jet to not have killed her. Lightning travel was equally impossible, as was surviving that lightning strike after he'd watched her get decimated. And it was impossible for actual snow—not hail—to appear at the current Floridian temperature, yet it *had* all happened.

He couldn't explain everything he'd seen, and he'd been quick to refuse to believe her words. But no matter how much he knew he was sure, he couldn't dismiss it without first doing research. Unfortunately, he didn't even know where to begin. He'd wanted answers for what'd happened in the sky, and it was almost as if Olivia had presented him with a handful of jigsaw puzzle pieces to solve instead.

He pulled his phone from his pocket and opened the search engine, entering air manipulation into the browser's search bar when the swift tapping of footsteps approached from behind. His chest tightened as something—or someone—zipped by before he could even glance over his shoulder. A familiar petite figure skidded to a halt and spun to face him, eyes wide.

51

"Dormouse!?"

Without a word, she whirled back around and fled down a side street, disappearing from view as quickly as she'd appeared.

Ferenc's first instinct was to reach for his back pocket and make sure his wallet was still present. With the object clearly able to be felt through the fabric, he then thought back to the expression of pure terror on her face.

It couldn't have been him she'd been afraid of. He remembered how she'd cautiously looked over her shoulder when she'd first stolen his wallet and how she'd also done so after giving it back. She'd never once appeared as panic-stricken as she had just now.

A deep, guttural growl reverberated behind him—so unnatural and otherworldly, he swore it came from the pits of hell. The hairs on his neck stood on end as he whipped around, squinting through the darkness toward a figure. The reflection from the streetlights barely glinted off its full-faced silver filigree mask, and a menacing pair of glowing red eyes flanked the individual on both sides.

Dormouse must've been running from them. He couldn't blame her, almost wanting to rush off as well, but he stood his ground. His natural sense of duty and compassion wouldn't allow them to get her, but there was something else too. Something he couldn't quite put his finger on.

He raised his cellphone, wiggling it in his hand. "I suggest you leave the little lady alone before I call the cops."

"I suggest you get out of our way," the person replied with a partially muffled, male voice.

"Or what?" Ferenc dared.

The masked figure lifted his hand, pointing to Ferenc, and the two sets of floating orbs lunged forward. Large black masses sprinted toward him, and he stiffened, surprised by their unnatural speed despite their long, gangly limbs and curled backs.

He glanced about for something to stop them with—anything—and beelined for a large garbage can down a side street while haphazardly shoving his phone back in his pocket.

As he skidded to a halt, he grabbed hold of the handle and heaved the metal can around with one arm, grunting from the weight. He sure wished he could use both arms . . .

The receptacle connected with one of the creatures, knocking it to the ground. It steadily rose back to its feet, luminous eyes narrowed to mere slits as it took a menacing step toward him.

Ferenc swallowed hard as he released the trash can, which clanged against the cement, and took a step back. He'd envisioned that happening differently in his mind, hoping to at least give himself a little more time to analyze the situation and make sense of whatever those *things* even were.

He eventually bumped against the solid brick wall of an establishment as he continued to back away. He had nowhere left to go. The monster approached with an alarming and otherworldly growl reverberating past a lycan-like maw full of clenched, jagged fangs. When a shriek tore through the night, Ferenc's blood curdled; Dormouse was in trouble.

A piercing whistle followed, and the creature turned back toward its master, who pointed off to the side where the scream's echo originated from. The beast lunged away from Ferenc, and in a beat, he followed. He had to stop these things, but he had to reach Dormouse first; his instincts outlandishly insisted upon it.

Of course, he couldn't keep up with the monster's unnatural speed, losing it from sight. He slowed to a stop, desperately looking for any sign of Dormouse or the creatures. He listened intently for footsteps, a growl, anything, but couldn't hear much over the sound of his own heart pounding in his chest and heavy breathing, and he couldn't detect much in the dark, despite the streetlights.

A knot formed in the pit of Ferenc's stomach as the spindly beast returned, on the hunt, straightening its freakishly long torso to freely scan through windows. The second creature wasn't too far behind, creeping low to the ground, its rangy limbs resembling some sort of monstrous spider straight out of a horror movie as it peeked around dumpsters and bins and stacked pallets. They were searching for something. Someone. Relief flooded through Ferenc; it seemed they'd lost Dormouse.

The beasts returned to their curved state before disintegrating as if a strong breeze blew them to nothing. It defied all sense, and Ferenc gawked.

"The chase has been suspended," a voice said from behind. "Lucky for you."

Ferenc reeled around to find the masked man lowering his arm, probably from having called off his pets. "Who the hell are you?" he demanded. "And what the hell were those things?"

The figure didn't answer. Instead, he walked away, fading into the night, leaving Ferenc to stare at absolutely nothing.

Finally, he grabbed his throbbing collarbone. "Son of a b—" he started through clenched teeth, holding his breath to lessen the pain.

He'd known lifting the garbage can would hurt, but it was excruciating now that the adrenaline started to wear off, and it was just going to get worse. But he couldn't concern himself with it at the moment.

"Dormouse," he hissed, not wishing to attract any unwanted attention from the new adversaries. He bolted down the side street the beasts had reappeared from earlier. "Dormouse!"

"Are they gone?"

Her voice was faint, muted. Ferenc paused, trying to figure out which direction her voice had come from, when something rummaged about inside a dumpster nearby.

The lid opened, and Dormouse appeared with dark, gritty filth smeared across her sweater and face, and something mysterious dangling over her shoulder, tangled in her hair. He released a long, pent-up breath and approached, holding out his good hand for her to take. Dormouse jumped out of the dumpster with ease before glimpsing about, skittish.

"They're gone," he assured her.

"Your shoulder . . ." she started.

"Yeah, that wasn't exactly a smart move on my part. Are you okay?" She nodded but kept her distance. He tried again. "What the hell were those things? Why were they chasing you?"

She disregarded his question and took a few steps back. "I gotta—I gotta go." With that, she fled.

Ferenc swiveled around to face the enemy but saw no one, not even when he turned back in the general direction in which Dormouse ran off. He was becoming as paranoid as her. He stepped out of the alley to return home, massaging his shoulder and keeping an eye open for Dormouse. Or trouble.

Things were getting stranger by the second. Now he found himself in a whirlwind of air manipulation, lightning travel, filigree masks, and whatever the hell those monsters were. He had to be dreaming. He was probably in a coma from the accident. There was no way any of it could be real.

He hated being ignorant. In the dark. Uneducated. Whatever one wanted to call it. Not only did none of it make sense, but it was going to be impossible to research, as well. He wasn't looking forward to that.

With a quick gander over his shoulder, he hustled toward his neighborhood. He hoped that whatever those dark, wiry creatures were, they weren't still chasing Dormouse.

He unlocked the door to his house, carefully monitoring both sides of the street before opening it. Everything seemed quiet and normal. He just hoped it was the same for Dormouse, wherever she was.

It was going to be a long night. His mind couldn't stop running back over everything Olivia had said, as well as the events with the beasts and masked person. There was also a perplexing sense of commitment over Dormouse's well-being he couldn't quite wrap his head around. He barely even knew her.

Between his fracture and his confusion, he foresaw a night of painkillers, frozen peas, and lots of research.

CHAPTER 11
Ferenc

Despite his fracture crying out in protest every now and again, his exhaustion swiftly pulled him back into a deep, dreamless slumber each time the pain woke him. His dog barking, however, was not something he could as easily ignore, and Ferenc jumped, startled, his eyes flying open.

The bright sunlight filtered into his bedroom from the roof windows in the kitchen and living room. When he'd been looking for a house, he'd wanted something with a lot of windows—to feel as close to the sky he loved so much—while Amy wanted something close to the water. He thought it lucky that he'd found it when he did, just waiting for him. He instantly fell in love with it before he'd even mentioned it to Amy and hoped she'd love it as much as he did. She didn't . . . but she liked it more than the other houses they'd visited.

Max barked again, sending an uncomfortable vibration through Ferenc's entire body. He'd fallen asleep doing some research while lying in bed; his phone was still in his hand, resting over his chest.

He'd looked up the possibilities of air manipulation and the intricacies of how lightning worked. His research even fell into ridiculous holes, such as whether elementals actually existed. Looking up silver filigree masks only pulled up costume opportunities. And those creatures? He didn't even know where to start with that research, but he wanted to know how everything linked together. The whole guardian and elemental thing was such a mystery that needed digging into, but he seemed to have misplaced the proper tools—whatever they were.

More barking occurred. "Max!" he yelled sharply, lifting his phone to check the time.

Max had never been that loud or agitated in the morning, even as a puppy. The barking continued, growing louder as the dog ran from the sliding door, passing his bedroom to rush down the stairs to the front door, then back up again. With a grunt from pain and stiffness, Ferenc stumbled out of bed, quickly slipping on a pair of gray sweats.

"Max!" he shouted again as the dog zoomed by. The golden retriever paused and looked at him with big brown eyes before persistently barking again. "What's going on?" he asked, the knot returning to the pit of his stomach. Clearly, the dog was alerting him about something. The first thing that came to mind was that the masked man and his beasts were back.

He followed as Max darted down the stairs and back to the front door. With a distinct click, he unlocked the front door and peeked out, but there was nobody there. He opened the door wider and stuck his head out, peering around and slowly surveying, but there was nothing.

Once he pulled back inside and shut the door, Max, who sat silently with its tail wagging wildly on the wooden floor, went right back to vocalizing while rushing back up the stairs to the kitchen. Ferenc followed as quickly as his aching body would let him and arrived as Max jumped up against the glass, fogging it up with each bark.

"Max!" he warned. "Jesus!"

He approached the sliding door, monitoring for trouble before opening it. The dog darted out into the open, then turned rather suddenly, skidding to the white fence. Max's determination was something fierce, Ferenc had to admit, and he followed the dog outside, watching from the porch.

Max got along great with all animals: cats, other dogs, hell, even the pesky raccoons. So there couldn't have been anything that'd rile the dog up on the other side as it barked at something Ferenc couldn't discern.

"What's the matter? What can you see?"

Max barked a few more times before sniffing around. Ferenc stepped down onto the stairs to see if he could get a better look, but he still couldn't spot what'd made the dog go into a frenzy. Max sniffed the ground and the air, gradually making its way back to the porch.

"Crazy dog . . ." he muttered to himself while shaking his head. The masked person hadn't returned after all.

With a yawn, he slowly extended his forearm to start his elbow exercises when Max barked again, darting beneath the porch. A great cacophony followed as one of the large and heavy garbage bins stored beneath fell over.

"Max!"

He rushed down the stairs as Max continued to bark. There, cowering behind the equally large recycle bin like a frightened and cornered animal, was Dormouse.

"Jesus Chr—" Ferenc started, snatching the dog by its red collar to save Dormouse. "Max!"

The dog barked and whined, tugging and pulling, but Ferenc wouldn't give in, despite the intensifying pain from his fracture.

"I'm sorry," he said, casting her an apologetic look, "Max normally isn't like this."

Max yanked with perseverance, forcing Ferenc to let go with a hiss of pain on his lips. Dormouse squeaked again as the dog playfully threw its front paws forward and its backside in the air before continuing with its barking. Ferenc wedged himself between the dog and the girl, grabbing Max's collar again.

"Get out from beneath the porch," he instructed Dormouse. She scampered out, pressing herself flat against the fence, eyes wide. Ferenc lost his grip, and Max darted for her again. Dormouse clamped her eyes shut and shielded her face, but Ferenc lunged to stand between her and the dog once more.

"Max! What is your problem? Get back in the house!" he scolded. Head down and tail between its legs, the excitable dog obeyed.

A jarring jolt of pain coursed through Ferenc's body, originating from his fracture that pulsed with displeasure. He swallowed down the pain as best he could before turning to Dormouse, her arms still raised defensively. There she was, safe and sound.

Her eyes shot open, and slowly, she peeked up past her arms at him.

"Are you all right?" he asked. Dormouse only nodded, her breathing shallow. "I'm sorry about Max. She's never done that before . . ." he added, running his fingers through his hair and glancing back at the dog, who straightened and wagged her tail excitedly when she met his gaze.

"She?"

"Yeah." His hand dropped down to his side to ease the suffering in his collarbone as he turned back to her. "My ex got me a dog for Christmas one year. We named him Max, but later found out that he was a she. We kept the name, though. Short for Maxine, I guess." He grinned.

The corners of her lips tugged slightly in an attempt at a smile but quickly caved in as she retreated in her invisible shell like he'd seen her do a few times now. Her attention fell to the side, and she brought her hands to her shoulders, hugging herself.

"I . . . I should go," she started.

He really wanted to ask why she'd been sneaking around his house, but he figured she'd probably run off without so much as an explanation. Something unidentifiable stuck to her hair, more than likely from when she'd hidden in the dumpster from the strange monsters. His heart skipped a beat, and his brows drew together in concern.

"Are you hurt?"

She didn't answer, which caused his heart to start racing in fear. The masked figure must've returned after he'd left. He raised a hand and ever so gently hooked his index finger beneath her chin to get her to look at him. She flinched as her focus darted to him.

"Dormouse, did they hurt you?"

She pulled her head away. "No. I just . . ." She shut her eyes.

Ferenc let out a breath in relief. So, the creatures hadn't returned. Or, if they had, they must not have found her during the night. His mind reeled with countless questions and thoughts, but eventually came to a pause at a specific idea.

"How about I make you some breakfast?" he suggested with a gentle smile.

She flicked her attention back to him before flitting it toward the dog at the sliding door. Her fingers found her lips, and she began chewing on her nails.

"She meant no harm, I promise. The way she moved, she was just really excited and wanted to get your attention."

Dormouse tilted her head some, as if weighing her options.

"I can lock her in the laundry room, if you want," he added. He wasn't too fond of the thought, but if it would make Dormouse more comfortable, he could compromise—and make it up to Max later.

"No, it's—it's all right. She doesn't need to be locked up."

Relieved, heat radiated through his chest, but it still didn't change the fact that Max made her uneasy. He'd have to keep a close eye on the dog. He climbed the steps, turning to make sure Dormouse followed.

"Go lie down," he said to Max—who'd gotten up from her seated position, tail wagging like never before—as he approached. He repeated himself a few times before Max finally padded through the kitchen and down the stairs into the living room.

He then turned back to Dormouse, who stood near the top of the stairs, chewing on her fingernails while staring into his home.

"What would you like for breakfast?" he tried.

There he was with that small talk again. He'd always hated it and couldn't figure out what it was about Dormouse that was making him do it.

She didn't answer, however. He could see how either Max or entering a stranger's house could be a little disconcerting. But when he took a step toward her, she flinched.

Ferenc lowered his voice. "I don't want to force you into anything that makes you uncomfortable."

He could tell it was a hard decision for her to make, and his heart sank when she glanced over her shoulder, the gesture becoming more familiar to him now. Her hand dropped away from her mouth, and she flexed her fingers before forming fists. That was it: shoulders tense, determined gaze, foot lifting . . . she'd chosen to run.

But when she stepped forward instead—toward him, toward his home—his mind went fuzzy in surprise before he stepped aside, allowing her inside.

"Right," he said, reeling his mind back in as he followed, shutting the sliding door behind him. "A little bit of everything, then, for breakfast."

CHAPTER 12
Ferenc

There was nothing quite like a home-cooked meal when there was someone to share it with. After putting on a T-shirt and downing his pain killers, Ferenc had cooked up some fluffy scrambled eggs, thick, chewy bacon, and buttered wheat toast, which he'd set on plates with thin slices of tomato and sharp cheddar. He'd also brewed a fresh pot of coffee, which he'd offered alongside a pitcher of orange juice.

He'd even started some small talk again while he moved about the kitchen—first going on about the weather, then shifting to the food and people at the diner, which finally got Dormouse joining in on the conversation.

Once served, she'd attacked her plate in silence just as quickly as she'd eaten the cheesecake the night before. With the bag of frozen peas resting atop his collarbone, Ferenc poked his fork in and out of his scrambled eggs with an unfocused stare.

"I haven't made this kind of big breakfast in a while," he said, a faint smile tugging at the corner of his lips before it vanished. "I used to make it every Sunday."

"Why'd you stop?" she asked, barely audible, her mouth full of toast.

The memories replayed in his mind: Amy, sitting across the table from him in nothing but a pair of white panties and one of his T-shirts she'd claimed as her own, thick brown curls dancing over her shoulders as she threw her head back in raucous laughter at something he'd said. Her laughter was always so infectious, and he couldn't help joining in every single time. They'd spend hours in the kitchen on the Sundays he was home, enjoying one another's company as they ate, told stories, had water fights while doing dishes . . .

His brows knitted together in a frown. He couldn't, for the life of him, figure out what had gone wrong. She'd claimed it was his love of the sky and how he spent more time there than with her, but he'd been like that long before he'd met her. He inhaled deeply before answering.

"Because she left me." Dormouse said nothing, but he didn't need her to. "Suddenly, cooking breakfast for two didn't matter anymore. Even cooking breakfast for myself was a challenge. But here we are—it's Sunday, I've made a big breakfast for two again . . ." He looked up at Dormouse for a moment, but all he saw was a ghostly image of Amy overlaid atop of her. "And I have court tomorrow because of her."

Amy had known of his obsession with the sky, and for years, he was convinced it'd never bothered her. She'd never said anything. It was as if she'd woken up one day with less love, excitement, and interest. Their relationship struggled from that point forward; her indifference only grew from there, and it eventually broke everything apart.

Dormouse muttered something. Ferenc blinked, slowly pulled from his thoughts as though wading through sludge, until the overlaid image vanished, and he stared at his petite homeless guest instead. "I'm sorry, what?"

"The food." She pointed to her empty plate. "For something you haven't made in a while, it's good."

He cleared his throat before letting out a faint chuckle. Had he been making her uncomfortable while lost in his memories? "Thank you," he replied with a genuine smile.

They fell back into an awkward silence as he finished his breakfast. His mind raced as she brought her nails back to her teeth. What could he possibly start talking about now? She'd seemed comfortable talking about the diner earlier, but before he could speak more on the subject, a soft mutter escaped her.

"Could I . . ." she started.

She occasionally wrinkled her nose and ping-ponged her gaze everywhere, avoiding eye contact in her internal conflict.

When she pulled her fingers away from her mouth in favor of fidgeting with a scratch on the surface of the table instead, he gently set a hand atop of both of hers. She stiffened as her focus finally fell back on him.

"Don't be afraid," he reassured her with a soft smile.

"I'd like to borrow . . ."

Her words were painfully slow and drawn out, and he could only imagine how she must've been trying to pick and choose the correct words. But he wasn't impatient with her in the least. He didn't rush her or try to put words in her mouth by attempting to guess.

"I need . . . water," she finally said. "To . . . to wash up. Please."

She skewed her face in obvious discomfort. He lightly squeezed her hands before getting to his feet.

"Of course you can take a shower." He set the bag of peas on the table and offered her his hand to help her up. "Come on, let me show you to the bathroom."

He led her down the stairs and into the hallway, to the first door on the left. He grabbed navy-blue towels and a washcloth from the linen closet door on the opposite wall, then found her chewing her nails once more as she openly stared, silently taking in the immense bathroom.

An amused smile crept to his lips as he set everything down on the marble countertop. He found the unidentified object caked in her hair, and his gaze traveled down to her filthy clothing as images of the previous night—how she'd hid from the beasts by covering herself with garbage from the dumpster—flashed through his mind.

"Would you like me to wash your clothes?" he offered. "Unfortunately, I don't have any that will fit you as Amy took every last piece of hers with her, but I can lend you a shirt and another towel that you can wrap around as a—"

"No, that's . . ." she started, pressing her elbows into her sides to make her body as small as possible.

"Nobody's going to hurt you, Dormouse. I won't let them. And I won't hurt you either. You're safe here. Okay?" She dropped her attention to her feet. "I don't want to force you to do anything you don't want to do. I'll leave you alone to clean up or take a shower or whatever you want to do. If you'd like me to wash your clothes, just leave them outside the door, and I'll get them, all right?"

She nodded without lifting her eyes, and he stepped away, heading back to the kitchen.

He grabbed his cigarettes and lighter and called for Max, who bounded up the stairs excitedly. Once outside, he sat in his chair, wincing in discomfort from his sore muscles, and for once, he willingly allowed his thoughts to go into overdrive since his accident.

His mind replayed everything he'd said and done during breakfast, recalling every detail about Dormouse he'd remembered when looking at her instead of the food.

He liked that she hadn't anxiously looked over her shoulder once since entering his house, despite Max's earlier strange behavior. She'd been so relaxed, despite the awkward silence, small talk, and discomfort in asking for a shower . . .

A soft chuckle escaped him when he'd caught himself smiling, as if he'd enjoyed every moment. And he had to be honest—he had. It'd been a while since he could genuinely admit it to himself.

When he returned inside, Max on his heels, a small pile of fabrics lay crumpled in front of the bathroom door. The familiar sprinkle of the shower grew louder as he approached, and he picked up her clothes before continuing to the last room down the hall.

After spraying the stains and tossing them in the washer, he grabbed a short-sleeved checkered shirt hanging nearby and a folded towel stacked atop the dryer, setting them where the discarded clothes had previously been.

He thought about knocking on the door and asking if she was all right, but he decided against it. He'd told her he'd leave her alone, after all. He moved on to the living room, where Max lay curled up on the rug, and slowly dropped himself onto the leather recliner. He grabbed the book of crossword puzzles and blue pen laying on the coffee table next to him and began filling one page out.

The shower water finally stopped about halfway through his puzzle, and he was about three-quarters done when the bathroom door creaked open ever so slightly.

He carefully leaned over the arm of the chair to peek out down the hall, but all he saw was a slow and careful hand pulling the shirt and towel inside the bathroom before the door shut once more. The corner of his mouth quirked upward, and he engrossed himself back into his puzzle.

He returned to the back room when the washer finished and placed the tiny load in the dryer. As he stepped by the bathroom on his way back to the couch, the door opened.

He paused in his steps as the sauna-like heat and steam radiated out of the room. Dormouse wiggled her toes as she turned her feet inward. He slowly followed up her stick-like legs to the towel that hung below her knees, up to the loosely buttoned shirt, and to the wet, wavy strands of hair hanging past her shoulders. When his eyes finally met hers, it was only for a split second as she looked away, her cheeks flushing.

"Can I get you anything?" he asked. She shook her head, and he gently added, "Come. Let's have a seat until the dryer's done."

He led her to the living room, where she sat on the edge of the couch, as close to the armrest as she could. Her hands fell in her lap, clasped together, and she fidgeted with the hem of the towel.

"Do you feel better?"

Dormouse neither reacted nor replied, to which his stomach knotted up. She was still acting like something was wrong. He'd missed something.

"Are you all right?"

With a barely detectable nod, her lips twitched upward, but her hand soon covered them as she bit at her nails once more. "I was as red as a lobster. I was afraid to come out," she stated, looking everywhere but at him.

He kept a straight face as relief washed over him, but all he really wanted to do was laugh to hide his embarrassment. He'd misjudged, gone overboard. And as someone analytical, it was highly unlike him. A hand combed through his hair before he spoke again. "Amy used to take hot showers. She'd only get out once the hot water ran out."

"What happened between you and Amy? If y-you don't mind telling me."

Memories of Amy danced around in his mind, making it their home until forcefully evicted when he could handle it no more. "I . . . I'm not sure." His voice went quiet for a moment before returning. "Everything was going fine, and then it wasn't. Or maybe it never was, and I was just oblivious." With a sudden lack of energy, his chin dropped to his chest, and he stared at his empty hands. "She said I was never around, even when I was."

Dormouse muttered an apology, and he swiftly shook his head, his focus back on her.

"No, you have nothing to apologize for. You didn't do anything. It was all me, apparently." He frowned for a split second, then changed the subject altogether. "So," he started, clearing his throat before continuing. "What are your plans for the day?"

65

"I have no plans. I just do stuff. Go places." She shrugged. "And watch my back."

His lips drew into a thin line. He'd hate to need to watch his back constantly. It must've been exhausting. And with whatever the hell those creatures were, he wasn't sure he'd last very long.

He watched her in silence, his mind going a million miles a second as she continued to fidget with the navy towel. Being homeless, there must've been a safe place for her to stay, somewhere beasts or people couldn't find her. He licked his dry lips, carefully formulating his question.

"Can I take you to your next destination?"

She lifted her attention to him for a second before it fell back down into her lap and her fingers found their way back to her lips.

He wanted her to be safe. She seemed comfortable enough there with him, inside his house. At least, he hoped she was. And so, opening his house to her only seemed logical.

"You can stay here as long as you want. There's a spare bedroom down the hall—"

"No." Wide eyes flicked back to him before her expression contorted. "No, I . . ."

He couldn't blame her for being as quick to decline as she did. After all, they were still strangers to one another. Acquaintances, at best.

"Remember, I'm not forcing you to do anything. It's just an offer. I don't know what those things were or why they were after you, but you're safe here." Or so he hoped. "Listen, I'll set up the spare bedroom for you. I'll even leave the sliding door unlocked at all times. You can come here whenever you want, all right?"

Dormouse didn't answer. Her thick brows pulled in, and she shut her eyes, trailing her hand from her mouth to her forehead to rub at it.

There was that internal battle of hers again, clear as day. He didn't know what else to say to convince her he wasn't a dangerous man, that he had no interest in harming her or taking advantage of her. Maybe she'd feel better about it if she earned her stay instead.

He parted his lips to make an offer, but a rather loud and obnoxious buzzer interrupted him. Dormouse jumped—skittish as ever—but Ferenc offered a reassuring smile as he stood.

"Your clothes are ready."

CHAPTER 13
Ferenc

The faint creak of the bathroom door sent a flood of relief rushing through Ferenc's body and mind. Dormouse was still in his house . . . and she was still alive.

She'd returned to the bathroom to change back into her own clothes, but after ten minutes, she hadn't reemerged.

He couldn't blame her. That face-scrunching internal battle she'd been having with herself had probably been made more complicated with the offer of staying for as long as she liked. She was probably still torn about it.

After fifteen minutes, a stray thought had ventured through his mind: was she even still in the house? Maybe she'd escaped through the window so she didn't have to face him again. But as quickly as the thought had appeared, he'd dismissed it.

At the twenty-minute mark, he'd contemplated knocking on the door and checking to see if she was still breathing. He hadn't thought to ask if she was allergic to any of the food he'd made or the detergent or fabric softener, and he didn't know about any underlying health conditions.

But he'd promised to leave her alone. He knew she needed space . . . but what if?

So when she'd finally emerged twenty-five minutes later and made her way back to the couch, he set his book and pen down and watched her in silence, hoping his reassurance wasn't outwardly visible.

She sat with her hands clenched in her lap, never once meeting his gaze, before bringing her arm up to her face.

His stomach dropped in dread. She must've taken so long because she'd been crying. "What's wrong?"

She finally looked at him before muttering, "It smells good. The clothes, I mean." Ferenc's tense body relaxed as she continued. "It's been a while since I've smelled freshly cleaned clothes. When mine get too nasty for me, I just steal myself something new. It never smells this good, though." She surreptitiously sniffed the fresh rain fragrance once more.

"Aren't you afraid of getting caught?" he asked.

She shrugged her tiny shoulders. When he raised a suspicious brow at her nonchalance, unconvinced by the act, she was quick to look away once more, flushing pink in the cheeks.

"I am," she admitted, barely audible. "But I'm less afraid of that than I am of . . ."

She trailed off, chewing at her fingernails again, her other palm restlessly rubbing against her jeans. He didn't need to imagine what she was referring to.

He'd tried not to talk about it during their breakfast earlier—he hadn't wanted her to run away—but the burning questions had been eating at him since he first saw the masked man and unearthly creatures the night before. He *had* to know.

"Who are they?" he finally asked. "*What* are they? And why were they after you?"

She shut her eyes, and he could have sworn her breath came out in a shudder. "I don't know." Her trembling voice barely came out above a whisper. When she opened her eyes, tears threatened to fall. "I don't know where they came from, and I don't know why they're targeting me because I didn't do anything. I don't have any money, and I don't—"

"Have you filed a police report?"

"Who would believe me?" she squeaked. "They'd lock me up for being delusional, and who knows how far this person's power extends!"

His brain stumbled at her words as she suddenly stood, startling Max, and paced through the living room. He'd never even considered the possibility of some sort of criminal infiltration. He probably would've deemed her paranoid—delusional, even—had he not seen the uncanny chase for himself. The beasts, controlled by the masked individual, were adamant about hunting her down. Unable

68

to think up any options or ideas at that moment, Ferenc got to his own feet, causing Dormouse to pause in her steps.

"You're safe here. You know that, right?"

Dormouse's glazed expression proved she was in her own head and hadn't heard a word he said. He reached out and gently placed a hand on her shoulder, causing her to flinch back so hard, she stumbled into the wall.

"Whoa! Hey! It's okay!" His own hands innocently flew up near his head, and he gritted his teeth in pain from his own sudden movement. Even Max had jumped up, huffing at the commotion. Ferenc bit down on the pain in favor of calming her down. "I won't hurt you," he reminded her. "I won't let anyone or anything hurt you."

She trembled like a leaf, staring at him with wide eyes. At least she was out of her head, but all he could do was offer a soft smile. He couldn't convince her any more than he already had; she'd have to trust her gut.

"Let me get you a glass of water."

He took a few steps backward before climbing the stairs, where he was quick to fill a tall glass with tap water from the kitchen. When he returned, she was sitting on the couch again, and Max sat so closely, they were almost touching. He handed Dormouse the water, then scratched Max behind the ear.

"See? Even Max is willing to protect you." Dormouse took a slow sip, the water barely wetting her lips. "Are you okay?" he asked, his brows knitting in concern. She nodded ever so slightly before dropping her attention down to her lap.

There wasn't much more he could do. He couldn't keep pushing her to trust him, and he couldn't keep up with the small talk anymore. It was his turn to pull into his mind and get lost in his thoughts.

"I'm gonna go do the dishes."

Ferenc almost allowed a sigh of defeat to follow his words, but he held strong, for her sake and his own. With a single nod—more to himself than anything—he returned to the kitchen.

It took a half hour for the area to be spotless once more, and in all that time, Dormouse hadn't once joined him. He forced aside his current thoughts to focus on her once more, hoping everything was well.

When he reached the living room, he found her napping, curled up on the couch with Max still at her side, keeping watch. A fond smile found its way to Ferenc's lips. She must've been exhausted. He approached, gently pulling down the woven throw that hung over the top of the couch and covered her with it. She stirred slightly but became quiet again.

He watched her sleep for a few minutes, her body gently rising and falling beneath the throw with each breath. She seemed so peaceful. He couldn't imagine having to sleep with one eye open every night. He'd be worn out and weary only after a couple days. She deserved better, and the least he could do for her was allow her to rest for as long as she needed.

He quietly made his way to the deck, leaving the door open to listen for Dormouse, or in case Max wanted out. He allowed more of his thoughts to flow as he stretched his elbow a few times, as per his physical therapist's request.

He'd really gotten himself into something. There had to be a reasonable explanation for the monsters, but no matter how he analyzed the scene repeatedly in his mind, no matter how much research he'd done the night before, he couldn't figure it out. Maybe he needed to ignore it and move on.

No. He couldn't do that to Dormouse. He couldn't explain why he felt such a supernatural attachment to someone he'd just met— such a sense of protective duty—but he knew he *wanted* to keep her safe. It was the right thing to do.

After his cigarette, Ferenc returned to the living room to check on her. Nothing had changed. Satisfied, he headed for the upstairs bathroom, where he washed up, shaved, and changed out of his T-shirt and sweats for something a little more proper.

He'd just sat down in his armchair, pen in hand, ready to continue to fill out more puzzle grids, when a gasp came from the couch, followed by a panicked whimper. His gaze shot to Dormouse as she flailed beneath the throw.

"You're safe! I'm here."

She continued to struggle, her breaths turning shallow in her panic, before scampering to her feet after finally having escaped. Ferenc jumped up, arms extended out protectively as he kept his distance.

"Dormouse," he tried again, "it's just me."

70

His words fell on deaf ears as she seemed blinded, lost in her mind. She lunged at him as if she were a trapped animal.

He blinked in surprise, caught off guard by her sudden urge to fend him off. Not wanting to fight back in case he accidentally hurt her, he took a few steps back until his heel hit the wall behind him. He didn't want her to hurt *him* either, what with his broken collar-bone.

He had to do something, and quickly.

In one swift motion, he snatched her wrist with his good hand, pulling her into himself before wrapping his arms around her—one snaking about her back, the other holding her head up against his chest.

"It's okay, you're all right," he said, wincing from the pain. "It's just me."

She froze in his grip. Her body was so tense, he could've sworn she'd turned into a statue. Still, he continued to hold her until she forcefully pulled away. Unfortunately, he was met with flaring nostrils and a scowl.

"Why are you so nice to me?" She stepped away from him, bringing her arms up to her shoulders to hug herself, clearly on the verge of tears. "You've paid back the kindness owed by saving me last night. Isn't that *enough*?"

At first, Ferenc didn't know what to say. He was nice to her because being nice was the good, human thing to do.

"Is that what this is about? Equivalent exchange?" He reached out for her, but she swatted his hand away as she took a step back. "I wasn't even thinking about paying your kindness back when I tried stopping those creatures from chasing you. All that mattered was your safety because that's who I am. I would've done the same thing were it anyone else." He purposely left out how he also felt a strange sense of commitment toward her.

"No, you're indebting me! I can't—I can't afford to pay you back!"

"Dormouse . . ." he started.

Tears streamed down her cheeks, and she looked insulted, as if he'd just slapped her in the face. He tried reaching out for her again, but she darted away toward the stairs.

"Dormouse!"

He barely snatched her wrist, which stopped her dead in her tracks. She spun back around with the deadliest of glares, full of loathing and hatred, before her face turned more pallid than it already was, and she began trembling.

"Let go of me," she pleaded, her voice tremorous.

His hand immediately released her as his heart skipped a beat at what he'd done. He parted his lips to apologize, but she immediately scampered up the stairs and into the kitchen, where she slid the glass door open and ran out, leaving him standing alone, confused, and worried.

He wouldn't chase after her. He told himself he'd give her space. Hell, he told *her* that, yet there he'd been, snatching her wrist, trying to stop her. He needed her to figure out on her own that he wasn't the bad guy, that he would never hurt her, and that he only wanted her safety.

Max whined beside him, pulling him back to the moment at hand. With a groan, Ferenc ran a hand through his hair before rubbing around his throbbing fracture. He needed painkillers and a cigarette.

CHAPTER 14
Olivia

Olivia was being stood up. She'd abandoned everything on a crazy whim—her home, her friends and family, her job—and had come all this way . . . and for what?

She'd wanted to give him time to mull over everything she'd said. In those few hours after checking out of her hotel room that morning, she'd homed in on her tug—purposely following it or pulling back, testing it, experimenting with the sensation deep inside.

And now she sat alone on that large piece of driftwood along the quieting beach, the pull no more active than it'd been in the last two hours.

To be fair, Ferenc had practically told her he'd stand her up when he'd asked what she'd do if he didn't show. She'd gotten frustrated by his words—had thought the whole thing was ridiculous and impulsively stormed off in anger—but she was stubborn and headstrong. She couldn't just abandon this idea, this *urge*.

Wherever Ferenc was, it was nearby. The closer she'd gotten to the ocean from the hotel room, the more that invisible draw had strengthened. At first, she thought he was already at the beach, but she never felt that same indescribable and conscious awareness she'd had when he'd run her over with his jet or when he'd touched her shoulder the night before. Her search was thinning; she'd eventually find that needle in the haystack.

She slipped her bare feet back into her flats and downed the rest of her cooled coffee. The increasingly bitter taste made her miss the spicy Mexican mochas from back home. Olivia stood from the washed-up log and headed toward the main street along the beach, tossing her empty cup into the plastic trash bin along the way.

She followed the tug, slowly turning down side streets, testing the pull until she got closer and closer, until that feeling was nearly suffocating.

Finally, while down in a very California-like neighborhood that screamed *more-money-than-one-knew-what-to-do-with*, she paused in front of a huge, well-kept property and a large two-story house with numerous wide windows that allowed as much access to the sky as possible.

Olivia's heart hammered against her chest whenever she tried to urge herself to move forward. Her imagination ran wild with possible scenarios, from her being completely wrong and it not being his house, to the reason he stood her up was because he'd thought her certifiably crazy and wanted nothing to do with her antics.

She swallowed hard. No, now was not the time to second-guess herself. She'd always been confident. At least she'd always been *before* finding out she had special abilities.

It was now or never.

As she marched closer to the house, the flutter in her stomach grew stronger, and a flicker from behind caught her attention. She paused and looked over her shoulder, but there was nothing out of the ordinary, so she continued on.

Her feet firmly on the concrete platform just outside the front door, she raised a hand to knock, but the flicker occurred once more. She spun around as every single streetlight blinked up and down the street. A brow raised before her eyes narrowed.

The fluctuating brightness matched the nervous palpitations of her heart, and just as she went to move and inspect the strange occurrence closer, the front door opened. She couldn't tell if the startled scream that escaped her was because of Ferenc's sudden appearance or because of the lights shattering all along the street.

"Jesus Chr—" he started, grabbing at his chest. "You scared the crap out of me."

"I scared *you*?" Her heart practically pounded right out of her chest as she whipped back to face him.

"The lights were going haywire in the house, so I came to see what was going on, only to find you standing out here. What the hell happened? What are you even doing here? How did you find my house?"

74

"I . . ." she started, her mind whirling over everything from the last few seconds. She then cleared her throat. "I told you to meet me at the beach, but you stood me up, so I followed that feeling I get all the way here." Olivia peeked over her shoulder at the shattered streetlights before adding, "As for that, I *think* that was me. I think it was from my own personal electric field."

"Your own personal *chaos field* is more like it." He eyed her suspiciously before he moved to the side, allowing her to step inside. "Let me grab the candles."

She heard his movement but quickly lost sight of him in the darkness until a soft glow danced along the walls. Ferenc reappeared, setting a plate of white tea lights onto a small wooden stand by the door.

"Are you ready?" she asked.

Ferenc blinked in confusion. "For what?"

"To ask me anything."

He brought a hand up to comb through his hair before it trailed down to the nape of his neck. "Are you kidding me?" he said, exasperated.

"No." A knot formed in the pit of her stomach. It seemed he'd definitely had no intention of following up with her, that he had no interest in anything she'd said the night before and had simply been humoring her.

That irritation she'd felt when she'd stomped off the previous night returned, boiling and churning inside of her. It wasn't Ferenc she was annoyed with—it was the situation in general and her helplessness around it. But it wasn't like she could ignore her newfound abilities and the urge that'd brought her all the way to him.

"Look . . ." Ferenc started. "I'm sorry. I have a lot on my mind and haven't really thought about our conversation much. Come on in."

He picked up the plate of candles, and Olivia followed him into the living room, where a golden retriever stood with its tail wagging excitedly and a stuffed toy in its mouth.

"That's Max," he introduced, as he motioned for her to take a seat.

The candlelight intensified the coziness of the living room, and she couldn't help but smile as she sat on the pale leather couch nearest him and his armchair. Her eyes traveled past the large roof windows on the adjacent side to the potted palm next to the loveseat,

75

then to the flatscreen sitting atop a wooden entertainment center opposite where she sat, the model airplanes on the shelves overtop, and finally to the ceiling-to-floor window next to everything.

"Wow," she said, truly in awe. "Nice place."

"Thanks."

Max dropped the toy at her feet, and she smiled, petting the dog's head. Her attention then went back to Ferenc, and her lips had parted to speak, but she stopped herself. He was fidgeting, focused on smoothing out folds in his pants as his heels bounced.

This wasn't like him. Granted, she didn't really know him, but based on his observant and analytical style the previous night, something was bothering him. She didn't doubt it had to do with her and her abilities.

"What's on your mind?" she asked, tilting her head.

"Don't worry about it, it's—it's nothing."

It wasn't nothing. That much was clear.

Ferenc stood back up and disappeared, leaving her alone with the dog. She didn't know if she was supposed to follow. He rummaged about elsewhere in the house, and when she got to her feet to check, he'd returned with a frozen pack of peas slung over his shoulder.

"I can help with that," Olivia said, pointing to the makeshift ice pack.

"Help how? Unless you can miraculously heal fractures, then there's not much—"

"But I *can* heal fractures," she cut in, stepping toward him. "I mean . . . it's not instantaneous, but it'll heal faster. And after a few rounds, you'll be good as new."

This was it. This was her chance to pull him back to her side. If she could use her abilities *on* him instead of in front of him, maybe he'd not only believe her, but maybe he'd also remember being a guardian.

It was worth a shot. She didn't know what else to do or where else to go. She was stuck in her mission until either the guardian side of him returned or she found the elemental.

Olivia gently reached for his hand, her pinky finger making contact with his skin. Tiny bolts of static followed her finger as she hooked it around his, keeping him steady as she felt him pulling away.

"Relax," she said, a smirk tugging as he furrowed his brows. "I'm not coming on to you; I'm going to help heal you."

"It's kind of hard for me to relax right now."

"I know. You have a lot on your mind."

Maybe he could benefit from a good calming session as well. He was no help to her without remembering his guardian side, and without a clear mind, she'd continue getting nowhere.

Her fingers slowly trailed up his hand and forearm, and Ferenc's attention fell to her movement. A red trail and little electrical currents followed her touch like a plasma ball. She continued to trace her tingling fingertips up toward his shoulder as her free hand removed the bag of peas, dropping it onto the coffee table.

She gently ran her fingers over his collarbone beneath his white T-shirt, pausing at the fracture. Shifting her ability, she allowed electromagnetic fields of low frequency to pulse across the break.

He was still tense, standing still as a statue. She could practically feel his stare, but she refused to look at him until she shifted her abilities and resumed the static trail. She could almost see the gears turning until his eyes fluttered shut and he gave a shuddered exhale when she reached the nape of his neck. The tension in his body instantly melted away, and she gave a small smile as she used her other hand to trail down the other side of his neck.

He'd needed this.

Her fingers continued across his shoulder and down his arm, focusing once more on the task at hand. She loved how aware of everything she was: the snaps from the static, the warming of her blood, the current coursing through her veins. She wondered if Ferenc could feel it as well since his arm hair stood on edge, his flesh blanketed with goosebumps.

When she finished trailing down his arm to his hand, she pulled away, severing the connection. The tingle in her fingertips faded as Ferenc swayed, his eyelids heavy as he tried to open them.

"Was it good for you?" she asked, her lips tugging in one corner.

The only answer Ferenc could give was a mixture of a sigh and a moan and maybe a yes in there somewhere.

"I gave you a little more than you needed, but . . ." Her touch was no longer electric as she took both of his hands in hers, leading him forward. "Come. Let's get you to your couch before you fall over."

She helped him onto the couch, where he instantly fell asleep. She hoped it worked.

"Sleep well, Guardian. I'll see you tomorrow."

CHAPTER 15
Ferenc

He couldn't remember the last time he'd had such restful sleep. Even his muscles, usually so stiff since his accident, were soothed and quiet. Ferenc slowly opened his eyes, staring out the large roof windows that revealed a cloudless blue sky.

His mind tried to rewind over the events of the previous night as he sat up, slowly and carefully stretching his arms over his head. His fracture didn't hurt as much.

All at once, it came flooding back: Olivia had done something to him. She'd worked some sort of unbelievable and unexplainable magic.

"The power came back on shortly after ten last night," came a woman's voice.

His heart skipped a beat, and he jumped up from the couch, startled, as his mind sluggishly tried to associate the voice with a face. He found a familiar freckled person looking down at him from the railing in the kitchen, and he brought a hand up to his spinning head, allowing his guard to drop once more.

"What do you want, Amy?"

"Wow," she replied. "Cranky, much?"

With a frazzled frown, he tried to wrap his mind around everything. "How long have you been here?"

"Since you missed our court hearing."

His stomach dropped as panic seized him, adrenaline shooting through his system. He must not have set his alarm. And if anyone had called to check up on him, he hadn't heard it. He'd never slept through everything like that before.

79

He instantly reached into his pant pockets, only to come out empty-handed. His chest felt suffocatingly tight as he shot his gaze to the small table next to his recliner, relief only partially soothing him as he found his phone. Ferenc snatched it from the table and hissed his discontent to find his phone off.

It had either died, or Olivia's electrical mojo had fried it.

"Your phone was going straight to voice mail," she said, after having descended the stairs.

He held the power button, and his phone started right up, vibrating to life from a few missed calls, voice mails, and dozens of text messages. He didn't remember shutting off the device, and his heart pounded as his mind dizzily raced at how he was going to have to somehow explain all of it to his lawyer.

Amy came to a stop in front of him, her brown eyes hard and one hand on her hip. "I stopped by to see what was going on when I saw the front door wide open. I was worried . . ."

His attention darted to the front door, which was closed. He didn't understand how it'd been left open. Olivia must not have shut it properly when she left.

"Worried about me?" he asked as he looked back at her. She'd been so cold toward him lately that worrying about him almost seemed foreign.

"No!" She huffed. "About poor Max! She could've run off and gotten lost!"

He rolled his eyes and stepped past her, heading for the kitchen. Of course she wasn't worried about him. He grabbed his cigarettes and lighter from the counter and reached for the handle of the sliding door. When he pulled, the door didn't budge.

With all the strange things that'd happened in the past few minutes, he knew with one hundred percent certainty that he hadn't locked the sliding door just in case Dormouse came back. He turned to face Amy, who was close behind.

"Did you lock this?"

"Um, yeah," she replied in a matter-of-fact tone. "You in the habit of leaving doors unlocked, now?"

Ferenc took a deep, calming breath before unlocking the door, then sliding it open and stepping outside. She was grating on his last nerve, which never happened, but he deemed it because he was still frazzled about her sudden presence in his house. His lawyer had instructed him to avoid taking the bait and being drawn into any kind of conflict or arguments with her. Naturally the quiet type, it hadn't been a problem for him, especially as he'd always had a tough time outwardly dealing with his emotions. And Amy knew that.

After setting everything down onto the wicker table, he lit himself a cigarette and took a well-deserved inhale.

"At least you're still smoking outside."

He was unsure if her comments were a scolding or a praise. They could've even been a threat. He didn't know anymore. "Why do you even care?" he retorted, and instantly regretted it.

"Wow, you *are* cranky. Go back to bed."

She wheeled around to go back inside, but Ferenc shot out his good arm, grabbing her by the wrist before he could even utter his apology. The glare Amy shot him when she whirled back could have killed him on the spot, were they lasers. And he almost wished they were.

"Get your hand off me before I have to file a restraining order against you." Her voice was laced with poison.

He instantly released her, but he had to do a double take at her words. "Excuse me? Need I remind you that *you* broke into *my* house?"

"I didn't break in. I have a key, remember? And what part of 'the door was wide open' did you not understand?"

He stared at her long and hard as he took another drag. She'd claimed the door was wide open but had also told him what time the power had come back on. Living in the next city over, she wouldn't have known the power was even out. And with how vehemently she hated him, he couldn't see her randomly driving by. But if she had, she should've seen the open door then.

"I'll be taking that key back," he finally said after blowing the smoke away from her, holding his palm out expectantly.

Amy took a step back, her mouth falling open, appalled, before her thin brows pinched together in disgust.

Ferenc heaved a heavy sigh as he scrubbed a hand over his scruffy face. There was that self-loathing regret that usually came with dealing with his emotions, especially those revolved around Amy not being happy. And he'd always had a tough time coping with his feelings.

"I'm sorry," he said. "Look, I just—this has to end. Whatever *this* is. I'm sorry I hurt you."

81

"Do you even know why you're apologizing?" she snapped, stomping back into the kitchen for her expensive white purse, retrieving her keys to give back the one to his house.

"No," he replied from the deck, taking another long drag. There wasn't enough nicotine in the world to cope with his current stress level. "Truthfully, I don't. I never did know what I did, or didn't do, or whatever. All I know is that I accidentally hurt you, and you're turning that back on me tenfold."

"Sorry doesn't cut it." She marched back over to him and shoved the key against his chest, which he almost dropped as he fumbled to catch it.

"Amy, I love you . . ."

"And I *loved* you, Ferenc. You have no idea how much I did."

She brought her arms to cross over her chest, but she rubbed at them instead, hugging herself and looking ever so vulnerable. He didn't think there were any pieces of his broken heart left to reciprocate in her sadness, but there she was, tugging at his heartstrings again.

He missed the way the mole on the corner of her lips danced whenever she'd laugh, or how he liked to count every single freckle that graced her beautiful complexion. He missed tangling his fingers into her curls as he tasted her lips. No matter how much he enjoyed his personal space, he'd never stopped loving her. He must've made some mistake to make her change her mind and turn so cold.

He took one final drag of his cigarette, extinguishing the butt in the nearby ashtray, never once taking his eyes off her. He then reached his hand out, slowly, gently, to caress her cheek, but she turned her head away, denying him.

Ferenc shut his eyes and drew in a long breath in irritation before loudly calling out, "Max! Come see your mother before she leaves!"

She huffed at his words and stormed back inside. Ferenc massaged his temples, and Amy's squeal and baby talk toward the golden retriever pulled him from whatever dark thought his mind tried to sneak into.

He grabbed his things, setting them on the counter before shutting the door and making sure to keep it unlocked. He watched Amy smother Max in hugs and kisses and pettings, which brought a sad smile to his lips.

"Do you want to take her for the weekend? I'm sure she'd love it, and it would allow me to rest and—"

"Oh, no," she cut in, waving him off. "Richard's allergic—" She suddenly paused.

It only took him a second to fit that puzzle piece together. "Richard? As in Richard Moyon?" His suspicions were correct when she didn't answer. "What the fuck, Amy, you're dating your lawyer?"

"Marrying him, actually, but it doesn't matter because it's none of your business." She stood back up to face him.

"Is that why you keep bleeding me for all this nonsense every now and again? You talk bad about me, and he looks in all his lawyer books to see what ridiculous loophole he can get away with pulling against me? I should tell my lawyer to mention it to the judge and have Richard recuse himself."

"But you won't."

"And why not?"

"Because you still love me, and you're a nice guy. You wouldn't dare spitefully break my heart like that."

Ferenc blinked, taken aback. He couldn't believe she so freely admitted to playing him that way. His mind went haywire, wondering how long they'd been dating that she'd so quickly get married. He even surprised himself by wondering if she'd been cheating on him.

Just as he parted his lips to retort, he paused, his thoughts screeching to a halt. "Is that what this is about? I never asked you to marry me?"

"You would *never* marry, Ferenc. Let me spell it out for you. The sky always mattered more than I ever did. Fuck, have you seen this house? With these windows, it can't be any more obvious than this! You were always so isolated and detached for days after flying, always ignoring everything and everyone. Getting you off that high and out of that lovestruck desire to return to your *sky mistress* was impossible."

The figurative dagger she'd plunged and twisted deep into him left him winded and dizzy. "Amy . . ." he started, shaking his head. Everything she'd said couldn't have been further from the truth.

"Goodbye, Ferenc." She grabbed her belongings and turned to pet Max, her tone instantly changing. "Bye, baby! You be good for Mommy, okay?" She then headed for the front door. "I'm sure your lawyer will fill you in on the repercussions for failing to show up this morning," she added over her shoulder.

And with that, she walked out.

Ferenc's eye twitched uncomfortably, and he took a breath as if it was the first one he'd taken in hours. He was going to need another cigarette.

His legs felt like they were trudging through waist-deep mud and refused to move despite only being a few steps away from the sliding door. Amy's final words weighed heavy on him—he dreaded knowing what his repercussions would be—but it was her scolding that rang loudest in his mind.

He'd been distant. That's why she'd left. He'd alienated himself so much that he missed out on his relationship with her. He rested his head up against the glass door and shut his eyes. His body began to shake as his hands formed into fists. His breathing became shallow, and his exhales trembled along with the rest of his body. He could've sworn the glass from the sliding door vibrated as well, but maybe that was his imagination.

He took a breath, then another as her words played over in his mind. His emotions pulsed until something inside his broken heart snapped. He then punched the door.

The glass shattered, crashing to the kitchen floor and spilling out onto the wooden deck. Ferenc's eyes shot open as his collarbone pulsed hot and angry, but it was quickly silenced by his bloodied fist demanding his attention.

Despite the agony, he didn't move as his heart skipped a beat and his gaze suddenly locked onto Dormouse scampering out from beneath his deck like a frightened animal, clutching herself protectively, eyes bulged in terror.

CHAPTER 16
Ferenc

He'd never felt so relieved, yet so horrified all at once. Ferenc's mind reeled as his fractured collarbone throbbed and his trembling knuckles shot sharp jolts through his arm.

Dormouse was safe and sound and alive, and he couldn't be happier about it. But if she'd been hiding beneath his deck the whole time, she must've heard his conversation with Amy. And now she'd seen his temper flare and would likely flee, never to return, fearing him the violent type.

"Dormouse, wait!" he called out, before wincing in pain.

She flinched at his words and twitched as if about to run like a frightened animal, but she didn't. Her wide, frightened eyes softened some before hardening, and she pressed her lips together as she inhaled deeply through her nose, then exhaled with a shuddered whoosh.

Her head held high in sudden determination Ferenc had never seen before, she slowly approached the deck, cautiously making her way up the steps until she reached the top.

His legs threatened to give out from beneath him as his blood sugar dropped from the adrenaline high, and he parted his lips to speak, but he didn't even know where to begin. He should begin with an apology, but he didn't know why he needed to apologize. All he really wanted to do was tell her how relieved he was that she'd returned.

He swallowed hard, and his voice barely came out above a whisper. "I was so worried about you."

She stared at him in silence, bringing her nails to her lips. He recognized that internal battle going on in her mind; she was going to run off again.

"You're hurt," she finally said, her voice no louder than his had been. The glass crunched underfoot as she carelessly approached, her petite and gaunt frame easily squeezing by until she was inside. "Where is your first aid kit?"

"I . . ."

Ferenc couldn't concentrate. He tried to be present, but his mind was retreating. It wanted to be alone. Too much had happened in such a short time, and he hadn't yet had time to process anything. Part of him wanted to drop everything and just focus on Dormouse, while another part of him wanted to walk away from it all.

Air. He needed air. He needed to be high in the sky without a care in the world. But that was what'd pushed Amy away.

The shards poking through sent an uncomfortable burning pain through his bleeding knuckle, which brought him back to the matter at hand. He licked his dry lips. "There's a kit beneath the sink," he said, tilting his head toward the kitchen counter.

Dormouse headed for the sink. Ferenc clenched his jaw as he pulled out a shard protruding from his skin in
one swift motion. He thought his teeth might shatter much like the glass did as he bit down harder to not cry out in pain.

"Sit down," Dormouse instructed as she set the red nylon bag down on the kitchen table.

It was strange to see her so firm when she usually made herself yielding, but he didn't need to be told twice. Carefully sidestepping any glass on the floor, he sat in the closest chair as Dormouse scrubbed her hands with soap and water before unzipping the kit and rummaging through the contents.

He watched her expertly pick things out, donning latex gloves before opening anything. She cleaned the tweezers with a cleansing wipe and slowly lowered herself down in the chair closest to him, reaching for his wrist.

It was Ferenc's turn to flinch, but her touch was gentle as she lifted his hand by his wrist, turning it and inspecting it in the sunlight as the glass glinted like diamonds.

"Looks like you've done this before," he casually mentioned.

Her gaze rose to his for a moment before she returned to work, grabbing the tweezers from the table. "I was a primary care nurse."

86

Ferenc stared for a moment. Dormouse had stayed instead of running, had been firm instead of yielding, and now, she'd actually broken down her defensive wall and opened up to him—albeit ever so slightly—instead of hiding behind it. A soft, satisfied smile began to form, but it was interrupted by her next words.

"So, that was your ex."

And there it was—clearly changing the subject away from herself, hiding back behind her wall.

"How much of the—*ow!*—conversation did you hear?" he asked, as she pulled a shard free.

"Enough of it. She must've made you really angry." She pulled out another piece of glass.

Amy hadn't been the one to make him angry. Sure, she'd pressed his buttons and he'd been highly irritated, but it was his self-loathing that triggered the punch. He was angry at himself.

Everyone had different ways of showing their love. Ferenc didn't need to constantly touch, kiss, or hug; he showed his affection with small actions—cooking breakfast, taking on some extra chores to free her up, filling her car's gas tank. Amy had always known that about him, but unfortunately, it seemed to have eventually pushed her away.

"There," Dormouse eventually said, removing the gloves. "I think I got it all. Go wash your hand and let me know if you feel more glass. Where's your broom and dustpan?"

"In the laundry room at the very end of the hall downstairs," he replied as he stood up and made his way to the kitchen sink.

Ferenc stood with his eyes shut, allowing the water to run over his wounds as the mixed aromas of opened antiseptic wipes and citrus-scented hand soap fought for dominance in his nostrils. The pain had dulled significantly, and for that, he was grateful. He opened his eyes to the sound of footsteps rushing up the stairs, and he watched her begin sweeping right at the first step.

When he noticed himself smiling, he turned his attention back to his hand and grabbed the soap.

It didn't take long before they were seated back at the table, most of the glass in the kitchen swept into a pile against the sliding door's frame, and all the glass in his knuckle removed from his hand. Dormouse applied ointment as he finally asked what he really wanted to know.

"How have you been? *Where* have you been? I was worried."

"I've been around." She shrugged. "The farther I ran from here, the more I realized that I shouldn't have and that I was wrong. So I came back to apologize but couldn't bring myself to just walk inside like nothing happened."

"You don't need to apologize for anything. You have every right to question the motives of a complete stranger."

"Yeah, well . . ." she started, finishing with the ointment and applying the bandages. "There's questioning your motives, and then there's falsely misjudging them. Besides, you're not a *complete* stranger. You opened up to me a hell of a lot more than I did to you. And you're so generous and nice and . . . and I feel safe around you, I don't know why."

He'd wondered why he cared so much for her safety while barely knowing her as well, and it was interesting to know there was a similar connection on her end.

"There," she said, finishing up. "How does that feel?"

His bandaged hand was all neatly and professionally wrapped. It didn't hurt quite as much as it had—his fracture was currently screaming the loudest—and he appreciated her expertise, however she'd learned it.

"Feels like I'll never do that again," Ferenc said matter-of-factly, glancing back to the frame. He was going to need a new door. "I'm about ready to pop some pills for my fracture, so I'm sure it'll get rid of what little pain's left in my hand." His thoughts traveled to whatever Olivia had done the previous night. If only he could get his body to quiet down like she'd done. "I'd love to have Olivia use her magic touch like she did last night. That felt great."

Dormouse's eyebrows raised high on her forehead, and she sat back into the chair, looking away uncomfortably.

"No, wait, not—it's not what you think. Whatever she was doing was like some hybrid . . . electric shock treatment."

"Who's Olivia?"

It was a complicated answer, and one he couldn't just blurt out. If anything would make Dormouse run, that would be it, so he had to ease into his reply as much as possible. But he had to start somewhere.

"Do you remember what I do?"

"You're a pilot," she replied, and he nodded.

"I met Olivia before my accident. And 'met' is a very relative term, here." A flash of her green eyes as she landed on the nose of

88

the jet burned itself so uncomfortably in his memory that he rubbed at his forehead with his unbandaged hand. "I was flying in a storm. I've done it many times before. And this is going to sound crazy, but Olivia quite literally appeared out of thin air."

Dormouse had leaned forward in the chair, focused on him as he spoke, and her mouth fell open at his words. She probably didn't believe him.

"I'm thousands of feet in the air, and there she is, on the nose. How she managed to—to *stick* there at the speed I was going, I . . ."

Ferenc trailed his hand up from his forehead, combing his fingers through his hair. She'd claimed it was air manipulation—hell, she'd *shown* him air manipulation on the beach—but it didn't make sense. People couldn't just control the air at will.

"The jet had already been having issues that I'd been recording. But then I lost a stabilizer, which sent the jet spinning. I tried to regain control while keeping an eye on her . . ."

Reliving the events of that day was just as traumatizing. Even though Olivia was perfectly fine—with a crazy explanation on how she survived—it'd still scarred him. He'd blamed himself, even though there'd been absolutely nothing he could do.

"She fell," came Dormouse's quiet voice.

Ferenc concentrated on steadying his breathing before he continued. "There was nothing I could do. And then lightning struck her. When the flash of lightning passed, there was nothing left: no stray limbs, no skeletal flaming body . . . nothing."

He shut his eyes as his mind replayed the events—from the spinning, to the lightning strike, to having to eject, and getting tangled in his parachute.

"I had to eject. The jet crashed, and I walked away with a fracture at worst, but . . . I was convinced she'd died on the spot. And I couldn't get that image out of my mind. I gave my statement, but everyone dismissed it as
a figment of my panicking imagination." He frowned before opening his eyes again. "You have to understand; I don't panic in the air. Ever."

"So what happened when I found you?"

"I was having a double flashback because, as it turns out, I saw her walking down the street. I chased her, but I lost her. Do you have any idea how it feels to see somebody you thought was dead? I blamed myself."

He knew there was nothing he could've done. All his ideas and what-ifs weren't even a blip in his mind at the time everything was happening.

"But she's alive, and she came here . . ." Dormouse's eyebrows squished together as she tried to understand what he was saying.

"Yes. After you and I—after those creatures . . ." Dormouse flinched, but he quickly shifted his train of thought to make sense to her. "I needed to clear my head, so I went to the beach, and she was there. She explained that—it's crazy, but—she can travel via lightning." Dormouse gasped, and Ferenc laughed nervously in response. "I know, right? She explained how it worked and even showed me this unbelievable thing where she controlled the air, making it hot, then cool . . ."

Ferenc paused when he'd noticed her gripping the edge of the table so tightly, her knuckles were white. She stood from the chair, her gaze darting everywhere in fear.

"Dormouse?"

"I . . ." She bolted for the sliding door. "I have to go."

"No, wait, please don't leave again! What—what happened?"

She vanished from sight, and his chin dropped to his chest in defeat. The conversation had been going as well as it could, or so he thought. It had to have been something he'd said. And here he thought she felt safe around him. That's what she'd told him, after all.

He retraced over everything he'd said that might've scared her, and his thoughts fell on Olivia. Maybe Dormouse thought Olivia was one of those masked people. He couldn't see it, but it was a possibility.

Before his thoughts could go any further, a knock occurred at the front door, and Max barked in warning.

"I know, Max." he said as he descended the stairs.

When he opened the door, he found himself staring into a familiar pair of green eyes, much like he had thousands of feet in the air. Olivia wore a smile on her lips, however, which quickly vanished as her gaze fell to his bandaged hand.

"Um," she started. "Is this a bad time?"

CHAPTER 17
Olivia

A re you sure you didn't punch that hard?"

Olivia eyed the swept-up pile of glass in the kitchen and the mess of shards still scattered about the deck. It must've been quite a feat to accomplish.

Ferenc had allowed her inside—though he appeared somewhat displeased about it—and had given her a simple "I punched the door" reply when she'd asked what had happened, as if it were the most obvious answer in the world.

Unlike the comfortably cool air-conditioned temperature from the night before, the inside of his house was just as hot and humid as it was outside. And when she'd followed him up into the kitchen, she'd seen why.

His demeanor shifted away from irritation, becoming calmer. And she even detected a hint of sadness.

"I don't even know anymore," he replied through an exhale, defeated.

"Well," she started, before pursing her lips and placing her hands on her hips. It wasn't how she'd intended to spend her time, but she knew she had to take it one step at a time with him, and if that meant helping clean up, then that's what she'd have to do. "Let's get to picking this up, shall we?"

"Oh, you don't have to—"

"But I *want* to," she said, turning away from the mess to look into his honey-colored eyes. "Come on."

She carefully maneuvered herself around the shards as she stepped onto the deck, cautiously plucking up the biggest pieces and setting them in a pile as Ferenc swept the pile from the kitchen into the dustpan.

"Listen," he started, and Olivia glanced up to look at him. "What do you know about Dormouse?"

He never looked at her as he spoke, focusing on his work, but his eyes were narrowed as if bothered. She raised a brow at his strange question. "Dormice? I don't know much about rodents."

"No, Dormouse, the person. I don't know her real name. She's tiny, black hair . . . She seemed terrified when I mentioned you."

Her heart skipped a beat at his last words, and a plethora of reasons why someone would be terrified of her flooded her mind. She was almost afraid to know what exactly he was saying about her. He himself knew how crazy everything sounded when she'd tried explaining it to him, but she had good reason to: he was a guardian.

"Well, of *course* she'd be terrified!" she said, exasperated. "You can't just go around telling people about what I can do! Even *you* barely believe it!"

"She became nervous even before I mentioned it."

"But I've never met her."

"Are you sure? You both forced yourselves into my life right around the same time."

She had no answer for this. She'd been extra vigilant in making sure nobody saw her use her abilities—outside of Ferenc, obviously. And how somebody could be afraid of her by name when she didn't even know anyone in Florida was beyond her.

"Are you sure you don't know of any girl fitting her description?" he continued. "You don't have any filigree masks lying around or weird creatures working for you, do you?"

She scrunched her eyes shut, holding her hands up to stop him from continuing with this outrageous nonsense. "Okay, what? No! I don't know anyone here but you. I traveled here as you see me now, not even with a cell phone or a watch because the lightning would just fry them. As for weird creatures . . ."

She flipped through her memories, much like the organized files in the work folders she always kept so tidy, for any type of beast she'd recently seen that she'd consider weird and came up empty-handed. Olivia shrugged before returning to cleaning up the shards.

They picked up as many of the fragments outside as they could—for Max's sake, more than anything—cleaning beneath the deck once they were done with the surface. As time went on, Ferenc slowed down, rubbing the area around his fracture with his bandaged hand and stretching his arm muscles.

She hated seeing him like that, and the more he did it, the more she cringed on the inside as her own muscles tensed with sympathy pains.

"Hey," she eventually said as he winced, holding his breath. "Let me help."

She stepped over to him, wiggling her fingers as the tingling began buzzing through them. And as she reached up, he snatched her hand. She jumped, and a gasp caught in her throat.

"Did you leave the front door open last night?"

She blinked, her mind rewinding back to her actions from the previous night. She wasn't the type to just leave doors open, whether it was her house or not. Olivia shook her head with confidence.

"No, I shut it behind me. I don't know about you Floridians, but in California, leaving the door wide open is an invitation you don't want to be a part of."

"Did you shut off my phone?"

Her brows couldn't lift any higher off her forehead in her confusion. "Why would I do that?"

He studied her in silence, and she could've sworn she saw the gears in his head turning. It seemed he still didn't fully trust her, and to be honest, she couldn't blame him. She'd appeared out of nowhere, called him a guardian, and began doing illogical things his analytical mind couldn't compute.

Finally, he released her hand, dropping his arm limp at his side. It was Olivia's turn to watch him for a few seconds, weighing whether she should continue trying to help. He'd continued to remain skeptical, even after all the proof she'd given him: the lightning travel, the air manipulation . . . hell, even the low-frequency electrical stimulation. She then internally scolded herself. Of course she should continue trying to help. She wasn't heartless. And so, she gently placed her hand atop his collarbone, resulting in a slight flinch, but that was to be expected.

"Shouldn't we do this inside?" he asked. "In case somebody sees, or I fall over?"

A partial smirk of amusement made its way to her lips. "I gave you a little something extra last night, to calm you down. This is just electrical stimulation. The pulses can't be seen, and it's too bright out to see the static."

She lightly traced over his collarbone, running her fingertips back and forth over the fabric of his shirt. He eventually closed his eyes as he stood perfectly still, and she continued to work her magic.

There was a heaviness in the pit of her stomach—regret for what had happened to him. He couldn't have known she was coming. There was no way he could've prepared for it. And though he'd run into her, she'd broken his concentration, resulting in his jet spinning out of control.

He might not have believed her, but she knew he'd been controlling the air around him. She'd felt it.

She pulled her hand away. "Better?"

He slowly opened his eyes and nodded as he carefully stretched. "Yeah. Much better, thanks."

"I can heal that too, if you'll let me," she added, prodding her chin toward his bandaged hand.

His arm slowly fell to his side once more, and he continued watching her. Eventually, his attention fell to his injured hand while his other one ran through his sun-bleached hair. He was clearly weighing his options, and she wanted to help sway him in the right direction—the direction where he'd finally trust and believe her.

"It'll be fun!" Olivia said with a grin. "I get to show off a new ability, and you get to use both hands again." He tilted his head in question, and before he could say anything, she quickly added with a wink, "Might want to do this one inside, though."

She made her way up the deck stairs, glancing over her shoulder to see if he'd follow. He stood where he was while his eyes reluctantly followed her.

She approached the kitchen sink to wash her hands. It hadn't taken quite as long as she thought it would for Ferenc to follow, and she bit down on the inside of her cheek to prevent a knowing smile from appearing on her face.

"Do you have anything to board it up with?" she asked.

He pulled a dish towel out of a drawer and handed it to her to dry her hands. "I can't board it up."

"Why not?"

"That's how Dormouse gets in."

Dormouse again. She smiled gently, setting the towel on the counter. There seemed to be more going on between him and this girl than he was letting on, but that was none of her business.

"Give me your hand," she said, reaching out to meet him half-way.

It took a beat, but he finally raised his injured hand out to her. Ever so carefully, she undid the bandage, impressed with the professional wrapping job. There was no way he could've done that himself.

Cuts and gashes ran along the knuckles, though amazingly well cleaned. They'd be easy enough to heal.

"Are you ready?" she asked.

When he nodded, Olivia took a deep breath, reaching into her core for that special something.

And then she gently blew on his hand.

The icy chill from her own breath tickled her fingertips as she continued to hold his hand in her palm, and she had to force herself to keep concentrating when he gasped. The cuts wiped away as if they were never there, the gashes mended from the inside, seemingly filling up with his own matter before closing, and the scabs left behind crumbled away into nothingness with the last of her breath. She took a proper gulp of air afterward.

Ferenc pulled his hand away, inspecting it with his mouth agape, flexing his fingers as she caught her breath again.

"That's . . ." he started, still in awe.

"'Impossible'? No." It couldn't be impossible, as she'd clearly done it. "That's just another air ability. I can only do that with surface or open wounds. Unfortunately, I can't fix your fracture that way."

"How do you know how to do all this?"

"Funny story, that. I burned myself while cooking and blew on it and—"

"So, you don't actually know what you're doing? The mechanics behind each action? The rationality?"

It was a harsh but fair question. "No, I suppose I don't. Just like that gut feeling to come find you." At this, he rolled his eyes, and she hastily added, "I know it's there, whatever 'it' is. And I don't actually know how to do anything until I just so happen to do it. Pure chance or intentional."

95

Why she, of all people, had these abilities drove her as crazy as that tug she'd eventually followed all the way to Florida.

"Have you ever had that sensation deep inside where you just can't explain why you know something or why you feel a certain way?" It sounded stupid when she put it that way, but she couldn't even seem to formulate that feeling into words.

Ferenc seemed contemplative of what she'd said, however, distantly staring out past the deck. "Yeah." He returned to reality as his attention fell to his healed hand. "There's an unexplainable feeling I get over Dormouse. I worry about her, I'm protective of her, and I don't even know why. I barely know her."

Olivia smiled. He seemed like such a pure, kind-hearted man with that answer. Those types were hard to find in this day and age, and she appreciated having run into him—or, quite literally, the other way around.

With a tilt of his head, he beckoned her to accompany him down into the living room. She followed and lowered herself onto the couch, but he remained standing, his gaze bearing down on her to the point she almost shrunk down in discomfort, thinking she'd done something wrong.

"All right, let's go then," he said, clasping his hands together, momentarily checking his healed hand.

Her mind reeled over their past conversations, trying to recall if they were supposed to go somewhere.

"If you're so convinced I'm the guardian, then let's go. Teach me something."

The gears in her brain came to a screeching halt, and she blinked in shock. She'd expected to have a lot more resistance from him. She parted her lips, stuttering as she tried to restart her brain.

"Where would you like to start?" she finally asked.

"How about with that air manipulation?"

There was no better reply than to nod. She lifted her hands to form that invisible box she'd shown him on the beach. Ferenc imitated her.

"To contain the element so you don't end up with a nasty surprise, you have to first imagine a box, as wide as your hands. Make sure it's closed."

She waited for a beat. It was simple for some to envision certain things, but not for others. Olivia wasn't sure in which category

Ferenc fell into just yet. He focused on his hands, then looked up, silently prompting her to continue.

"You can see it? All right. Now, imagine something hot inside that box."

"Like summer?" he asked.

"Not quite."

"A cigarette burn, then?"

"Close," she replied. "I meant something more physical, like fire. Think of fire between your hands, inside that sealed box."

He focused on his box once more, but nothing happened. Nothing that she could see or feel, at any rate. But that didn't stop Ferenc from looking up at her expectantly.

"Am I doing it?" he asked.

She crossed her arms over her chest and shook her head. "No."

"What do you mean, no? My campfire was awesome."

"Awesome in your mind, perhaps . . . but not in the space between your hands. You can't just think it, you have to manifest it."

He dropped his hands and shot her a deadpan look. "You didn't say anything about manifesting it."

"I was getting there . . ."

"Look, I don't do that manifestation New Age crap. I don't believe in it."

As much as she liked a good debate, now wasn't the right time. The whole concept had nothing to do with it. "You don't have to," she replied. "This manifestation isn't about belief. Well, not directly."

He pressed his lips into a fine line, and she almost thought that was the end right then and there, but he just sighed.

"Look, I—" he started, his hand trailing up the nape of his neck, scratching through his hair in frustration. "I thought I'd researched all I could about all this stuff, but . . ."

Olivia's posture sagged some. Ferenc had seen and experienced a few impossible things since running her over with his jet. And just when it seemed as if he'd finally dismissed the possibility of having imagined it all, he reerected that previously demolished wall of resistance in an instant.

Though not nearly as analytical as he was, she understood where he was coming from. It had almost been impossible for her to wrap her head around as well. But at some point, she'd accepted it. He would too. He just needed help.

97

"You don't need to do more research."

"You don't understand—" he started, but she cut him off.

"Oh, trust me. If anyone understands what it's like to *not* understand what's going on, it's me. Don't you think I've tried doing my own research? There's only so much of it you can do before you're going in circles."

He stared at her with narrowed eyes, but her own gaze held strong in a silent challenge. She wasn't afraid of confrontation. Sure, she hated how mentally and physically exhausted she felt, but she couldn't do anything else other than call him out. She couldn't give him any more time. He needed to trust his gut.

Part of her thought this was all a mistake and she needed to give up, but the other part of her was stubborn and driven. If only she could detect the elemental . . .

Olivia finally broke eye contact as she shut her eyes, searching her core for that pull. It was there, as it always had been, reacting to Ferenc as he stood before her. But there was something else, something she'd never felt before.

Her brows furrowed, and she delved deeper. It was faint—barely detectable over Ferenc's presence—but she could've sworn the tug felt different, almost like there was a second one layered over it.

Olivia's eyes flew open, and her gaze darted everywhere, trying to find which direction the new pull came from. Excitement bubbled inside of her, nearly drowning that new sensation.

Ferenc reached out, alarmed. "What's wrong?"

She jumped to her feet as she hushed him. She couldn't lose that new lead. When she thought she had a good handle on it, she finally looked back at him with a grin. "I feel something! Something other than you!" She rushed to the front door. "I'll be back. I have to—"

"Hey!"

She stopped in her tracks before swiveling her head to look over her shoulder.

"Thank you," he then said, lifting his healed hand and pointing to his collarbone. "For this."

With a smile and an acknowledging nod, she stepped out of the house, shutting the door behind her, and followed the new sensation.

CHAPTER 18
Ferenc

The entire World Wide Web was at his fingertips, yet he hadn't been able to find any believable information about Olivia's abilities. Every search led him through fiction rabbit holes—movie effects, fantasy novel characters, even New Age *magick-with-a-K*.

Ferenc had even dared look into manifestation, only to find what Olivia had said about it not *directly* being tied to belief actually made sense. Not that he believed what he'd read—which, in the end, was the whole twisted point. He'd gone full circle with that information, just like she'd said he would. And as someone who loved learning and researching as much as he did, he hated that she was right.

The figurative puzzle pieces laid out before him should have been easy to assemble now that he'd seen and experienced all these new things over the course of the last few days, but being the factual person he was, he still struggled with everything. He'd never been into jigsaw puzzles anyway, preferring crossword puzzles instead. He clearly pictured the word *guardian* inside the boxes in his mind—mentioned by Olivia a few times—but aside from eliciting a dozen more questions on whether that explained his actions and attitude toward Dormouse, no amount of analyzing the puzzle pieces was getting him any closer to actual, factual answers.

He needed to get some air . . . and he needed a new sliding door. After forcing down a quick bite to eat and getting an earful from his lawyer when he called back, he hopped in his car and made his way to the home improvement store.

He allowed his thoughts to roam as he leisurely drove the metallic-red sedan down the main street, going back over everything Olivia had said and done as well as every tab of his research, trying to piece it all together differently. Maybe there was something he just wasn't seeing.

He pulled up to a red light and slowly applied the brakes, his eyes dropping to the now-healed hand gripped about the black leather steering wheel. He couldn't explain it. Ferenc flicked his gaze back to the light, which was still red, then glanced at the mixture of maple, oak, and palm trees interspersed between warehouses along the road, when something—no, *someone*—darted out from behind a nearby building: Dormouse.

Adrenaline shot through his entire system as he snapped his focus to the unmistakable creatures giving chase. A horn blared behind him—the light had turned green—and with his heart in his throat, he stomped on the gas pedal and turned the wheel hard, peeling down the other street as his car went from zero to sixty in five seconds flat.

He had to catch up. He didn't know how much longer Dormouse would be able to outrun them.

Tires screeched as he came to a stop in the empty parking lot, and he jumped out of the car, leaving the door wide open as he sprinted to follow.

"Hey!" he called out, trying hard not to lose them as they approached a tall chain-link fence. "Hey!" he tried, louder. Anything to grab the attention away from Dormouse.

One of the two beasts slashed out at the girl, and the tear of her sweater in between his pounding footsteps was as harsh as if it was his own, even as far back as he was. His hammering heart skipped a beat, dread roiling inside as Dormouse continued to run.

She scaled and jumped the fence with such impressive ease that Ferenc's jaw dropped. But reality came crashing down on him as the monsters followed—but they didn't leap over the top rail. Instead, they dispersed like smoke upon reaching the fence and reappeared whole again on the other side, giving Dormouse a tremendous disadvantage. The closest creature lunged, knocking her to the ground.

Her shriek triggered rage within him so sudden and intense that he saw red.

"Get off her!" he bellowed.

He was beyond the point of wanting to kill whatever those things were. Now he was out for whatever blood-like substance was inside the creatures. His vision tunneled so thoroughly that he didn't see the black car with tinted windows skidding to a halt near the beasts and Dormouse until he'd come to a sudden stop at the fence.

A broad figure in a crisp shirt and tie jumped out of the passenger seat, and Ferenc's body stiffened. His grip on the chain links tightened at the sight of a full silver filigree mask—identical to the one he'd seen the other night—upon its face.

The monsters dissipated into nothingness, and panic seized Ferenc once more as the masked individual approached Dormouse and grasped her tiny neck with a massive hand.

Despite the height difference, Ferenc scrambled up the fence with much more difficulty than Dormouse had. Something tore on the way down—whether it was his clothes or skin, he didn't know, nor did he have time to care. He stumbled awkwardly to his knees in landing and fell onto his bad shoulder, yelping as pain seared through him.

His blood curdled when Dormouse's shrieking picked back up. Despite being as in shape as he was, he struggled to get air into his smoker's lungs as he got to his feet. The person's fist was practically as big as Dormouse's head, and she flailed her feet wildly when he lifted her up, hefting her as though she weighed absolutely nothing.

"Stop fighting, you won't win," came the muffled, deep bass voice behind the mask before he turned and opened the vehicle's back door, flinging Dormouse inside and slamming it shut behind her.

"Hey!" Ferenc called out between coughs, his legs wobbly as he darted for the masked man, but the car took off even before the man had finished getting into the passenger side.

That was it. There was no way he'd be able to catch up to a speeding car, no matter how fast he ran. He slowed his pace to a stop, his eyes darting around in desperation as his lungs burned. He needed something—anything—to stop the car.

The black sedan approached a large maple tree, and Ferenc wished with all his might that it would topple over, blocking their way. If only Olivia were there with him now; she could use her lightning powers to help.

He almost scoffed as his mind went to Olivia's manifestation lesson, but he couldn't just stand by and wait for a miracle. And so, he imagined the tree falling—but nothing physically happened. He tried harder, tried to reach deeper inside, but the maple remained standing, and the car was about to pass his only remaining hope. He tried again, gritting his teeth and closing his hands into fists, but the results were the same.

"Come on!" he snarled, desperate.

As if on command, lightning cracked through the mostly sunny sky, striking the tree and felling a thick branch, which fell atop the vehicle's roof as it sped by, crushing it beneath its weight.

He froze in shock. He couldn't believe he'd made it happen. And even if he could believe it, he couldn't figure out *how* he'd done it. His thoughts shifted to Dormouse, and he set off in a sprint once more. He wasn't the religious type, but he implored to every deity he knew the name of that Dormouse would be uninjured and alive in that back seat.

Both the broad man and the driver—also donning a silver filigree mask—climbed out of the car, black handguns pulled and aimed at him while dark wisps swirled dangerously at their sides to form what Ferenc only assumed would be more unwanted trouble. But instead of throwing his arms up defensively and taking cover, he narrowed his eyes as he lunged, shooting his arms forward, palms out. Two large bursts of lightning shot out, sending both men flying and the churning creatures dissipating into the air.

Had he not already been surprised and questioning the bolt that had hit the tree, his new actions definitely would have had him curious. But he didn't have time for that.

Ferenc skidded to a halt at the back door of the car and yanked it open, peering inside past stray leaves and the scent of burning wood. "Dormouse!"

Relief flooded through him at the sight of her, but she squeaked and recoiled as if he'd burned her. She swiftly retreated to the other end of the back seat, curling up in the fetal position as far away from him as possible.

"Dormouse, it's me," he tried, as gently as his winded breath would allow. "Quick, we have to get out of here," he added, looking over his shoulder, much as she'd done in the past, to make sure the masked people were still down for the count.

She continued to grip herself tightly, trembling like the leaves from the fallen branch, staring at him past the caved-in roof and swiftly shaking her head. "No!"

His brows drew together. "Please, we have to hurry. I don't know how hard I hit them, so I don't know how long we have—"

"No!" she shrieked. "Get away from me!"

"Dormouse . . ." He paused, taken aback. She was terrified of him, but she was supposed to feel safe around him. This was not how he wanted things to go. "Is it—is it because of what I did? Are you afraid of me now?" She didn't answer. "Are you afraid that I'm working with them and that I'm after you?"

She still didn't reply, and his heart sank. That was enough of an answer for him. He shot another quick peek over his shoulder, then back to her before taking a few deep breaths for his own benefit.

"I'm trying to help you, and I have been since day one. I don't— I don't know how I did it. Frankly, I'm not even sure it came from *me*, but I'm one of the good guys, and I've wanted nothing more than your safety from the start. And if we don't leave now, I'm not sure I'll be able to stop them again when they wake up."

Ferenc held out his hand for her to take, but she still didn't move. Snatching her and carrying her kicking and screaming over his shoulder would probably add fuel to her fear, but at that point, he was ready to face the unfortunate consequences if it meant she'd be safe. As he peeked back over to the unconscious men, Dormouse lunged forward. But instead of attacking like a cornered animal, she instead clung to him, her arms wrapped around his torso and fists tightly clutched to his shirt. He stumbled backward, surprised, but quickly embraced her trembling form in return.

Even though he could've stayed like that forever, they needed to get out of dodge, and fast. "Come on," he said, helping her out of the car and to her feet.

Ferenc slid one hand in hers, gripping it tightly as he pulled her to run, but he quickly stopped.

"Wait here a minute."

He released her hand and cautiously approached one of the downed men, unsure if he was dead or simply knocked out. Once he got close enough, he slowly crouched, reaching for the closest pocket.

"What are you *doing*?!" Dormouse squeaked past her fingertips as she bit down on her nails.

"Trying to see if I can get any clues as to who they are—ah. Here we go."

He pulled out a wallet before standing back up and jumping back until he was out of physical range. Being that close to a guy *that* big unnerved him. He opened the wallet and flipped through it to find plenty of twenty- and fifty-dollar bills, credit cards, a driver's license revealing the massive man's name to be Duane Cordell . . . and a business card with a symbol Ferenc instantly recognized.

"Son of a . . ." he started, pulling the card out and tossing the rest of the wallet next to the unconscious body.

"What is it?" Dormouse squeaked, taking a few steps back as if she was ready to bolt.

"I'll explain later." He hurried back to her, grabbing her hand once more. "Let's go!"

He rushed back to his car with her in tow and bailed out of the parking lot as fast as legally possible.

The tight discomfort in his chest from being short of breath blended with the agony of his fracture, thrumming through his entire body. But Ferenc endured and briefly turned what little focus he could muster toward Dormouse before looking at the road ahead once more.

"Are you hurt?"

She shook her head, though he was unconvinced. "You?"

He went to shrug, but the pang that instantly stung his clavicle was warning enough to not continue through with the action. "I'll live," he finally replied.

A gasp escaped her, and his heart skipped a beat. He clutched the steering wheel even tighter, and his gaze flicked to the rearview mirror to see if they were being chased.

"Your hand!" she squeaked.

Instinctively, his eyes fell to his hands. He couldn't see anything wrong with them—thanks to Olivia—and that was when it hit him: Dormouse had cleaned his hand from the glass and had wrapped it . . . and there it was, healed like nothing had ever happened.

"Dormouse, I promise you that when we get home, I'll explain everything to you, but right now is not a good time."

He gritted his teeth in pain. He needed painkillers, he wanted a cigarette even if his lungs had almost killed him moments ago, and he couldn't think straight as what little focus he could muster always went back to the symbol on the business card: Richard's law firm.

CHAPTER 19
Ferenc

By the time they pulled into the driveway, all Ferenc wanted to do was die. He was pretty sure it was the only way to end the pain—which had lessened from white hot to an unfortunate and uncomfortably dull heaviness. It coursed through his entire system, fraying every nerve until he wasn't sure what his body was trying to tell him anymore.

Frankly, he thought it was a miracle they'd even made it home. With the number of times his body had distracted him, he was pretty sure he'd accidentally done a few illegal things on the road. Dormouse hadn't ever said a word about it if he had, but that didn't entirely comfort him.

A shuddered exhale escaped him as he put the shifter in park and leaned his head against the headrest of his leather seat, shutting his eyes. Now that he didn't have to focus on driving, his other thoughts made their appearance known.

He wanted to know how the creatures had found her again. Maybe she frequented the same places often. Maybe she'd done something to make them so adamant about chasing her and only her.

He also owed her an explanation about what had happened, but frankly, he wasn't sure he could give her one. Part of him wasn't convinced he'd been the one to do all of that—it was physically impossible! But on the other hand, Olivia had been performing some pretty *physically impossible* things of her own, and he'd been a witness to a lot of it.

He opened his eyes and turned his head toward Dormouse. She chewed on her nails again, staring ahead at the house. He wished he could read her thoughts because he couldn't read her expression; that wasn't entirely because of the pain, though. He'd always had trouble with that.

"Are you all right?" he finally asked.

She flinched at his words, flicking her gaze in his direction before focusing forward once more. She lightly nodded her reply, but he didn't believe her. The masked men and strange creatures kept chasing her, and as if that wasn't distressing enough, she'd watched him perform some inexplicable miracles. He'd be traumatized too, if he were her.

"Please don't run."

She lowered her hand down to her lap. It took a few seconds before she whispered, "I won't."

Ferenc turned the car off and opened the driver-side door, which prompted all other doors to unlock. She was quick to get out of the car, and a sudden coldness hit his core. She'd said she wouldn't run off . . .

Thankfully, after shutting the door behind herself, she remained near the car.

His weak sigh of relief shifted into an agonizing hiss through gritted teeth as he forced his body to move because willing it to was getting him nowhere. He got out and shuffled to the front door, keys in hand.

She followed him, which was a good sign, and he managed a soft smile through the pain. "Max will be excited to see you when I let her out of the laundry room. Think you can handle it?"

Her only answer was bringing her nails to her lips. They stepped inside, and she remained at the front door as he made his way to the last room down the hall. Max huffed enthusiastically on the other side, and that concerned him. Dormouse hadn't done too well the last time Max was overly excited. Granted, the golden retriever had been significantly calm the last time Dormouse was over, so it could go either way.

He placed his hand on the doorknob, then turned to Dormouse. "Tell me when you're ready."

She backed into the door as if trying to meld into it, but eventually gave a determined nod after a few deep breaths. It was now or never.

Max was nothing but a blur as Ferenc opened the door, darting directly for Dormouse, who squeaked and squeezed her eyes shut, defensively throwing her hands up in front of her face. But before Ferenc could call out, Max skidded along the hardwood floor, parking herself directly at Dormouse's feet, happily panting while her tail wagged violently. Ferenc sighed with relief as he approached them.

"Good girl, Max," he said, petting her head and scratching behind her ears.

Dormouse slowly opened her eyes, peeking down at Max before lowering her arms and straightening her posture, a deep exhale escaping her.

"Come on, let's go outside," he said to Max, before adding to Dormouse, "I'd like you to join me too. I have some explaining to do."

The retriever didn't wait for him—what with his shattered sliding door—so Ferenc downed a painkiller with a glass of tap water, grabbed the frozen peas from the freezer, and made his way to the deck.

Once as comfortably seated as possible, he gently slung the peas onto his fracture before lighting his cigarette and taking a long drag. Dormouse joined him soon after, seating herself on the edge of the other chair, hands clasped in her lap nervously.

"I don't know what I did," he admitted. "I mean, I have an idea, but . . ."

He knew it was something guardian-related, that it had something to do with what Olivia spoke of. But he couldn't explain it to himself, let alone to Dormouse. He licked his dry lips, then continued.

"All I know is that I wanted you safe, and I'd have done anything to keep you out of harm's way. I'd do it again in a heartbeat. I can't explain it any better than that."

She said nothing in reply, and he surprised himself to be the first to drop his gaze, looking at his healed hand as his mind played back the impossibilities.

Dormouse was probably right not to trust Olivia, but he just couldn't see her being one of the masked people. She was assertive, sure, but she seemed as lost and confused as he was, just way better than him at handling it.

"I know you don't trust Olivia, but if you'd seen what I saw . . ."
Ferenc trailed off, lifting his attention back to her, only to find her
flinching. He flexed the hand he'd used to punch the sliding door,
every muscle working painlessly. "For her to do this, for her to heal
me . . . I don't think she's one of the bad guys."

Dormouse stared at his hand while wringing her own in her lap.
He wished she'd say something. He wanted her to tell him she totally understood and was all right with everything. What Olivia had
done was technically no different from those unexplainable beasts
that formed from nothingness and dissipated just as quickly. It was
just as unnatural.

He really wanted to know what the masked figures wanted with
Dormouse and how they kept finding her. Maybe they'd been se-
cretly keeping an eye on her.

He pulled the business card from his shirt pocket and held it
between his thumb and middle finger. He flicked at it with his index
finger before setting it on the table between them.

"This is what I found in the wallet. The symbol belongs to Amy's
lawyer's firm."

Dormouse froze, her wide eyes flicking back and forth between
the card and him. "What does that mean?"

It was the first thing she'd said that whole discussion, but he
couldn't answer her. He didn't know what it meant. It could've been
a coincidence, for all he knew. But one thing was for certain: he was
going to look into it as soon as he could.

"Listen, I can't keep you here against your will, but I think—I
think staying here is your best bet at remaining safe. I have the
spare bedroom set up, there's plenty of food . . ."

Ferenc's stomach growled at his words. He hadn't eaten much
at all yet, and he was sure her situation was the same. Eventually,
she nodded ever so faintly, and he cocked his head, unsure what she
was agreeing to.

"I'll stay," she managed to whisper, and what little tension in his
body he could feel past the pain and numbness vanished.

"Great." He grabbed his phone from his pocket. "I'll order a
pizza, and if you want to feel useful—but only if you want—you can
help me board up the sliding door. Deal?"

"Deal," she quickly replied, her eyes sparkling. "Pizza sounds
amazing right now."

With a smirk of amusement at her childlike glee, he struggled to get to his feet as he called for Max, who lazily came padding up the stairs to the deck, followed by Dormouse. As they got settled, Ferenc flipped through the pizza app on his phone, but the pain his body felt in anticipation of any kind of work only made him wish for Olivia's swift return even more.

CHAPTER 20
Ferenc

Ferenc's eyes flew open before quickly squinting from the sunlight that pooled in around him. He was disoriented for only a split second thanks to the familiar roof windows of his living room.

His fracture loudly lamented the fact he'd fallen asleep on the couch by sending throbbing jolts of searing pain through his entire body, and he hissed past clenched teeth.

After Dormouse had retired for the night, he'd waited for Olivia to return, but she never came back. Shielding his vision from the bright sunlight, his eyes swept around the room just in case she'd been quietly sitting by, but there was no sign of her, and his stomach churned. He hoped she hadn't gotten herself into some kind of trouble.

His mind reeled back to the events of the previous day. Dormouse had helped him board up his sliding door, barely able to reach up farther than his own fracture allowed. But she'd proven herself resourceful as she'd grabbed a kitchen chair and climbed atop it.

A smile found its way to his lips as he remembered how determined she'd been to help, as well as her excitement when the pizza arrived. The smile then instantly dissipated, and his stomach dropped. Dormouse was prone to running off, and he worried she might've done so in the middle of the night. He shot up from the couch, lightheaded both from the pain and his sudden movement, and dashed for the spare bedroom in a rush of panicked adrenaline to make sure she was still there.

The door was slightly ajar. He peeked through and found Max staring back at him before lazily resting her head back down as she returned to napping at the foot of the bed. The tension in his body instantly slackened. There Dormouse lay, curled up atop the covers, sound asleep. He softly smiled before quietly stepping away to take his painkillers and grab his peas and cigarettes.

Ferenc opened the front door, calling for Max as quietly as he could, and when the golden retriever slowly padded in his direction, they both stepped outside.

With the peas over his shoulder, he lit his cigarette as he watched Max sniff around in curiosity, but his mind was elsewhere. Dormouse had thankfully stayed the night, but now Olivia was missing. She'd never said exactly when she'd be back—and was under no obligation to come back at all—but he couldn't help overanalyzing. Those masked people could've been after her as well. Sure, with her air-based skills, he was certain she could easily handle herself against them . . . but those creatures? That was a different story.

His mind returned to the card he'd pulled from the man's wallet and the symbol of Richard Moyon's law firm. It made no sense how Richard tied in to all of this, and it frustrated Ferenc enough that he wanted to pay the lawyer a visit.

The front door opened, pulling him from his thoughts. A drowsy Dormouse stepped out and shut the door behind her before protectively crossing her arms around herself.

"Well, good morning," he said with a smile. "Sleep well?" He took one last puff of his cigarette before putting it out on the edge of the slab.

"I did once I was finally able to."

"Can I get you anything?"

She brought her fingertips to her lips and shook her head at his words, nervously averting her gaze. Maybe it was because they were outside, where those beasts might see her. He watched her for a moment before opening the door.

"Come on," he said to Dormouse as Max trotted inside. "Let me make you breakfast."

He made his way to the kitchen, and she followed him inside. He placed his extinguished cigarette butt in the ashtray on the counter, then washed his hands before gathering all the items and ingredients for breakfast.

112

"Are you all right?" he asked, as she quietly sat at the kitchen table, fiddling with her fingers.

She didn't give a verbal answer, nodding ever so faintly instead.

"I was afraid you'd leave again." Ferenc turned a burner on, watching her from the corner of his eye.

"I thought about it," she admitted. "Many times."

"I'm glad you didn't follow through."

"I just . . . I remember you said that you might not be able to help me next time. Not that I feel indebted to you, but . . . I kind of do."

He froze at her last words. They echoed in his mind, and he pressed his lips together before speaking again. "I didn't do it for debt. I did it because I like to think that I'm a genuinely nice person and that you desperately needed help."

"I wasn't desperate," she shot back with a glare.

"That's not—that's not what I meant." He cleared his throat, re-turning to the pan. "I meant you no longer had the situation han-dled. And I'm glad I stepped in when I did because they had guns. Things could've gone south very quickly, and I'd be . . ." He glanced over his shoulder. "I would care if you got hurt or worse."

Dormouse looked away again, and Ferenc turned back to the food. There was an uncomfortable silence despite the sudden sizzle of bacon, but he really didn't know what else to say. Everything he'd said was true.

"I'm afraid of trusting you," she suddenly said, hugging her arms. "What if you're on their side, trying to make me believe that you're not?"

"That's not something I can convince you of. You're just going to have to trust me."

"I know . . . That's what I was fighting with myself over before I finally fell asleep last night."

Ferenc smiled softly to himself. He was glad she'd eventually decided to trust him enough to get some sleep. She must've been exhausted after everything that had happened. He definitely was.

He still needed to know *what* had happened, though. The day before, and before that, and even before that. He couldn't imagine she could've done anything to make those masked figures interested in her, but the questions were begging to be answered. Unfortu-nately, every time he asked those questions, she ran.

He couldn't keep it inside any longer as he flipped the bacon in the pan. "So," he started, as casually as he could. "What happened yesterday?"

"I . . ."

There was silence once more, and it was killing him on the inside. He desperately wanted to turn around and look at her, but as much as he wanted an answer, he didn't want her to think he was pressuring her for one.

"I was walking. Minding my own business."

Minding one's business hardly seemed worthy of giving chase. He bit his tongue to prevent from asking the millions of questions that arose with her answer, but something else had to have been at play. His mind methodically ran through each new question, such as where she might've been walking to, where she'd come from, and whether she'd stolen anything belonging to the ones chasing her. He silently scolded himself for thinking that last question, but he couldn't help that it was unfortunately in the realm of possibilities.

"I thought I saw one of them, and I—"

"One of the masked men?" He spun around to face her, blinking in surprise.

"A man in a suit was walking down the street, and I thought—I hid from him before he could see me, but then I screamed when someone touched me."

"Who touched you?" His stomach dropped before the scent of something burning swiftly drew him back to the pan.

"It was an old man, asking if I was all right. He startled me. But when I continued on, I—before I knew it, those—those *things* were after me again."

After sliding the crispy bacon onto a plate, he quickly scrambled a few eggs, poured them into the pan, and put the bread in the toaster, his mind back on the way the beasts had dissipated through the fence like plumes of smoke. But he knew they were solid. He'd hit one with a trash can.

"There are so many of them now!" she squeaked, as Ferenc grabbed plates, filling them with food as it became ready. "At first, there were just two of them. Now, I swear there are at least a dozen, if not more, and I don't know what they want with me!"

He set a plate down in front of her, and she flinched. "Hey," he tried gently as he set his own plate down. "I won't let them touch you."

114

"What if you're luring me into a false sense of security? What if you're trying to gain my trust, just to turn around and give me to them?"

He didn't know how else to prove he was every bit the nice guy she'd seen him be to date. "I would never do that. I know there's nothing I can say that will make you believe me, but . . . You just have to believe me."

She brought one hand up, biting at her fingernails while she flexed her fingers in clear agitation with the other hand. There was that internal battle again. He was going to lose her; he just knew it. He took a careful step toward her, but she shot up from her seat, a trembling hand extended to stop him, and a wild and harried look about her features.

"Don't come near me!" she screamed.

His hands shot up defensively, and Max barked at the sudden commotion. "It's okay," he tried.

"Why are you so nice? What do you want from me?"

"I want nothing more than your safety and well-being. You know that."

"Why? Why do you care so much?"

"I—" Ferenc paused. He really didn't know why he cared so much. It was a sensation deep inside, something he couldn't explain. "I don't know."

"Do you do this for all strangers? Invite them into your house without knowing them and cook them breakfast? Do you do this for all *women*?"

His hands dropped to his sides, and a long, inaudible sigh escaped him. "No, I don't normally let strangers into my house, and I definitely don't invite all women in either. I'm not trying to take advantage of you in any way. I just—I don't know. There's something inside of me that says you need a helping hand. That's it. Simple as that."

Dormouse's trembling intensified, and her breathing hitched. Tears filled her eyes until they rolled down her cheeks like miniature streams. She blindly reached for the chair to sit back down but couldn't seem to find it and grew even more frantic.

Ferenc reached out his hand for her to take, and she froze when she touched it. He remained still. He wouldn't push her. "Just a helping hand," he reminded her. "Nothing more."

She suddenly collapsed to the floor, sobbing. Surprised, Ferenc swiftly knelt at her level.

"I'm sorry!" she managed through her sobs. "I—"

"It's okay. Trust me." He hesitated before placing a hand on her shoulder, rubbing it gently. "It's okay."

When he felt she wouldn't pull away, he wrapped his arms around her, and she allowed him to. Shutting his eyes, his stomach in knots, he just allowed her to cry.

CHAPTER 21
Ferenc

The closer Ferenc got to the law firm, the more the tightness in his chest grew, until he could barely breathe. His knuckles turned white from his grip on the steering wheel—despite his fracture's protests—and every worst-case scenario flooded through his mind. He wanted answers.

No, he *needed* answers.

He'd consoled Dormouse until her sobs had become hiccups, until she'd eventually calmed down entirely. She hadn't run, which was a bonus, and had actually smiled while eating the reheated breakfast. She'd fallen asleep on the couch while he'd done the dishes, and he'd taken the opportunity to quietly leave after writing her a note that he'd return with a new sliding door. Of course, he'd left out the part where he'd stop in and visit Amy's lawyer first. Dormouse didn't need to know that part.

He steered into the imposing building's parking lot, pulling up as close to the door as possible. In and out. That was his intention, anyway. Many of the concocted worst-case scenarios in his head took a little longer. He hoped none of them would come true.

As he stepped out of the car, adjusting his arm and shoulder back into his brace—mostly to ease the pain, but also to garner a little sympathy in case things went south—part of him wasn't just frustrated about the strange situation with Dormouse. Of all the lawyers, Amy had chosen the richest, most prestigious and grandiose in all of Florida. His own lawyer probably didn't compare with experience or money, and definitely didn't compare status-wise.

117

A low hum of chatter greeted him as he walked into the lobby toward the alcove with the elevators, past pacing clients venting on calls and slouching ones in gray leather chairs, scrolling on their smartphones.

Ferenc arrived on the fifth floor and approached the counter, where an older woman with her black hair in a neat and tidy bun eyed his sling and brace before greeting him with a wide smile that pulled at the wrinkles around her eyes.

"Can I help you?"

"Hi. I need to speak with Richard Moyon, please."

Her smile never left as she gave her automated reply. "Do you have an appointment?"

"No. I just really need to speak with him right now. It's really important."

"I'm afraid I can't let you see him without an appointment, honey. Would you like me to see if I can get one of the other lawyers to—"

"No." Her smile finally faltered, and he forced a weak one of his own. "No, it absolutely has to be Richard Moyon. It'll only take a few minutes. It's really important."

He hated doing this. Under different circumstances, he'd have waited, but the longer it took to get his answers, the more an inexplicable fire roared inside of him; but most importantly, the sooner Dormouse would awaken and have the chance to run away again.

"Let me take down your name and number—"

"Look . . ." He squeezed his lips together, his mind reeling. He was quickly losing control of the situation. "Can you call him? Tell him it's Ferenc Janos."

"Sir, I—"

"If you mention I'm Amy's ex, I'm sure he'll—"

"Sir, I—"

Ferenc raised a hand, slamming his fist onto the counter. "Call him," he demanded. "Right now." The receptionist took a sudden step back from his actions, her palms flying up defensively, and the lobby fell silent, save for the talk-show host on the TV screen along the back wall.

His stomach dropped, slightly taken aback by his own behavior, before running his fingers through his hair in irritation. He didn't have time for this. He needed his answers, and he needed them now.

"I'm sorry. I—I just—" His frustration, which was already pretty deep at that moment, grew as the words refused to come. "I really need to speak with him. Right now."

She stared at him a moment before finally reaching for the phone. Ferenc's hand fell to rub at the nape of his neck while she dialed. None of the scenarios in his head had included the receptionist wasting his time, and that was highly annoying.

"Hi, I'm sorry to bother you," she started, an ever so faint tremor in her voice, "but there's a gentleman here by the name of . . ."

"Ferenc Janos," he said.

"Ferenc Janos, who is adamant about speaking with you right now." She nodded during the pause—not that Richard could see her—and her fearful gaze never left him as she replied to the voice on the other side. "Yes, I told him that, but he—"

"It'll only take a few minutes!" Ferenc clamored insistently, making sure the lawyer would clearly hear him on the other end of the line.

"Thank you, I'll let him know," she then replied, and Ferenc could feel the knot in the pit of his stomach as she hung up, cleared her throat, and straightened her white blouse.

"Mister Moyon will be with you shortly," she finally said to him, with impressive professionalism after his little outburst toward her.

He thanked her and started pacing like the clients he'd seen when he first walked in, even though they'd sat down long ago, failing at hiding their quick glances and whispers to one another.

"Thank you, Edith," a gravelly and confident voice said before the wooden door next to the reception desk opened.

Ferenc locked eyes with a pair of russet-brown ones. Richard stepped into the lobby, adjusting the silver cufflink on one of his crisp, expensive shirt sleeves. He appeared neither angry nor bothered—the perfect stone-faced lawyer. Richard swiftly scanned the lobby before looking at Ferenc once more, propping the door open with an oxford shoe.

"Mister Janos," he greeted curtly. "I'm a little surprised to see you here without your lawyer present."

"This has nothing to do with Amy," Ferenc replied.

There was no change in Richard's expression—ever the professional. "Well, then. Let's take this to my office, shall we?"

He followed Richard back toward the elevator. As they slipped inside, Ferenc bit his tongue, refraining from going off on the man

119

by focusing on the salt-and-pepper coloring in Richard's dark hair. In a way, he was glad Richard was pulling him away from potentially causing another scene. But at the same time, the more people around, the less likely Richard would weasel himself out of the matter at hand.

After a quick and silent elevator ride to the very top floor, the door slid open to a surprisingly small windowless waiting room with a set of large double doors at the end. Richard sauntered ahead while Ferenc followed, his attention trailing over the two leather armchairs stationed around a low coffee table accentuated with a couple magazines. With a key card, Richard opened the doors to a large corner office with such a gorgeous view of the beach in the distance that Ferenc almost forgot why he'd needed to talk to Richard in the first place.

He accompanied Richard inside, walking by sleek, contemporary tables, chairs, and something that resembled a couch—Ferenc wasn't entirely too sure—until he reached the floor-to-ceiling windows.

"Can I get you a drink?" Richard asked, but Ferenc simply shook his head.

Not only did the view take his breath away, but he found himself pining something fierce for that open air. The urge to fly again buzzed through his entire being—fingers, toes, brain—until a single thought formed, triggered by it: Richard had brought him up to his office.

While a wealthy lawyer wanting a sea-view office was nothing out of the ordinary, Richard could've easily pulled him into an empty meeting room on the lower floors. This must've been to throw him off. As Amy's lawyer, Richard knew of his love for the sky.

His train of thought suddenly jumped tracks, veering along the path concerning his ex. If only he'd known Amy preferred him to have enough money and a corner office with a view . . .

"Quite the sight, isn't it?" Richard pulled Ferenc from his thoughts. "How's your shoulder? Amy told me about the accident."

Of course Amy would've told Richard about the accident. And Richard would use that against him in some way, to make his life more miserable in whatever the hell was going on legally between himself and Amy. He didn't even know anymore. But it still bugged him how Amy had even found out.

"How can I help you, Mister Janos?" Richard said suddenly, standing right next to him. "If this isn't about your current case, then what was so important?"

Ferenc blinked back the fog in his mind, clearing his throat. That's right: he was there to talk about the business card. His anger reignited, he glowered at the man before him.

"I need you to tell me why the hell your men are chasing my friend."

He reached into his pocket and pulled out the business card, practically shoving it into Richard's face. Other than taking a step back from the sudden proximity, Richard's expression never changed. There was no realization, no fear, no anger . . . it was the same stoic, professional expression he always had. He was *good*.

Richard looked at the card, then back to Ferenc. "I don't understand what you're getting at."

"Yes, you do. I found this on one of the guys that was chasing her."

Richard leisurely walked to his desk nearby. "My employees would never chase down anybody. I'm sure if there were any type of business cards on the people you
speak of, regardless of how you've acquired them," he added with a slight pause, "it's likely they may be clients."

"I doubt it."

"I don't know what else to tell you, Mister Janos. I'd give you the names of all my employees and their exact locations at any given moment while on the clock, but you'd need a warrant, as I'm sure you're aware—"

"Richard?" Amy opened one of the double doors, and Ferenc's heart skipped a beat.

"You're early, darling," Richard said as he faced the door.

The term of endearment coming from her lawyer added salt to Ferenc's already-opened wound, where his shattered heart barely hung on by a thread.

"I know, I couldn't wait to try on the dresses—what's going on?" she asked, pausing in her actions. "What's he doing here?" Her eyes hardened instantly.

"Mister Janos and I were just having a friendly discussion, darling. Nothing to be concerned about."

Friendly? Hardly. Ferenc fought the urge to roll his eyes, and Amy was clearly unconvinced as well. She frowned as she shut the door.

"What the hell are you doing here, Ferenc?"

"Blaming your boyfriend."

"Fiancé," she corrected, storming forward, her curls bouncing from her movement. "And why the hell are you blaming him?"

"His goons are chasing a friend."

She stopped next to Richard and gave a humorless, dry laugh. "Goons? Richard doesn't have any goons. You need to leave." She pointed to the doors.

"That's not your call to make," Ferenc replied. "And I'm not leaving until he tells me why one of the guys chasing my friend had one of your boyfriend's business cards in his pocket."

"Did it ever occur to you that maybe they're a client?" she spat. "Geez, you've become delusional!"

"All right, that's enough, you two," Richard interrupted, stepping between Amy and Ferenc. "Darling, I hate to see you upset." He rubbed her shoulders and kissed her cheek. "Let's go to lunch so I can see your smiling face again before you go try on dresses. And you," he added, turning to Ferenc, "you have exactly thirty seconds to get out of my office before I call the police for harassment."

Ferenc raked his fingers through his hair before growling in annoyance. He shoved the business card back into his pocket, then glanced at Amy one last time before he stormed out of the office and firm.

Ferenc was still in a foul mood once he pulled into the driveway and put the car in park. Even after going to the hardware store and purchasing a new glass door for the deck—to be delivered, as he couldn't transport it in his car—his drive home only allowed his thoughts to simmer to boiling point.

A loud and high-pitched, continuous beep came from the inside of his house, as well as Max's frantic howling. He dashed forward, opening the door to the pungent odor of something burning.

"Oh, come *on!*" Dormouse groaned from the severely smoky kitchen. She rushed for the stove just as Ferenc bounded up the steps.

"What are you—?"

He swooped in, lifting the overflowing pot and placing it on the back burner before flicking the closest burner off. He then grabbed the oven mitt from the counter and pulled a pan of something blackened and crispy from the oven, dropping it onto the empty area on the stove.

"I'm sorry!" Dormouse squeaked, frozen in place. "I wanted to make you something for lunch so you didn't have to do all the cooking . . ."

"It's all right." Ferenc hastened through the house, opening all the windows before waving the oven mitt around the smoke detector to silence it.

"I'm so sorry," she repeated, a tremble in her voice from behind her fingers.

Out of breath, he made his way back to the kitchen. He wasn't upset in the least about her almost burning his house down. He was just glad she hadn't run off when she'd woken up. She had no idea how relieved he was about that.

"Hey," he tried soothingly with a warm smile. He tentatively reached out for her shoulder, and she flinched, as he'd expected, but he continued through with his cautious movement until his hand was on her shoulder. He gave it a light squeeze. "It's all right. No harm done."

"It's been a while since I've cooked anything . . ."

He chuckled, his attention on the charred mess on the pan from the oven. "Let's go out to eat," he suggested as he turned off the oven. "I think we both deserve it, and neither one of us has to do any cooking."

CHAPTER 22
Richard

R ichard wasn't listening as Amy talked on.
He poked at one of the scallops of his coquille Saint Jacques with the tines of his fork while tracing the curves of the shell-shaped plate with his other hand. Far too preoccupied with his earlier confrontation with the guardian, the deep loathing he'd kept contained after all these years threatened to break free entirely too soon.

While his firm's business cards were plain white and professional—the logo in black on the front, and the names, phone numbers, email addresses, and the firm's address and website on the back—the one Ferenc had shoved in his face was for special clients only—ones Richard personally chose.

Richard was an excellent judge of character and quite charismatic. These two traits combined were dangerous and *usually* got him what he wanted—especially when it came to "goons," as Ferenc had called them.

He picked out the desperate, those with both nothing and everything to lose, and handed them a single black card with the logo emblazoned in silver. If they accepted the call, they were blessed and became his soldiers, his spies, his pawns. In exchange for their power, Richard was granted a portion of the darkness, that desperate energy, inside of them. And with that, he raised a different army entirely—one that was, quite literally, *out of this world.*

"Richard?"

The sound of his name interrupted his thoughts, forcing him back to reality. He was suddenly acutely aware of the classical music lightly mixed with ambient chatter in the pleasant atmosphere.

"Honey, is everything okay? You're not thinking about what Ferenc did, are you? Because I swear, I'll—"

"You'll let the lawyers handle it." Amy appeared taken aback when he finally looked up from his food, and he quickly continued, changing the subject. "I was simply reminiscing."

Amy relaxed and cocked her head. "About what?" she asked in a gentle tone.

Richard moved his hand away from his plate to rest it atop of hers. "Do you remember when we first met?"

Her eyes twinkled, and a playful smile flickered across her face. "Are you talking about when you walked into the antique store to buy furniture polish, stole the owner away from me for fifteen minutes, then asked for my forgiveness before leaving, or the time you claim I dropped oregano from my shopping cart, and you chased me down the cereal aisle to return it?"

He chuckled. He'd actually swiped it from her cart while she'd reached for some tomato sauce on the bottom shelf. "I still can't believe you remember me from the antique store." The antique store was only the first step of his plan, however. He'd been watching her for a while.

He'd been lucky enough to recognize Ferenc in passing. Being that close to the guardian meant the elemental had to be nearby. Searching for her was risky if the guardian aspect in him was awakened, but if he could keep Ferenc occupied and out of his way long enough, he might get away with it. And to make that happen, the woman Ferenc was with had instantly become his target: Amy.

"I was only thinking about how lucky I am that you'd actually turned around and gave me the time of day in that cereal aisle," he continued, and Amy blushed. "From stranger in a grocery store to my soon-to-be blushing bride." He gently pulled her hand across the postal blue tablecloth toward his lips and placed a light kiss against her knuckles. "Now . . ." He looked at his luxurious steel watch. "You'd best hurry. You don't want to be late for your dress shopping."

Amy's eyes widened as she glanced at her slender smartwatch. "Mm!" She snatched the white cloth napkin from her lap and dabbed at her lips before getting to her feet. "I'm sorry for cutting this short, honey."

Richard slowly stood. "Nonsense. You have nothing to apologize for."

"I love you!" She leaned in, and he met her halfway, giving her a peck on the lips before pulling back with a soft smile.

"Enjoy yourself, darling."

Richard watched her rush off through the fancy dining room of the upscale restaurant before the vibrating holster hooked to his leather belt grabbed his attention. He pulled the smartphone from it, read the awaiting text message from his apprentice, and inwardly grinned.

"Check, please," he said to a passing waiter with hands full of food. The man nodded and continued on his way.

Richard's eyes fell back to the text message. Two more people had joined his cause. His army was growing. Now, he just needed to permanently get the guardian out of his face.

He'd lured Amy into his false world with every bit of natural— and unearthly—charm and charisma he had, and it hadn't taken long before she'd been swept up hard . . . hook, line, and sinker. He'd planned to run into her while grocery shopping. At the gym. Even at a red light outside of the elementary school she taught at. From that point on, her indifference toward Ferenc steadily grew, and when she'd left him, Richard swooped in to execute the next parts of his plan.

He had her keeping tabs on Ferenc. The fact she could get so close to him for sabotage while leaving him completely oblivious to it all was a bonus Richard had quickly used to his advantage. And using every obscure legal trick in his lawyer books to keep the guardian too busy to awaken was not only the icing on the cake, but it was fulfilling a satisfaction deep inside Richard never knew he needed.

After paying for his food and leaving a hefty tip, he made his way to his ritzy white sedan. It was time to pay his new initiates a visit. He hoped they were more competent at locating a single homeless girl than the others had been so far.

CHAPTER 23
Olivia

The Florida humidity made Olivia's skin hot and sticky, and she hated it. She missed the dry California heat, especially while beneath the scorching mid-day sun by Ferenc's front door, waiting for him to return.

She'd tried his sliding door, only to find it boarded up with plywood, which she'd found odd, as he'd wanted it left open for Dormouse.

Part of her regretted not immediately returning after she'd lost the pull—which hadn't taken long at all—but she hadn't wanted to bombard him. She'd known he'd need time to process everything, and she'd wanted to give him space to do that, but he was taking too long. Restaurants and hotels depleted her savings more with each passing day.

Now she was left in the dark even more. She didn't know where Ferenc was, or why or when he'd boarded up the deck door. Sweat beaded along her forehead, and she wiped it with the back of her sticky arm, only making it worse. She scrunched her nose, attempting to dry her arm on her saturated leggings as she wondered how long he'd be gone for, and whether she should go looking for him.

Her eyes fluttered shut, and she reached deep inside, searching for that familiar sensation that would connect her to him. It was easy to find now that she was accustomed to it, and her eyes shot open when she realized the tug was particularly strong, as if he was nearby.

Laughter came from the left, and she shot up from the slab she sat on, her attention falling on Ferenc walking up with a petite

black-haired woman. The oversized gray hooded sweater she wore
made Olivia sweat even more.

Before she could react, the strange images returned to the forefront of her mind: that same battlefield, the same strange giants, the
same armor and weapons. She took a step back, dropping the sword
and shield again, then brought her fingers to the lightweight breastplate she wore. A burning boulder exploded overhead, thrown by a
colossal being made of molten lava.

Olivia remembered this. She'd had this vision before. Her attention darted to the one who had saved her—to Ferenc.

"Protect the elemental!"

There were those muddled words again before he lunged forward, sending shock waves toward an oncoming enemy . . . or
maybe they were powerful gusts of wind.

She remembered the vision had faded when she'd tried to get a
good look at the elemental last time, so she reeled around to find a
towering, wispy, smoke-like being attacking oncoming fiends with
lightning. With a gasp, she stumbled back.

"Holy sh—"

The scene switched in the blink of an eye before she could finish
the words, back and forth, superimposed until she was no longer on
the battlefield staring at the towering sylph, but in a grand throne
room, gawking at a pale woman with cascading black hair in an off-
the-shoulder flowing gown that shifted between pure white and the
color of oncoming rain. The gentle smile on her lips was familiar.
Soothing.

"Olivia!"

The voice pulled her from the vision until she recognized Ferenc
before her. It took her body a moment to catch up, to realize someone was shaking her shoulder.

"Olivia!"

She rapidly blinked back the hallucination, bringing a hand up
to her forehead. The vision felt like an out-of-body experience—not
that she had knowledge of how that felt, but it was the closest thing
her mind could relate it back to.

"I'm okay," she said. Even her own voice sounded partially distant before reality came loudly crashing back.

"Jesus! What the hell happened?"

She found Ferenc's features etched with concern. Breathless, Olivia pulled her hand away from her forehead and rested it atop of his.

"I'm okay," she repeated.

Her gaze then shifted past him, to the woman nervously biting her fingernails, and all Olivia could do was laugh. The elemental had been with her guardian the whole time. That explained Ferenc's concern for the woman, as well as why she couldn't feel a separate tug. The pull for both the guardian and the elemental had been practically atop one another.

"What's so funny?" he asked.

"She's the elemental." Olivia prodded her chin toward Dormouse, who took a step back. "You've been with her this whole time."

Ferenc looked over his shoulder at the girl, then shook his head before turning back to Olivia. "No."

"I saw it, Ferenc. Me with my weapons, you in your armor, and her . . ." She couldn't describe what the air elemental even was—perhaps a cloud, or maybe even a tornado. "With her stormy dress," she continued, choosing the easier of the two forms to describe.

"Dormouse, this is Olivia," he cautiously introduced, stepping to the side where he could see them both. "She won't hurt you; she's one of the good guys . . . right?" He gave Olivia an expectant look, and she nodded in response.

"It's nice to finally meet the air elemental—"

"Stop," he warned. "Not now."

She frowned, taken aback. She didn't understand what he meant. He wasn't the one who'd been pulled all the way from California because of a dream. He wasn't the one who didn't know how to continue on until he found out *why* he needed to find them. "But she—"

"Where the hell were you?" he interrupted, clearly changing the subject. "You said you'd be back."

"I'm here now, aren't I? I figured you needed more time to process everything, so I gave you your space."

His expression changed from annoyance to concern. "I sure could've used your help yesterday."

A knot formed in the pit of her stomach. "Why? What happened?"

129

"Let's talk about this inside." He turned his attention to Dormouse again. "I won't let anything happen to you, I promise."

Dormouse's eyes flitted from Ferenc to her, and Olivia raised her hands near her head to show she held no ill intentions. She wished she could remember the elementals from her visions, though, and wondered if the air elemental had always been this skittish. Dormouse constantly appeared ready to dart off at any second, and Olivia felt exhausted for her just by *looking* at her. Finally, Dormouse nodded.

Ferenc shot Olivia a look in warning before unlocking the front door. She didn't move a muscle as she waited for Dormouse, who took forever before finally following him into the house. Olivia then stepped inside, shutting the door behind her.

Max sat pretty by the door, tail wagging excitedly, looking up expectantly at Olivia with big brown eyes. She gave the dog a few pets; satisfied, Max got up, following the two others into the kitchen.

To stay out of everyone's way—especially skittish Dormouse—Olivia sat on the couch in the living room. She tried not to pry as Ferenc's mumbles found their way to her ears. He was probably comforting Dormouse, and she couldn't blame him. He'd said Dormouse seemed terrified of her even before explaining what she was able to do. But she didn't understand why the girl was afraid—they'd never met prior to now.

"How do you take your coffee, Olivia?"

She was pulled from her thoughts to find Ferenc standing in front of her. "I'm sorry, what?"

"Coffee," he repeated. "How do you take it?"

It took her mind a second to process, to see beyond the thick fog that separated her thoughts from reality, but she finally answered. "A dash of cayenne pepper if you have any. If not, black, please." She missed her favorite spicy coffee from back home so much, she could almost taste it.

He nearly choked at her answer. "Cayenne pepper? Are you serious?"

"Yes." She grinned. "It might seem odd, but the flavor blend actually works well together."

He raised his brows, impressed, and gave her a halfhearted nod before returning to the kitchen. As soon as he was gone, her thoughts pulled her right back in.

Ferenc kept changing subjects whenever she mentioned the air elemental, which piqued her curiosity. Maybe Dormouse didn't know who she was. The desire to find out whether that was true or not shifted into excitement—the elation of Dormouse possibly helping her figure out what she had to do next building up, expanding into her entire being until she thought she'd literally burst.

Ferenc entered the living room, followed by an apprehensive Dormouse, who set down a navy-blue mug on the coffee table next to the recliner before returning to biting her fingernails. Olivia was afraid Dormouse might chew the tips of her fingers off completely if she continued any longer. Max brought up the rear, trotting along and parking protectively at Dormouse's feet once she slowly lowered herself onto the edge of the loveseat at the far end of the room. Ferenc handed Olivia a steaming white mug with the words "I'm just plane crazy" on it before running a hand through his hair.

"We have a problem."

Her heart skipped a beat, and instead of that buildup inside of her popping like a party favor, it deflated like a balloon. Those were never good words to start a conversation with. Her mind instantly ran through a dozen scenarios involving guardians and elementals before he continued.

"And by we, I mean Dormouse has a problem, and I'm helping her."

"Okay . . .?" Olivia blinked in confusion. She was totally lost.

"Remember those strange creatures I told you about? And the people with the filigree masks?"

She remembered. She'd been completely confused then too, as he accused her of being in league with them. "I do," she replied, tentatively.

"Well, I found the beasts chasing Dormouse again. And the masked group almost succeeded in kidnapping her, until I . . ."

She studied him quietly, waiting for him to continue with bated breath. "Until you . . . what?" She glanced at Dormouse, but she was focused on picking at the fabric of her jeans, revealing absolutely nothing.

"I don't know," he replied. "Lightning struck the tree, and it crushed their getaway car. I don't know if that was some fluke, or— and then they came at me with guns, but I . . ."

He slowly pushed his free hand forward as if moving a heavy, invisible box, his lips in a thin line, before combing his fingers through his hair once again and shrugging. She had no idea what that was supposed to mean, so she looked back to Dormouse for some sort of clue, but she continued to be invested in a single spot above her knee.

Olivia tried to piece everything together, from Ferenc's words to his actions. "You called forth the lightning?" she asked, wording it carefully.

"I just wanted to stop them. I couldn't let them take her."

She didn't understand how any of it was a problem, and that excitement she'd felt earlier returned. "Of course you couldn't!" She beamed. "You're her guardian."

His exhale came out shuddering as he looked at his hand before bringing it up to rub around his clavicle. Olivia's gaze fell to his sling, and her breath caught in her throat in realization. He must've strained himself while trying to protect her. She shot up to her feet.

"Do you need me to . . .?" she started.

He groaned in relief but quickly cleared his throat, his attention turning toward Dormouse. She sat stiff with wide eyes, one hand tightly gripping the arm of the loveseat while the other gripped the seat cushion.

"I won't hurt him," Olivia said reassuringly.

"She's right," he added, ever so gently. "It doesn't hurt at all. It actually helps."

"Think of it like a form of electrical stimulation, but with pulses. With a few sessions, his fracture will be good as new."

She approached him, wiggling her fingers, activating the tingling sensation while observing any adverse sign from Dormouse. Ferenc removed his brace and sling, and Olivia focused on Ferenc's collarbone hidden beneath his shirt. She raised her hand and lightly traced over the area while he kept eye contact with Dormouse.

"See? I'm fine," he said, but Olivia tuned him out as she focused on the sensation buzzing within.

When she finished, there was one important question at the forefront of her mind. "What did these creatures look like?"

Ferenc slowly and carefully stretched his arm. "Like nothing I've ever seen. They're animal and human, solid and gaseous—"

Olivia raised a brow. "Gaseous?"

"Solid enough for me to knock over with a trash can and for them to pin Dormouse to the ground, but immaterial enough to dissipate into thin air when needed. I'm . . . not sure how else to explain it."

They didn't seem like anything real, nor did they sound like any elemental she'd read about in myths and legends. "Are they after Dormouse because they know she's the elemental?"

"She's not the elemental," he retorted.

Olivia wondered how many times she was going to have to explain to him that she could feel it. Dormouse was an air elemental, Ferenc was her guardian, and they were the ones she'd been pulled to look for.

"She is! I can feel—"

"Olivia, stop. You're scaring her."

It was irritatingly unfortunate that neither one of them seemed to remember what they really were, meaning she was still stuck in a stalemate of not knowing where or how to proceed. But she continued to hold on to the hope that by teaching them a few moves she knew, they'd eventually remember.

"I'm trying to help, Ferenc!" She stomped back to the couch, where she begrudgingly picked up the mug of coffee. "I know you're the research type, the kind of person who needs credible evidence, but none of this stuff is tangible. You're out of time to hesitate. If you want to protect her like I know you do, you need to learn how to harness what's inside. Both of you do," she added to Dormouse before taking a sip of her coffee. There was nothing but a disappointing hint of cayenne.

Ferenc scratched at his cheeks and rubbed his forehead in apprehension, casting a glance to Dormouse every now and again before he finally said, "No."

Olivia set the mug down, almost choking on her beverage. "What do you mean, *no*?"

"Because she's terrified of all of this! Of them, of you, of—of me. I promised her I wouldn't let them hurt her. I want to keep her safe from all this ridiculous nonsense."

"I—" Dormouse started.

"You're not protecting her, Ferenc, you're sheltering her. Smothering her. Are you going to keep her locked up in here? What happens when they come crashing through your house to get to her? Are you going to be able to keep that promise?"

"I—" Dormouse tried again.

"They won't come here," he replied.

"Oh, you know that for a fact, do you? You've done your research on how they keep finding her?"

"Listen, I won't do anything to risk her running off again, so unless she gives me the okay, then I won't do it."

"*Enough!*"

Both Olivia and Ferenc shot their attention in the tiny screech's direction. Dormouse stood, her hands clenched into fists at her side as her shoulders rose and fell from her rapid breathing.

"I am standing *right here*," she said much more quietly, with a tremble in her voice and tears in her eyes.

"Dormouse—" Ferenc started.

His tone was as remorseful as the knot in her own stomach, and Olivia dropped her gaze to the floor.

"Let me finish, please. I *am* scared. I'm afraid you're both faking this and will turn me in to them, and I have to keep reminding myself that what you did—whatever it was—you saved me, and I'm more afraid of what . . ." She paused to compose herself, and Olivia looked up once more as Dormouse wiped the tears from her eyes with the sleeves of the gray hoodie. "I'm more afraid of what they might've done to me had you *not* done what you did." She swallowed hard. "So please . . . do what you have to do."

"Are you sure?" Ferenc combed his fingers through his hair. "I saw how scared you were. You wouldn't even let me touch you, and you needed a lot of convincing to come with me. I just want to make sure you're safe."

Dormouse brought her nails back to her teeth, but she still nodded. Ferenc pressed his lips together as he stared at her in silence. Finally, he spoke.

"All right. Let's do it."

Now they were getting somewhere. Olivia was one step closer to figuring out what she needed to do next.

"We're going to need a place to train," she said. "Especially if you can do what you say you can. We'll need a wide-open space."

Ferenc crossed his arms over his chest. "Where do you suggest we do that?"

"I was hoping you could tell me, seeing as I'm not from around here."

Ferenc rubbed his jaw deep in thought.

"I know where we could go," Dormouse piped in, her voice so hushed behind her fingernails that Olivia had barely heard it.

"There's an abandoned furniture store not far from here. There are plenty of signs that prohibit trespassing, and it's monitored by the police, so we wouldn't be bothered . . ."

"I'd rather not get arrested and have to explain to the cops that I broke in to train a stranger in the art of air manipulation," Olivia stated.

"I—" Dormouse squeaked, before shrinking back into her seat.

"No, that's a great idea," Ferenc confirmed. "Just because the building is being watched, doesn't mean the parking lot is."

"They do have a huge parking lot," Dormouse confirmed.

Olivia watched them both, her eyes shifting from one to the other as the gears in her head turned. She didn't like the idea, but they didn't have much other choice. Eventually, she replied. "All right," she agreed. "Let's give it a shot."

CHAPTER 24
Olivia

Olivia still wasn't completely sold on the idea of using her abilities at an abandoned furniture store—especially one supposedly monitored by the police. She was no criminal. Her record was squeaky clean. The risk of running into vagrants, drug addicts, or criminals on the run didn't thrill her either, but she didn't know much about Florida, being a California girl. If anyone knew the risks, it was tiny little Dormouse.

They waited until well past sundown before heading out, piling into Ferenc's sleek red car. Following Dormouse's directions, they pulled into the parking lot, where the weeds had pushed through the concrete, forming somewhat of a grid on the ground.

"Whoa," Olivia said in bewilderment from the back seat, eyes on the massive building as she leaned forward to peek from between the front seats.

They parked and piled out, standing next to one another before the imposing structure. Ferenc whistled, impressed.

"What do you think?" Dormouse asked.

Olivia slowly pulled away from them, meandering along the length. It had to be close to two football fields in size. "I think it'll do," she mused aloud, but there was still that knot in the pit of her stomach that convinced her otherwise.

With an abandoned building this large, chances were slightly higher that someone else was trespassing and hiding out. The thought of what those people would say if they saw them using inexplicable abilities dried out her throat, but there really wasn't anywhere else they could practice away from prying eyes. Her gaze rose to the top of the building. It seemed flat enough.

"What's on the roof?" she asked.

Before anyone could reply, she made a twisting motion with her wrists and began rising in the air, a small twister at her feet propelling her upward to the roof to investigate.

Olivia landed, pressing her lips tight into a grimace in disappointment as she stared at dozens of beams. There went that plan.

"Roof's not a good idea," she called down to them.

Dormouse looked on in horror, her eyes wide and her hands covering her mouth. Ferenc was no longer next to her, having moved closer; he looked up at her with his head tilted.

"Okay," he started. "I want you to teach me how to do *that*."

She smirked in amusement. Having him go from overly analytical and unbelieving to curious and eager was a delightful change of pace. "Master air manipulation first, *then* I'll teach you more."

With that, she jumped from the roof, and Ferenc gasped, the curiosity written across his features instantly shifting to panic. The roof was at least six stories high, and the risk of survival was minimal . . . for a regular person. She flicked her wrists again, summoning another twister around her feet and slowing her fall.

Ferenc, who had been rushing to rescue her, slumped as he slowed his pace, a hand on his chest, his laughter shaky. "You almost gave me a heart attack!"

"I knew what I was doing," she replied with a smirk. "Are you okay?" she then called out to Dormouse.

Ferenc rushed back over to Dormouse, and Olivia's smile faltered and faded as she watched them. While Ferenc hadn't been afraid of her abilities, Dormouse exhibited the very reaction most of the population would have, and the knot in her belly intensified. Part of her regretted the decision to openly use her abilities in front of poor Dormouse, but at the same time, it needed to be done. Dormouse was the air elemental. The things Olivia did so far shouldn't have even surprised her the way they did. Hopefully Dormouse would remember who she really was, and soon.

"All right," Ferenc said, rubbing his hands as he returned to her. "Let's do this."

"And her?" she asked, pointing her chin toward Dormouse, who no longer looked terrified out of her wits, but still hugged herself comfortingly.

"Give her time," he muttered as he stopped in front of her. "She's been through a lot."

Olivia continued to study her. She could only imagine everything Dormouse had been through and hoped her recollection of being an elemental would be swift—both for her own sake *and* for poor Dormouse's.

She slowly turned her focus back to Ferenc. "All right. So, uh, air manipulation." She forced her thoughts to return to the task at hand and away from Dormouse. "What did you get out of your research?"

His shoulders slumped as he tipped his head back to look skyward. "Something about being an open, aligned channel. Like you said."

With a satisfied smile, she then swept her hand out toward him. "Then show me what you've got. Heat up the air."

He glanced over his shoulder toward Dormouse—who continued to hug herself but seemed visibly calmer—before bringing his hands together to form his invisible box.

"This feels . . ."

"Stupid? Ridiculous? It might be," she admitted, crossing her arms. "But once you get the hang of it, you won't need the box anymore. You'll be able to control it instead of containing it."

His eyes hardened as he listened to her, but he eventually got to work. He took a few deep breaths before focusing on his box, on his manifestation, but she could see—she could *feel*—that nothing was happening.

"Are you envisioning your fire?"

"Yes . . ."

"Are you feeling the heat?"

He tilted his head some, as if that might've been the missing ingredient, then gave a nod. "Yes."

But there was still nothing.

"Manifest it," Olivia prompted. "Be that conduit, that open and aligned channel."

Ferenc narrowed his eyes in concentration, gritting his teeth as his hands trembled in his frustration. Olivia wrapped her hands around his to calm him down.

"What did you do when you summoned the lightning?"

"I—I don't know!"

138

"Okay. It's okay," she said, lightly squeezing his hands. "How did you feel? What was going through your mind? What were you envisioning?"

He stared at her for a moment, thoughts churning behind his gaze.

"I . . ." Agitated, he cleared his throat. "I wanted to protect her. I wanted—I wanted the car to stop, by whatever means necessary. And the closer they got to the tree . . ."

His breathing grew swift, and he took a step back, trying to pull his hands away, but Olivia tightened her grip. He shot her a glare, but it rolled off her like water off a duck's back.

"Come on, Ferenc, feel it! Let it course through you!"

A faint crackle of thunder grumbled in the sky, and she grinned in excitement. The sky was clear, meaning the thunder wasn't natural, and her own abilities were under control, so the only explanation was Ferenc.

Sweat beaded his forehead, and his hands grew clammy in his apparent anger. His eyes hardened, growing colder as his breathing hitched, but suddenly his tense body slackened.

"I—I can't do this anymore," he whispered before dropping his chin to his chest in defeat.

"Okay." She gently released his hands, and he instantly crumbled in exhaustion, sitting on the ground. "It's a start. Good effort." Frustration bubbled deep inside at how quickly he'd just given up. He'd been so close. *She*'d been so close to finding out what to do next. "Okay," Olivia tried again, turning to Dormouse. The tightness of her throat caused a faint quiver in her voice as she forcibly tried to rein in her emotions. "Come on. Your turn."

Dormouse's body tensed. She took not one, not two, but *three* steps back as she brought her fingers to her lips.

"Wait," said Ferenc from the ground. "Please don't make her." He took a breath before he continued, a little louder. "It's okay, Dormouse. You don't have to do anything if you don't want to."

Olivia threw her hands in the air. "How else is she supposed to remember what she is?"

"Give it time, Olivia," he warned.

"You don't have time!" she hissed. "*She* doesn't have time! And I know *you* can control the air. Can you at least put in a little effort?"

His eyes fluttered shut, and he inhaled deeply. "Okay, time out," he said through his exhale before opening his eyes again. "I know

139

how important this is to you to get your answers. And I know I asked for your help, but you have to understand that this is—this is all *madness*. But I'm trying. I really am. Right now, though, I think we should all go home and get some rest. Body, mind . . . We can try again tomorrow, refreshed."

The heat of her bubbling frustration drowned out any feeling of guilt she might have had; so instead of apologizing or agreeing, she stormed off.

Olivia was at a loss on what she was supposed to do. Yes, she was helping Ferenc protect Dormouse, but there'd been a sliver of hope she held onto, one that saw either one of them remembering who and what they were and telling her what she needed to do next, where she needed to go . . .

"Olivia, wait!"

The quiet squeak made her turn around. Dormouse was the last person she'd expected to come running after her. Dormouse slowed to an eventual stop, keeping her distance. Her lips parted to speak, but nothing came out. She dropped her gaze, lightly kicking at the weeds with her dirty running shoes before finally looking back up again.

"I'm sorry."

Olivia shook her head. "You have nothing to apologize for." She continued on, though at a much slower pace in case Dormouse wanted to follow—and she did.

"I didn't mean to make you angry."

"I'm not angry with you. I just—I don't know what I'm doing or where I'm supposed to go. All I know is that I abandoned everything and followed some strange sensation all the way from California to here."

"You're from California?"

"Yeah," Olivia said with a proud smile. "Oxnard. West of Los Angeles. Have you been?"

"To California? No. I've never really been outside of Florida."

"Well, we'll have to fix that, won't we?"

Dormouse came to a sudden stop. "I don't know if you can tell, but I'm kind of hard on cash and . . . everything."

Olivia slowly faced her. She hadn't meant to insult her. She wasn't insinuating anything money related. In fact, she'd been thinking about traveling via lightning. As the air elemental, Dormouse could probably easily go wherever she wanted, whenever she wanted. But of course, she couldn't just casually bring that up without the risk of spooking her and having her run off—something she seemed prone to do, according to Ferenc.

She was pretty curious about what happened for Dormouse to be in such a situation, but asking would be ruder than her previous comment ever would be, and she definitely didn't want to open that can of worms on her own. Not unless Dormouse opened up about it first.

Dormouse sheepishly shoved her hands into the deep pockets of the oversized hoodie. "So, California, huh? What do you do for a living?"

Olivia watched her for a moment. She appreciated the fact Dormouse was trying really hard. It would've been so easy for her to just turn around and walk away. A soft smile made its way to Olivia's lips before she answered.

"I'm a personal assistant to a managing director in the transportation, logistics, and storage industry."

Or at least, she *had* been. After simply up and leaving without much notice, she hadn't returned once her vacation days had run out. It'd now been a few weeks. Maybe a month. Maybe two. She didn't have her cell on her, as it would've fried in her travels, and honestly, she'd been too preoccupied to even think about using the library computers to check her emails. But that was trivial compared to the matter at hand.

"Wow." Dormouse started walking again, and Olivia followed, easily keeping pace. "What does a personal assistant do?"

Olivia shrugged. "Oh, you know. Anything the director needs me to do. Drafting agendas; booking flights, hotels, and car rentals for business travel; preparing expense reports . . . stuff like that." How about you?" she tried, watching Dormouse out of the corner of her eye. It was the perfect opening. "What do you do?"

"I—" She stopped walking again. "I don't have a job."

"That's okay. What would you like to do?" Dormouse became skittish again, so Olivia tried to be reassuring. "If you could have any job in the world—without thinking of money, transportation, clothing, housing, whatever. If all of that wasn't a factor and you could have any job in the world, what would it be?"

She'd visibly calmed down, tilting her head as she thought it over.

"I don't know," she replied. "I thought I'd like to get back into nursing to become an LPN—a licensed practical nurse—again. I used to be a primary care nurse. It's something I'm good at and enjoy, but after what happened . . ."

"What happened?" Olivia was almost afraid to ask, but curiosity got the best of her.

Dormouse didn't answer for the longest time. She focused on the ground at her feet, a hardened frown on her gaunt features. Eventually, a squeak came out, so quiet and shuddered that she'd almost missed it. "She overdosed in the supply closet."

Olivia blinked in surprise as Dormouse wiped the tears from her eyes with her sleeves, taking deep inhales that became shuddered when she exhaled.

Olivia dared not ask who had overdosed and wished she could alleviate Dormouse's pain. "I'm so sorry," she whispered.

"She was always so depressed. And when I opened the door, she was just—" She covered her mouth for a moment. "I couldn't go back to work after that. And I just—" She tried regulating her breathing again. "I stopped showing up at work and on campus. I'd lost my purpose, my direction, my meaning . . . Eventually, I also lost my apartment, then my car. I was so messed up."

Olivia couldn't possibly imagine it. The poor girl had been completely traumatized, and it'd led to her homelessness. She watched as Dormouse wiped more tears as she sniffled, and she found a lump in her own throat as Dormouse continued.

"I couch surfed for a bit, but I didn't want to be a burden to anyone. I spent some time in shelters, but . . ." She shrugged. "People expected me to just 'come back to the real world.' Family, friends . . . But I couldn't. So I walked away from it all. On the streets, I didn't have to pretend to be more or less. And it's allowed me to regain a sense of peace after what seemed to be a lifetime of torture."

Olivia's eyes stung as she studied Dormouse, wondering how long it'd been since she'd told anyone her story, how long she'd been lost with no one reaching out to her. She'd been in desperate need of therapy, and probably still needed it. But she also appreciated the fact that Dormouse had shared such a vulnerable story after only meeting her once.

When Dormouse spoke again, the quiver in her voice had disappeared. "I remember what I used to like, what I used to want for my life, but now I'm not so sure anymore. So I don't know how to answer your question."

The faint laughter had escaped her before Olivia even realized it had. She shook her head when Dormouse frowned, and she wiped her own eyes before offering an explanation.

"I'd almost forgotten what the question was," she admitted.

Dormouse giggled in turn. Both of them whipped around when the sound of footsteps approached from behind, Olivia taking up a protective stance before sighing in relief at the sight of Ferenc.

"It's late," he said, stopping a distance away. "We should go."

CHAPTER 25
Ferenc

He didn't know what he'd expected. He should've been able to do something—anything—at this point, but all he'd managed to do was get a headache.

Ferenc sat on the concrete next to Dormouse, finishing his cigarette while Olivia kneeled next to him, working on his fracture and occasionally applying pressure to a certain spot on his forehead.

After dropping Olivia off at her hotel the previous night, he'd returned to his house with Dormouse. She'd been quick to retire for the night, but he hadn't been able to sleep. His mind wouldn't shut off, and he'd spent many hours pacing his property, smoking cigarette after cigarette, researching everything and anything on his phone.

Even when he'd forced himself to lie down to get some sleep, he'd found himself right back on his phone, deep in research, until the wee hours of the morning, still no closer to finding a tangible explanation for what Olivia could do.

"Better?" Olivia asked, pulling her hands away.

He nodded as he put out his cigarette by his knee. If wanting to protect Dormouse and help Olivia with her mission—whatever that was—wasn't motivation enough to learn how to do this air manipulation stuff, then wanting to know how to heal himself was definitely a factor. Olivia had the magic touch, and while he was grateful, he knew he couldn't have her doing it forever.

"All right," Olivia said, getting back to her feet. "Let's go again."

His eyes followed her for a moment, and he couldn't help but smirk. She was all work and no play. After stretching his arm a bit, he smiled softly at Dormouse before he stood up. Olivia looked expectantly at her, but Ferenc lightly tugged her sleeve to pull her away.

"Don't make her do anything she doesn't want to do," he reminded her.

"She doesn't have time," she replied, slightly sing-song, as they made their way toward the middle of the parking lot.

"I'm here, right?" He opened his arms out. "Isn't that enough?"

"For now."

His arms fell back to his sides. "Look, I'm trying."

"I know you are."

Once they'd reached a safe enough distance from the abandoned building—and from Dormouse, who'd remained seated but had turned to face them—they paused, and Ferenc lifted his hands to form his imaginary box.

He concentrated on everything Olivia had taught him so far: the fire, the heat, aligning with his emotions, recalling the flow of events that led him to summon a lightning bolt into the tree and blowing the masked figures away.

"Come on," she encouraged. "I know you have it in you."

"Isn't there some magical incantation or series of moves that would make this easier?"

Olivia crossed her arms over her chest. "I mean . . . if you want to have a mantra or an affirmation or choreographed patterns to help you, by all means, go ahead. But it's not necessary. I don't use any."

"That's not true," he said, dropping his invisible box. Olivia opened her mouth to speak, and he quickly continued with his train of thought before she thought he was being accusatory. "You do movements. Some are very slight, like how you wiggle your fingers before working on my fracture, or how you took a really deep breath before healing my hand . . . You even did some circular movement with your wrists when you flew up to the roof. It's no different from forming this box."

Olivia tilted her head some, both curious and impressed. "Huh. I guess I do. I've never realized it."

"Does it help?" he asked.

"I suppose it does," she replied with a smirk, before uncrossing her arms and playfully nudging his arm with her shoulder. "All right, Mister Observant, get back to making that heat, already!"

145

He chuckled before raising his hands and imagining his box to contain his fire. He focused on it, making sure that it was as clear in his mind as it was in his belief. And then he imagined his campfire, burning big and bright, stuffed inside the box, sealed tight.

In all actuality, sealing the fire would have snuffed it, killing off the oxygen, but he knew his box wasn't real. He knew that to make this work, to be able to use these abilities, help Olivia, and protect Dormouse, he had to be okay with believing in things that weren't real. He'd done it once before, and he *needed* to do it again.

"Come on. I know you can do this. Reach deep down. Feel what you felt when you summoned the lightning."

He was focusing so hard, he could feel the headache returning already. Part of him wondered why it was so difficult to do, but the other part of him—the skeptic—reminded him that it was impossible, that he hadn't summoned the lightning, that it'd been a freak accident. And Ferenc had to silence that part of himself entirely.

Maybe it wasn't that he'd really wanted to stop the car; maybe it was fear-based. If he hadn't stopped the car, he had no idea where they would've taken Dormouse and what they would've done to her. He never would've forgiven himself for not being able to rescue her.

Ferenc could feel heat, but he wasn't sure if it was his imagined campfire or his anger. He really wished he knew what the masked people wanted with Dormouse. He was convinced Amy's lawyer was involved but had no way to prove it. He had nothing but a business card. Richard had denied everything, and even Amy had gotten on his case about it.

"Ferenc!"

With his train of thoughts suddenly broken, he swiftly snapped his attention to Olivia. "What?" he asked.

"What are you doing? You're just staring at the space in between your hands."

His eyes dropped, and reality set back in: there was no invisible box, and he was just making a fool of himself. "This is ridiculous." He headed back to Dormouse, running his fingers through his hair.

"Wait, where are you going?"

"Smoke break," he said over his shoulder.

"You just had one!" she called back.

"Yeah, well, I need another one."

She huffed, and he felt a twinge of regret, but he didn't turn around. He knew they were out of time, that the masked people could return at any moment, but he needed to process, to apply, and to perfect it. Unfortunately, he just couldn't shove the realistic part of himself down enough to allow the other side to succeed.

Dormouse was absentmindedly pulling at the weeds when he sat down next to her, reaching into his shirt pocket for his silver case. She wiped her hands on her jeans, broken pieces of the various weeds strewn about her crossed legs.

"I'm sorry you have to do this."

"I want to do it," he replied, lighting his cigarette, taking a drag, and blowing the smoke away from Dormouse. "I'm still not convinced I'm this guardian she speaks of, but I know it means a lot to her."

Deep down, he wondered what she'd do if none of this worked. Maybe she'd give up and accept that he wasn't who she thought he was, or maybe she'd just keep fighting it and insisting that he become something he couldn't be.

Olivia joined them but kept her distance as she paced, stepping over the cracks in the concrete like they were wide gorges. She was frustrated again. He could tell. And that tightness in his chest tugged at him guiltily each time. He couldn't do anything more. This air manipulation stuff wasn't instantaneous, no matter how much he wanted it to be. For her sake, and for Dormouse's.

Dormouse reached over, snatching his lighter, and he raised a brow in amusement at her boldness. Pulling another weed from the ground, she flicked the lighter and brought the stem to the flame, setting it on fire. She did it a few more times when Olivia rushed over, dropping to her knees between them, startling Dormouse into dropping the lighter.

Ferenc pulled back. "Whoa, hey!"

"That's it!" she said at the same time, snatching the dropped lighter.

"What's it?"

"Your lighter! Look at it!"

She flicked it a few times, but he didn't understand what he was looking at. His lighter had nothing to do with this. Its tiny flame was nothing compared to a campfire.

"What exactly am I looking at?" he finally asked.

"The click. The—the flick. Or snap. Or whatever your lighter is doing to produce the fire."

"It's a spark, Olivia. When the friction of the flint—"

147

"Can you stop being super smart for just one minute?" Ferenc blinked at her words, insulted—though it was technically a compliment. "Listen to me. Your spark, as you want to call it, is the result of an action. Earlier, you were talking about affirmations and patterns and what have you. What if this is your action? What if you snapped your fingers, or whatever, as a sign to your brain to connect your action to your end result? Not actually producing fire, because that's not our element, but the heat of it?"

As strange as her train of thought sounded, it made sense. Snapping his fingers would act as the anchor to rouse, assist, or hold his energy. He hated that he knew about that, having stumbled upon it while researching manifestation, but it did make sense.

"All right," he said. "Let's give it a try."

Extinguishing his cigarette without having finished it, he jumped to his feet as Olivia handed Dormouse back the lighter. He let Dormouse have it, as it would keep her entertained for a while, and followed Olivia back to the middle of the parking lot.

"Remember, though: you still have to tap into that same sensation. You have to connect."

"Yeah, yeah. Easier said than done," he muttered.

They stopped at a safe distance, and Ferenc formed his invisible box. But instead of concentrating on how he felt while wanting the tree to stop the car, he focused on his fear.

His eyes slowly shut as he tried to home in on how he felt thinking he'd let Dormouse down, thinking he'd never see her again. But still, nothing happened. His brows wrinkled in frustration, so he went back over the events in his mind.

He wasn't able to catch up to the car on foot. Helpless and struggling to breathe, he couldn't stop the car. He'd wished that something would happen to the car, like the tree they approached falling atop of it.

The fear he'd felt, the irritation . . . He allowed those sensations to flow through him again, but his imagined campfire still produced no actual heat.

He remembered the car being on the verge of passing the tree and the panic he felt. The desperation.

His eyes flew open as an audible gasp escaped him. That was it. That was the feeling he'd felt when the lightning struck.

He tried grasping the sensation again, digging deep inside as the memory played over in his mind. And when he reached it, he snapped his fingers.

His imagined campfire exploded in that instant, and for a split second, it felt like he was on the surface of the sun. He couldn't breathe, and his skin felt like it had spontaneously combusted.

"Whoa!" Olivia cried out, jumping back.

Ferenc stumbled back as well. "What the hell happened?" he asked.

"You didn't seal your box!"

He parted his lips to protest, but he had no valid argument. With everything going through his mind, he'd eventually forgotten about the box. "Are you all right?" he asked instead.

She nodded. "Are you?"

"I think so."

"That was . . . impressive," she tried, cautiously approaching. "Want to try that again?"

"Not really," he admitted. He didn't want to feel like he was on fire again.

"Come on. You set your anchor, now it shouldn't be as difficult to use. Just remember to seal the damned box this time," she added with a playful smirk.

He chuckled before lifting his hands, making sure his box was there, as solid as he could make it in his mind—sealed and double-locked, just in case.

His campfire was in the middle, *not* snuffed out from lack of oxygen, and once his mind was clear, the feeling of desperation roiling deep inside his core, he snapped his fingers again.

This time, the heat was contained, though it was still intense enough to be uncomfortable, as if he was standing right next to an actual campfire.

"That's amazing!" Olivia mused, testing out the intensity by placing her hands at different distances.

Ferenc shifted his wrists, placing the invisible locked box into the palm of one hand, and let out his held breath.

"Okay, now how do I stop it?"

"Let go of the feeling."

He glanced at her through his invisible box. "That's it?"

"That's it."

149

He released the panic and desperation, and it dissipated, along with the intense campfire heat. His body then felt excessively heavy, and he winced as the acute pain in his head returned. But he'd done it. He beamed at Olivia, who grinned back, then turned to look at Dormouse. The smile and pride faltered as she watched from her seated position, chewing her nails.

Getting her on board wasn't going to be easy.

CHAPTER 26
Ferenc

Never in his life had Ferenc thought he'd be able to manipulate air. He often woke in the middle of the night from a dead, exhausted sleep thinking it all a dream, but night after night, they returned to the abandoned furniture store, and he learned to manipulate something new.

Olivia had also taught him how to do electrical stimulation. His fracture was almost as good as new thanks to her, and while that was cause for celebration in and of itself—he'd be able to fly again soon!—having to carefully navigate the hundreds of questions from his doctor and his physical therapist—and even Amy—had proven difficult.

Amy had rebuked him during their latest settlement, claiming he'd been faking the accident and injury the whole time. He couldn't fault her for thinking it—he'd even anticipated it. But despite Amy's venomous words, he realized that deep inside, that wounded love he clung on to for so long seemed to be resting under a surprisingly comfy cover of indifference. The intense fury toward her big-shot lawyer boyfriend, however, burned profoundly. He still couldn't prove Richard's connection to the masked individuals, but deep inside, he knew Richard was somehow involved.

"So . . ." Olivia started. "Is anything coming back at all?"

Pulled from one agglomeration of thoughts, he was immediately shoved into a different set. He mostly learned air manipulation to better protect Dormouse, but he also did it for Olivia. She was convinced he was the guardian to the air elemental and that maybe using all these abilities would trigger something inside him, but nothing came up.

"No," he admitted.

"I know you're going to hate this, but—"

"No," he cut in before taking a sip of his coffee—caffeinated, despite the late hour. "You try this every day, and you really need to stop."

"What else am I supposed to do?" she said through clenched teeth, throwing her arms in the air. "I'm stuck, Ferenc! I don't know what my next move is supposed to be. I need to see if it'll trigger something in her—"

"I know this is frustrating for you, but what if, like me, nothing happens? What then?"

She stood up from the kitchen chair and began pacing, and he moved his feet from his spot leaning against the counter to give her more room. "Then she knows how to manipulate air! I don't see how this is a bad thing."

"I meant for you. Ever think that maybe there is no next move? Maybe you were only supposed to train us—me." He quickly corrected himself when she came to a sudden stop and cast him a look.

"There's no way the pull was only to train you while leaving huge, unanswered questions everywhere. Who else is going to explain to me how *I* can suddenly do all of this? Who else is going to tell me the reason I just *had* to find the elementals and their guardians? How many more are there? And why me, of all people?"

"Hey," he said gently, setting his coffee down and pushing off the counter to approach her. He placed a hand on her shoulder and lightly squeezed to comfort her. "It'll be all right. We'll figure this out."

"I need her to remember."

"I know. But she wants nothing to do with this. She's been through a lot, and I won't put this stress on her."

"That's the guardian in you talking," she said, dropping back into the kitchen chair.

"No, that's the nice guy in me talking," he retorted, picking up his coffee cup once more.

The newly installed sliding door slid open, and Max barged in, followed by Dormouse. Olivia ruffled Max's fur briefly before getting back to her feet and quietly disappearing down the stairs and out the front door without another word.

Dormouse, still by the glass door, brought her fingers up to bite at her nails as she always did when something was wrong. He knew she felt responsible for Olivia's irritation, even if they spoke low enough that it was impossible for her to have heard anything.

"You did nothing wrong," Ferenc reassured her, before taking a sip.

"She really wants me to try . . ."

"You don't have to. I was pretty adamant about that with her. There's no rule that says you *have* to do it just because she believes you're an elemental."

Dormouse brought her nails to her lips again, chewing on them as her eyes glossed over, deep in thought. He watched her as he sipped his coffee, and when she finally returned to reality, she pulled her fingers down, hugging herself instead.

"I'm no one special," she said, dropping her gaze to the floor. "And I don't want to be special. I don't like the attention. I've had enough of it lately."

He stepped toward her, and she didn't move. She didn't even flinch, as she normally would've, which was a great sign. "While I don't agree with you on that first part," he said, slowly hooking his index finger beneath her chin and gently lifting it to meet her gaze, "I know you've been through a lot. I won't let them hurt you. And I seriously doubt she'd do it, but I won't let Olivia hurt you either, should you decide to join us. I think it's pretty safe to say she's one of the good guys. But ultimately, that decision is yours, and yours alone."

She swallowed hard and nodded, and he pulled away just as Olivia came back in.

"You ready?" he called out to her as Dormouse's eyes fell back to the floor.

"Waiting on you," Olivia replied back.

He downed the rest of his coffee to keep himself awake for the next few hours, but his eyes never left Dormouse. Her trust in him was growing stronger. She could keep eye contact longer, she wasn't so jumpy . . . He just hoped that she trusted him enough to trust Olivia by extension.

When Dormouse finally looked back up, Ferenc arched his brows—a silent question, asking if she was ready. She nodded in response, and after rinsing his mug, he made his way down the stairs.

"Let's go, then."

Ferenc's exhale was practically a sigh—the cigarette smoke mixing with the air around him—as he watched Olivia and Dormouse ahead, walking along the building together in conversation.

They claimed to be having nice, proper discussions, but an empty feeling in the pit of his stomach always made itself known whenever Olivia was alone with Dormouse. He knew Dormouse would quickly retreat if the conversation turned to something she couldn't handle, but knowing how quickly Olivia's irritation surfaced and the fact she was desperate to get Dormouse to start manipulating air, his muscles always twitched in anticipation of it happening sooner rather than later.

He dropped the cigarette butt and stepped on it, extinguishing it before joining them. He still couldn't fully grasp how he was able to manipulate air like he did. It wasn't physically possible, yet there he was, doing it like reality didn't even matter.

Olivia laughed up ahead, and a smirk formed on his lips at the soft giggle from Dormouse. He might've been nervous about Olivia's inevitable requests, but seeing Dormouse smile or hearing her laugh always warmed his heart. It made him light as the air he now manipulated. She deserved happiness with everything she'd been through.

"What's so funny?" he asked, his long legs easily catching up with them.

"That's between Dormouse and me," Olivia said over her shoulder.

"Yeah? Am I going to have to force it out of you?" Ferenc teased.

"You're welcome to try . . ." Olivia spun around with a playful smile, flicking her fingers at him, which caused sudden gusts to blow in his face. As small as they were, they quite literally took his breath away. Once recovered, he pulled his hand back in fun, readying something of his own, but she darted away. "But you'll have to catch me first!"

She dashed off, and he charged after her, quick to notice the flick of her wrists as she suddenly pushed up into the air, a small twister at her feet. So, she was going to cheat and take the easy way out, was she?

He hadn't been able to replicate that ability quite yet, and frustration mounted through his core. He wasn't going to let her win that easily. That wasn't his thing. Skidding to a halt, he followed her to the roof with his eyes.

"Giving up already?" she goaded, looking down at him.

His attention darted around. There had to be a staircase of some sort nearby . . .

He narrowed his eyes back at her as she mockingly watched on from the roof. He then took a few steps back and arched his arms, flinging them forward as if he were throwing a ball. She easily dodged the gusts, despite her hair flying everywhere, and grinned down at him.

"Is that all you've got? At this rate, you'll never find out if we were talking about you or not."

Being the center of discussion or not didn't really faze him. He was just curious about what was so entertaining to get Dormouse, of all people, to laugh. But now that Olivia was making a game of it, he was all about knocking her confidence down a notch. If she was going to win, the least he could do was level the playing field. If only he could find some stairs.

An idea came to the forefront of his mind—maybe he could create some himself. If he could somehow manipulate the pressure of the air molecules, he'd have a fighting chance.

Focusing on the space in front of his foot, Ferenc utilized everything Olivia had taught him about manifesting and channeling while throwing in some anchors to help him visualize. He curled his wrist like he was skipping a stone, then lifted his foot to test his theory.

"Whatcha doing down there?" Olivia asked.

When Ferenc put his foot down, he stepped on something invisible, yet solid above the concrete.

Perfect.

His attention shot back up to her, and he smiled mischievously. "Wouldn't you like to know?"

He darted toward the building, curling his wrists, flicking his imagined disks and climbing them toward the roof. The look of surprise on Olivia's face as her mouth fell open was so satisfying. He'd caught her off guard. His chest drummed in elation—or maybe it was the caffeine—but the feeling was short-lived as his next step missed.

His heart caught in his throat as his mind struggled to find a solution to lock on to. This was nothing like falling with a parachute, because he had none. There was nothing to latch onto, nothing to slow his fall . . .

"I've got you!" She snatched him by the wrists, a twister about her feet, and she gasped as she struggled to keep a hold of him. "Control the air around you, Ferenc! This isn't new to you!"

She'd told him before that he'd been controlling the air in the storm; even if he believed that, he didn't know *how* he'd done it. He couldn't summon a twister like she could, and he'd somehow, in all the excitement, lost his concentration.

Now that he thought back on it, that loss of concentration was what had caused him to lose control of his jet as well.

"I'll swing you up on the count of three," she said. "Just watch out; there's not much of a roof up here. Ready? One. Two. Three!"

Ferenc used her momentum as leverage, swaying along as she spun, swinging his arms out to balance himself as he landed on the edge of the roof after she released him.

She gripped him by the shirt to keep him steady—not like it would've helped—before she barked in laughter. "How did you—"

A panicked cry from Dormouse below interrupted her, and Ferenc's stomach dropped in dread. They both turned as a figure approached, nothing but a dark mass cloaked further by the night.

"Shit," Olivia muttered. "What if they saw what we did?"

Her fear was valid, but he was more worried about her other concerns from a few nights ago: drug addicts, convicts . . .

A glint caught his attention, and his hands formed into fists as the lights from the parking lot revealed a familiar sight: a silver filigree mask.

"Dormouse," he said with a silent gasp.

Before he could react, two more recognizable forms seemed to appear from the ground itself. The creatures, with their glowing eyes, snarled dangerously, making their way toward the only one of the three not on the roof.

The hairs on his arms and the nape of his neck bristled as his stomach dropped.

"Dormouse!"

CHAPTER 27
Ferenc

Just like when he'd summoned the lightning bolt to stop the car, Ferenc summoned another. He didn't even need to focus or reach deep down inside of himself to make it happen; it was instantaneous—a pure, panic-driven rush. He clenched his fists, and a bolt struck the ground between everyone, the crack deafening.

Dormouse screamed, but Olivia had swiftly jumped down before the strike, shielding the girl from the shock waves of the sonic boom. The beasts and masked figure braced themselves from impact, but they remained on their feet.

Ferenc growled dangerously as the monsters stood tall despite being hunched, looming nearby as if awaiting orders from their master.

Olivia turned to face their enemies, standing in a guarded stance with Dormouse close behind her. "What the hell are those things?" she cried out.

"Hand her over, and nobody gets hurt," came a woman's muffled voice.

The masked person took a step, and Ferenc was quick to lash out in warning. "Stay back!"

Before he could even think about the consequences of his actions—running on adrenaline and spur-of-the-moment questionable decisions—he jumped from the roof.

His stomach leaped into his throat as he realized he didn't know how to slow himself down. And much like when he'd lost footing trying to get to the roof to begin with, he couldn't concentrate enough to figure out what to do, to figure out what exactly he'd done to get to the roof.

There was no time; the ground was quickly approaching. He waved his arm beneath himself, creating a gust right before he hit the ground. It bounded him up clumsily, then Ferenc hit the pavement hard—but much softer than he would have otherwise. The momentum continued, and he tumbled and rolled, crying out in pain. He was quick to land on his knees, blinking away the dizziness so he could analyze the situation.

"Ferenc!"

He recognized Dormouse's trembled voice, and he raised a hand. "I'm all right," he said before taking stock of any injuries. His arm hurt—he must've fallen on his fracture again—but while running on adrenaline, he couldn't quite tell how injured he was.

Stumbling to his feet, he faced the creatures, who bared their teeth and hunched down to begin an assault.

He was at a loss of what to do. They had no formal training, no plan of attack, and there was only so far one could get on the defensive. Thankfully, they weren't too outnumbered . . .

Olivia shot forward, a twister at her feet and a rumble of thunder in the clear sky. She bolted for one of the beasts, which lunged back. Ferenc glanced over his shoulder toward Dormouse who was frozen in place.

He parted his lips to tell her to run, but he paused. Running while outnumbered, even slightly, was a horrible idea. And before he could change his thoughts to vocalize something else, she shrieked, "Look out!"

He turned his head, only to be knocked onto his back by the second snarling monster. Ferenc winced as he got the wind knocked out of him, but he then gripped the creature by the shoulders, heating the surrounding air until he cried out from the intense heat against his face. It was so hot, he could barely catch his breath before the creature gave an ear-splitting cry, dissipating just as Ferenc had seen them do before.

He scrambled to his feet, desperately searching for the masked woman, who thankfully hadn't moved. He rushed toward Dormouse, skidding to a halt in front of her.

"Are you okay?" he asked, but she seemed too terrified to answer.

Ferenc veered, following her gaze, and caught sight of Olivia tossing razor-sharp wind slashes toward the beast before firing what looked like bullets of compressed air. For someone still new and confused about this, she sure knew how to do a lot.

He turned back to Dormouse. "Stay here," he instructed. "Don't run off, under any circumstances. Understood?"

She didn't reply, but she flicked her attention at him briefly before returning it to the battle ahead. Taking that for a good enough answer, Ferenc lunged toward the masked person. If she left, he was certain the strange monsters would follow.

The creature that had previously dissipated materialized in front of the masked woman, and Ferenc cussed under his breath. He didn't know how to attack, but he'd promised Dormouse he wouldn't allow anyone to harm her. And this all had to end as quickly as possible because he didn't know what kind of attention they were drawing from the homeless, convicts, or even the drivers along the street.

Thrusting his hands forward, he shot a large gust of wind ahead of him. The beast braced for impact by digging its claws into the asphalt as if it were nothing but dirt, but the masked individual flew off her feet, landing on her backside with a cry.

The monster lunged at him, and it was Ferenc's turn to brace himself—but a sudden lightning bolt struck the creature, obliterating it.

Ferenc blinked away a flashback of him watching Olivia get decimated—or so he'd thought at the time—and he shook his head to regain his focus. He didn't have time to lose himself in memories. Olivia rushed to his side, ready to attack again.

"Where the hell did you learn to do all that stuff?" he asked her as the masked woman got back to her feet.

"I'm making this up as I go!" Olivia replied. "You think I spent my time learning how to do this in California?"

It wasn't the answer he wanted to hear, but he'd have to go with it because they were out of options.

The masked person thrust her hand forward, black spikes shooting out from her palm. Ferenc stepped back in surprise, but Olivia waved her arm to the side, blowing away most of them. She missed one, however, and it came dangerously close to piercing his face. Thankfully, he dodged it.

159

"Two can play that game!" Olivia growled before shoving her own hand forward, sending solid spikes of condensed air rippling toward the enemy.

To help Olivia and make things a little more chaotic for their adversary, he shot forth a gust of wind, speeding up the projectiles.

She imitated Olivia and waved her arm to stop them. A ripple effect formed from her hand but dissipated as she screamed. A spike impaled her shoulder; now was the time.

If Olivia and the woman were now imitating each other, the least he could do was to imitate the beasts—whatever they were. He concentrated on channeling his abilities, to create something that looked like the dark monsters. Unfortunately, whatever he was doing, it was slow.

The masked woman summoned the two dark creatures again, and Olivia sprang back into her battle with them. Meanwhile, Ferenc was getting irritated. He'd so far only managed to form two blobs, barely solid in both mass and color.

"Come on!" he urged, more to himself than anyone else, focusing—manifesting—these creatures to come to life.

Suddenly, the blobs he'd created seemed to explode into dozens of tiny insect-like beings. He ducked as the insects swarmed toward him . . . then past him, toward Dormouse.

"No!" he cried out as she screamed and dropped to her knees, covering her head with both hands.

Ferenc sprinted toward her, but the swarm, which circled Dormouse like an eerie wreath, suddenly beelined straight for him. He swatted at them before pausing as tiny humanoid forms made entirely of wisps of clouds floated there before him. They weren't insects at all.

It signaled to the others with a wave of its thin arm, and the swarm changed course for the masked woman. Ferenc took the opportunity to check on Dormouse instead of gawk, rushing over to her and dropping to his knees, grabbing her by the shoulders.

"They didn't hurt you, did they?" he asked, but before he could get an answer, another screech caught his attention, and his stomach dropped.

He feared Olivia had been hurt, but when he twisted around, ready to jump and save her, he instead found the swarm attacking the masked person. He wasn't sure if Olivia had defeated the beasts or not, but she was backing away from everything rather quickly, her movements stiff from fear.

"Stop!" Dormouse suddenly shrieked, and the pixie-like beings dissipated in much the same fashion as the dark creatures often did.

Ferenc slowly got to his feet, tentatively taking a step forward. The woman didn't move, and Olivia voiced his thoughts.

"Is she dead?"

He looked down at Dormouse, with her hands pressed against the sides of her head, then to Olivia. He didn't want either of them at risk, so he advanced to check himself. When the woman coughed, he came to a sudden stop. That was as far as he was willing to go; he didn't need to get any closer. It was proof enough that she was still alive.

He then backtracked, striding in determination toward Dormouse. "Let's get out of here," he said to Olivia in passing.

He scooped up Dormouse and rushed to his car, Olivia close behind. Once they were all inside, he raced out of the parking lot and headed to his house, tires screeching.

"What the hell were those things?" Olivia asked, breaking the silence.

"I told you; those were the creatures after Dormouse—"

"No, not those—the cannibalistic *insect* things! Those came from you!"

Ferenc honestly had no answer for what they were, why they'd swarmed around Dormouse in ring formation, or why they'd started attacking him but changed their mind. He'd wanted to replicate the beasts, but that was what came of it. He didn't know how he'd done it or what feelings and sensations he'd channeled. His blobs had simply . . . melted.

"They were just trying to protect me."

Dormouse spoke so quietly, he almost missed it. But his attention snapped to his rearview mirror just in time as her face scrunched up and a sob escaped from behind her hand.

Olivia turned, straining to look at her from the passenger seat. "Wait—who was trying to protect you?"

"The pixie things! They were protecting me, but she was writhing on the ground, and I couldn't just let them—" Dormouse burst out crying, covering her face with both hands.

His heart broke for her, and he felt helpless at the wheel, but her words made sense. Whatever they were called—insects, pixies—

they must have circled Dormouse *protectively* because she was the elemental of air. And maybe, *just maybe*, they'd stopped attacking him because they realized he was the guardian. And they'd vanished when the elemental—Dormouse—ordered them to stop.

"Hey," Olivia started, her voice sympathetic. "It's okay, nobody died. You stopped them. You saved her."

"She's been through a lot . . ." He found himself saying that often, lately.

"I know," Olivia replied as she turned back to him. "She told me about the overdose thing."

Ferenc's core grew cold. "The what?"

Olivia stiffened. "She didn't tell you?"

So that's what they'd been talking about. And while he was glad Dormouse had befriended Olivia and apparently formed a sudden connection, she still hadn't completely opened up to him after everything he'd said and done for her. Dormouse still didn't trust him.

"I'm sorry," Olivia whispered. "I thought—"

"It's fine."

She turned and apologized to Dormouse but quickly did a double take. "You missed the exit—" she started, but Ferenc cut her off.

"I'm not taking you to the hotel. Until we can form a plan, you're staying with us."

She thankfully didn't protest, nor did she make any more mentions of her and Dormouse's discussion. She simply studied him for a moment before turning back to Dormouse.

Glancing in his rearview mirror, he found Dormouse hugging herself with her head hung low. His body ached now that the adrenaline had worn off, but he continued to drive, occasionally casting quick glimpses at the back seat.

It hurt that she still hadn't opened up to him, and it was such a strange sensation; he wasn't really one for emotional sustenance.

"Everything okay?" Olivia asked quietly.

"No." He chased those thoughts from his mind, replacing them with more important ones, such as the masked people.

They'd been after Dormouse the whole time. They knew exactly who she was and were determined to take her, but Dormouse didn't seem to know who they were. The image of Richard's law firm flashed in his mind, and he gripped the steering wheel tightly.

"I wish I knew who they were. I don't even know what's going on. What you did, what I did, what they did . . . none of this makes any sense," he finally said.

She parted her lips to say something but seemed to think better of it, turning her attention ahead once more.

It was a good thing he'd had a coffee earlier. He sure had no interest in sleeping any time soon.

CHAPTER 28
Olivia

Nobody moved after Ferenc parked the car.

Olivia could see questions zipping through his mind as his eyes flicked to the rearview mirror again, trained on Dormouse.

She felt horrible for letting that information slip, for betraying Dormouse's trust and hurting Ferenc's feelings. She'd assumed, with all the time they'd spent together, that Dormouse had told Ferenc about her past. And she'd made a fool of herself by assuming.

"I need to let Max out," he finally said as he unfastened his seatbelt. He exited the car, leaving the both of them alone.

The awkward silence that followed gnawed at Olivia's insides, and she needed to be the first to break it. She unfastened her own belt and shifted freely in her seat to face Dormouse.

"I'm so sorry, I didn't—why haven't you told him? I thought—"

She'd thought they'd fully accepted and stepped into their roles, and that Dormouse would just completely trust her guardian without question, which had proven to be absurd.

"I guess I wasn't thinking," she added.

Focused on her lap, Dormouse muttered her reply behind her fingertips, but she'd faintly bobbed her head up and down as she'd spoken, so Olivia took it as a good sign.

"Let's go inside," Olivia then said, and Dormouse nodded more enthusiastically this time.

As Dormouse silently absconded to the guest room, Olivia joined Ferenc out on his deck, where he smoked while tossing Max's ball over the railing and down toward the back of the yard. She paused next to him and leaned against the top rail.

"How is she?" he asked.

"How are *you*?" Olivia countered. "What's going through that analytical mind of yours? You got really quiet when I mentioned . . . y'know."

"I'm always quiet." Max trotted up the stairs, and Ferenc took the ball from her and tossed it back across the yard.

"Yes, but this was different. There's your normal quiet, then there's brooding."

He took a long drag from his cigarette in silence, and she instantly knew he had no intention of answering her. Lips pressed into a fine line, her grip tightened against the wooden railing. She was a personal assistant, not a psychologist, but she really needed him to open up and talk to her. She couldn't lose them to misunderstandings—or whatever this was—because she needed them to help her figure out her next step.

Max returned with the ball, dropping it at her feet expectantly instead of Ferenc's. The thin white line that had been her lips loosened and curved into a faint smile, and she picked up the slimy tennis ball, tossing it back over for Max to chase.

She wiped her hand on her leggings. "Why wouldn't she have told you?"

"I'm the wrong person to ask," he finally managed to say.

He finished his cigarette, extinguished it in his ashtray on the wicker table, then descended the deck stairs and headed for the fence gate.

Olivia blinked in confusion. "Wait, where are you going?"

"I'm going for a walk."

Her heart skipped a beat. "Oh, no, you're not," she started. "Were you not paying attention while we fought that masked person and those—those things that were with her?" Ferenc slowed his pace to an eventual stop. "They want Dormouse, and they'll stop at nothing, as proven by tonight's events! I can't come to your rescue *and* stay here to protect your elemental at the same time. I'm not some *magical—*" She paused when he shot her a disbelieving look, then she sighed. "Never mind."

Ferenc brought one hand to his hip as he fully faced her from the ground. "Ever stop to think that maybe she's not *my* elemental, but yours?"

That was impossible. Though dressed in armor in her visions, following a tug toward someone else made no sense if she was an elemental or guardian. Her dream never once said to find *others like herself*. And while, as the biggest believer in justice, her mama-bear instinct kicked in to protect the weak, it was Ferenc who had that inexplicable urge to protect Dormouse, specifically.

"That's ridiculous," Olivia replied. "You're the one with the connection to her, not me."

"She's guarded around me. She opened up to you without a problem."

"Is that what this is about? You're jealous?"

"Not jealous," he stated. "Helpless." The hand on his hip fell limp to his side, and he continued to the gate in silence.

Realization dawned on her. "You're withdrawing again," she said.

Ferenc paused once more and inhaled deeply. He might've rolled his eyes, but she couldn't tell in the darkness, even with the porch light.

Olivia continued. "I might not know you that well, but what little time I've spent with you, I've picked up on your trends: you overanalyze everything and always need to know it all before starting something. You enjoy feeling capable and competent. And when that doesn't work, you withdraw. Isolate. Detach. Whatever you want to call it. Am I right?"

His exhale came out as a huff, and he turned back to her. "What's your point?"

"My point is that you need to let it go. You don't need to know all the answers right away. The world isn't perfect, so you don't need to be, either. Focus on what you *can* control. Right now, whether you believe it or not, your elemental needs you. *I* need you. We'll figure the rest out as we go."

Olivia didn't budge as Ferenc studied her in silence. Finally, he spoke. "You might think you can control all these outcomes . . ." His voice was calm, almost sympathetic. "But it doesn't work that way. You can't just insert yourself into every situation."

She opened her mouth to speak but firmly clamped it shut once more. She always got so defensive over criticism. As much as she wanted to snap back, it wasn't like he was rudely attacking her character or behavior.

166

"I don't know why she so freely opened up to me instead of you. You need to talk to her." Ferenc opened his mouth, but she didn't want to hear his excuse, so she quickly continued. "I know you're protecting her. I know you're treading lightly so she doesn't run off, but you need to focus on what you can control. If you're so concerned about why she's not opening up to you, maybe you should be vulnerable first."

When he didn't move—or speak—she sighed. She wasn't a mind reader either, and she was going to start taking his silence as criticism if he didn't open up. Her hands flexed open and shut in frustration, but her next words were calm.

"Look. We'll get through this, I promise. Together. The three of us. But right now, after all that craziness at the furniture store, I can't let you leave. So let's go inside."

His silence became overbearing, but she held back her irritation.

"You're right," he finally said as he doubled back for the deck stairs, pausing at the top. "About everything."

Her mind buzzed as her emotions shifted, and she managed to quirk the corner of her lips some. "I love it when you see things my way."

He headed inside. "Yeah, well, don't get too used to it."

Olivia held back the laugh that threatened to escape her, but the jubilation was still visible in the form of the wide grin she sported. It was a small win, but a satisfactory one all the same.

She called for Max, who lay exhausted in the yard, and entered the house. Things had gotten plenty interesting, and she just hoped they wouldn't completely fall apart before she found out her next step.

CHAPTER 29
Ferenc

O kay, let's run through the plan one more time."

Ferenc groaned as Olivia continued to pace the kitchen as she'd been doing for the past hour and a half. The caffeine had worn off—as did the adrenaline—and Dormouse was practically asleep at the table, with her head resting atop her crossed arms and strands of freshly showered hair cascading over her shoulders. Olivia hadn't had any coffee that he knew of. She must've been getting all that energy from some secret Californian reserve.

"We've gone over it a dozen times . . ." he started, running a hand through his disheveled hair for the umpteenth time.

Lips pursed, she spun around to face him. "But what if I screw this up?"

"You won't," Dormouse mumbled before yawning.

Olivia recommenced her pacing, and Ferenc rubbed his face in exhaustion. "You make your appointment with Duane Cordell, pull the info out of him with the cleverly curated questions you'll memorize, and if he doesn't suspect anything, then you continue to humor him until your appointment is over. If he does suspect, then you have a sudden emergency. We can iron out the smaller details in the morning after you make your appointment."

"But what if I blank on your 'cleverly curated questions'?" She made air quotes with her fingers, but before he could reassure her, she spoke again. "I'm not good with lies, especially complicated ones. What if Duane Cordell doesn't work there? Or he does, but not in a department we can handle? What if the firm is actually some villainous lair?"

Ferenc blinked at the left-field comment, and even Dormouse slowly raised her head to quirk a brow in confusion at Olivia. Ferenc's hands found their way to his temples. He needed sleep. They all did.

"Okay, now you're just being ridiculous. I've been inside multiple times, remember?"

Dormouse dropped her head back onto her arms, and Olivia clenched her hands into fists. She was getting frustrated again. Ferenc stood from his chair and gently touched her shoulder, forcing her to pause.

"I just—"

"Let's get some sleep and tackle this with a fresh mind tomorrow, all right? This whole situation isn't doing us any favors. You'll do fine; we have plenty of time to get into the nitty gritty before your appointment. But right now, rest is best."

She faced him, studying him for a moment before finally nodding. As she did so, her tension deflated, as if the exhaustion that she'd been keeping at bay finally caught up to her.

He pulled away to his room, where he prepared his bed with fresh cotton sheets. With the way the sunlight
pooled through the many windows in the living room early in the morning, he found it best to take the couch himself. As big as his house was, he only had one available guest room; the other was used for storage. And though Dormouse had opened up to Olivia, he doubted she'd so easily share the bed—even if it *was* full size.

When he shut his bedroom door behind him, leaving Olivia to her own devices, Dormouse was no longer in the kitchen.

Light shone beneath the closed door of the guest bedroom as Ferenc made his way down the hall. His body, which had tensed up in fear of her having run off, partially relaxed. He knocked ever so quietly. The shifting on the other side eased his fears, and the remaining rigidity in his body lifted.

The door opened a crack, and a single dark-blue eye peeked out at him. He couldn't help but smile.

"Just checking to see if you needed anything," he said.

She shook her head, her gaze dropping down as Max approached, nails clip-clopping peacefully down the hall. Ferenc's attention dropped just in time to see the retriever push her way into the guest bedroom as Dormouse squeaked and jumped back.

"Max, no!" he scolded, grabbing for the collar, but missing.

Max jumped atop the foot of the bed and promptly lay down, her big guilty brown eyes watching Ferenc.

"Come on, you crazy mutt," he started.

Dormouse giggled. "It's okay, she can—she can stay if she wants."

"Are you sure?"

Max continued to look at him with a sheepish expression, and Dormouse slowly sat on the edge, cautiously reaching out to pet the golden fur. "Have you always loved dogs?"

"Yeah, we had a few growing up."

Childhood memories surfaced, reminding him of simpler times. He remembered every single one of those dogs, from the first one when he was five—a black Lab by the name of Skip—to the sibling border collies, Luna and Bear, and the three surprise pups Luna ended up having with the neighborhood stray. His smile shifted as his memories veered to when Amy had gifted him a puppy.

"Amy wasn't big on dogs, but . . ." His attention fell back to Max. Memories of the last few days swirled through his mind: their pointless arguments, her saying goodbye to Max, him punching the sliding door. "Max grew on her." He internally braced himself for the oncoming heartache, but to his surprise, it didn't quite pack the same punch it usually did.

An uncomfortable silence instilled in the room, and all Ferenc wanted to do was go for a walk to clear his mind, but Olivia's words resonated in his mind: *you're withdrawing again*. It was true, and he hated how right she'd been. But he'd always had a hard time outwardly dealing with his emotions, and this was no exception.

Amy's voice now echoed in his mind from their argument a few days prior, especially the part about how difficult it was getting him out of his head whenever he'd return from flying.

Olivia had suggested he get vulnerable with Dormouse, and as much as Ferenc didn't want to, as much as he wanted to keep it all to himself, now was the perfect opportunity. Dormouse simply watched him. She didn't appear terrified or bored or anxious; she wasn't chewing her nails or looking everywhere but at him.

"Can I . . ." he started, before swallowing hard. "Can I tell you something?"

She nodded, and he ran a hand through his hair. He was suddenly acutely aware of a dull pain stemming from his healing fracture, and he brought a hand up to rub at it.

He didn't know how to say it. He didn't know where to start. Part of him deemed it a horrible idea, but he locked his knees in place to prevent his legs from walking away from the situation.

"I—whenever I fly, I feel . . . free. Like I can be myself and relax and not be subjected to the pressure of others or of—of myself. It's almost addicting. And while up there, I spend a lot of time thinking. A lot of time in my head. But I—" He paused and licked his dry lips, his mind going a million miles a second. He couldn't stop now. "I can't explain why I can't come out of that headspace. It baffles me. And as the type of person who needs to know everything, I . . . I hate not having all the answers."

There. He'd said it. He'd admitted it not only to Dormouse, but also to himself. His admittance thankfully hadn't chased her away, but that vulnerability screamed at him, and it almost felt like she sat there silently judging him. He stopped rubbing his fracture and dropped his arm to his side, ready to apologize for bothering her and taking up the time she could use to be sleeping, but Dormouse finally spoke.

"So," she started in a tiny voice, "I have a thought on this, but I need to ask . . . are you looking for advice?"

Ferenc ran a hand through his hair, studying her. He'd vented his frustration, he'd opened up to her, but he'd also opened up in general, for the first time in a long time. And not only had she listened, but she was considerate enough to ask if he wanted to hear her thoughts.

"Yes—of course," he stuttered. He'd never refuse anything from her.

"I think that . . . just like a great vacation coming to an end, you get disappointed when you have to return to reality. Maybe to the point of depression. So you cling to that sensation, that familiarity, for as long as you can."

He sucked in a breath, amazed, his body stilling. She'd effortlessly hit the mark. A spontaneous laugh escaped him as he shook his head in both shock and amusement, and he crossed his arms over his chest.

"Were you majoring in psychology too?" Dormouse cracked a smile in response, and he added, "How'd you figure that out?"

That smile faded as her attention fell back to Max. "Let's just say I've been through something similar."

"Care to talk about it?" he offered.

171

"Not really." She fell silent long enough for it to almost be awkward, long enough for Ferenc's mind to start wondering if being vulnerable had even been worth it before she finally added, "Not right now."

The panic that bubbled inside ceased—a false alarm—and he smiled a bit. So, it hadn't been a complete lost cause. He'd never push her to do anything she didn't want, but the ball was now in her court.

"I'm here for you when you're ready." She didn't reply, so he added, "Thank you for being a listening ear. I didn't realize how much I needed it." He did feel lighter, and he was grateful for it. He'd always been one to keep things to himself, but he hadn't recognized how much having someone to just listen to him when he did open up was good for him until he didn't have anyone to listen at all.

Until he no longer had Amy.

Dormouse met his gaze once more with a light smile as she ran her fingers through Max's fur again. Ferenc uncrossed his arms and took a step toward the door.

"You should get some sleep. We've had a rough day. Don't hesitate to wake me if you need anything."

"Thank you," she replied, barely above a whisper.

He then glanced down to Max and reached for her, scratching behind her ear. "You watch over her, you traitor. Got it?"

His words elicited a giggle from Dormouse, and he smiled warmly in response. With a playful wink, he then exited the room, leaving the door slightly ajar for Max, feeling as if a great burden had been lifted from his shoulders.

CHAPTER 30
Olivia

They'd gone over the plan multiple times and thought up every possible scenario, but it didn't stop the butterflies from fluttering inside Olivia's stomach as she stepped into the lobby.

She scanned the room; from the light gray of the walls to the dark wood of the bathroom doors, the textured carpet and leather cushions, to the woman behind the help desk and even the button lock of the door she assumed led to the rest of the firm.

The help desk attendant smiled widely as Olivia approached the desk. "Do you need help, honey?" she asked.

"I have an appointment with Louisa Irene on the fifth floor." Her throat was so dry, she practically croaked out her reply.

"Right through that door. You'll want the elevator on the right."

She followed the attendant's finger to the door that was hidden from the entrance. Olivia thanked her, then licked her parched lips. "Um, I called on Tuesday. I *really* wanted an appointment with a particular lawyer, but was told there was no such name . . ."

"Ah, yes! I was the one you spoke with. You were looking for a Cordell—"

"Duane Cordell, yes. Are you sure he's not here?"

She'd nearly fumbled the plan over the phone when she'd called the next day. Thankfully she'd placed the phone on speaker. She'd also been thankful for her ability to read lips as Ferenc had mouthed the next plan: booking an appointment with any available lawyer just to get past the lobby.

"Well, he's not on this floor, but I looked through the directory twice. Where did you see his name?"

173

"Oh, I could have sworn I saw it on the website," she lied. All part of the plan.

"Maybe he used to work here and doesn't anymore? I don't know. I'm sorry I can't help you, honey, but I'll definitely leave a message for IT to change the website."

"Thank you." Olivia gave a quick smile before heading toward the door across from the help desk.

It led to a tiny rectangular area with a dozen hexagonal mirrors scattered about and a flower arrangement sitting atop a console table against the far wall. Everything was far too artsy for her liking. A single elevator flanked each side of the room.

She entered the one on the right side as instructed, then tilted her head as she pressed the button to the fifth floor. It was a full number pad; not split into odd and even floors, like she assumed was the case between the elevators. The base of her neck tingled with her sudden urge to know where the other elevator led to.

The door slid open to a room similar to the one she'd just left, only there was no elevator on the other side. She opened the door at the end of the room and stepped into a lobby like the one on the ground floor.

The receptionist—a young blonde—smiled almost as wide as the older lady she'd just left. "How can I help you today?" she asked.

Olivia didn't get a chance to reply when the reception door opened, revealing an older woman with a big, puffy, 80s hairstyle.

"Olivia Gillies?"

"Y—yes." Her heart thrummed in her chest, and her throat got even drier, if that was even possible.

"Come on in. I have a room ready for us." Olivia stepped up to the golden-maned woman, who offered her hand. "I'm Louisa Irene."

"Nice to meet you," she replied as she shook her hand and followed the lawyer down the hall. Closed doors flanked from both sides, with an occasional cross hall. Finally, Louisa opened a door wide, and Olivia stepped in.

"Have a seat," Louisa instructed, shutting the door behind herself.

Olivia did as told, though much slower than she should have. Her mind spun as she tried to grasp onto the plan she and Ferenc had discussed but came up blank.

174

2

Louisa sat down across from her and began a well-rehearsed introduction to what her job as a divorce lawyer entailed, but Olivia hardly paid attention. Her gaze flicked around the room as fear practically froze her in place. She was never good at complicated lies, and this one ran deep. As her mind reeled, it returned to the other elevator. She needed to find out where it went.

"I'm sorry," Olivia interrupted rather suddenly. "I just—I really wanted help from Duane Cordell."

Louisa briefly poked her tongue inside her cheek in confusion. "There's nobody in this firm by that name."

"Are you sure?"

"Positive. Maybe he's a lawyer for one of the other firms?"

"Maybe." Olivia stood up. "Sorry to waste your time."

"Wait!" Louisa called out, and Olivia paused before she reached the door. "I can still answer your questions! My qualifications—"

"I don't think we'll be a good fit, but thank you."

Olivia slipped out of the room, shutting the door behind her, and beelined back to the elevator. The door was sliding closed, so she rushed ahead.

"Hold the door, please!" she said. She wanted as much distance from Louisa as possible. The fewer questions she had to answer, the better.

The man in the elevator jumped, startled, before grabbing the door, preventing it from closing. Olivia slid in, quickly pressing the button to close the door once more.

"Is everything okay?" he asked.

Olivia smiled sheepishly. "I'm going to be late for another meeting." She bit her tongue, preventing herself from saying anything more. It was maddening to be so easily capable of lying on the spot but to be unable to follow up with a well-rehearsed plan.

"Not with me, I hope!" He barked a laugh. "I'm running late too. Thursdays are my busiest days."

"Oh no!" She tried to make her laugh as equally friendly as his, but it came out more nervous and forced than she would've liked to admit. Thankfully, they reached the bottom before she could make a bigger fool of herself.

"Good luck on getting to your meeting on time!" he said, and before it crossed her mind to thank him, he was out the door and into the lobby.

Then she was alone. Perfect.

She stepped to the opposing elevator, and the door slid open almost immediately. Cautiously stepping inside, she quickly pressed the button to shut the door, then paused, tilting her head in confusion and wonder. Aside from the buttons to open and shut the door and the emergency stop, the operating panel contained only three buttons—ground level, eighth floor, and basement three—and a key lock to access it all.

It was unfortunate that she didn't have a key. She had to contain the mounting curiosity that bubbled inside her, almost overflowing. They had such a massive parking lot, so the fact they needed a basement was odd. And to only have a basement three in one elevator while the other didn't have access to the first and second ones was just as puzzling. Her eyes roamed around the small box to see if there was anything else, but she came up empty.

With a frustrated growl, she reached for the button to open the door when the elevator jerked and began moving down. She quickly gripped onto the rail for safety. It looked like she was going to get her answer after all.

The elevator came to a stop, and she shut her eyes to halt the elevator-induced dizziness, but she quickly opened them again when the door slid open. She nearly jumped out of her skin as she came face to face with an expertly groomed, dark-skinned man, who took a partial step back in surprise before his eyes hardened.

"What are you doing in here?" he asked.

Olivia's mind raced as she blindly grasped at straws for something believable to say. "I, uh, I'm looking for Duane Cordell. I must've gotten on the wrong elevator . . ."

"There's nobody here by that name," he said, fully stepping inside.

If she could've taken a step back, she would've, but she was still pinned in the corner, right where she'd been on her way down. She swallowed hard, trying to give her typical reply to such a claim but came up empty.

The man hit the button to shut the door and inserted a keycard before pressing the button to the ground floor. He then faced Olivia, his eyes colder than anything she'd ever seen or felt in California in comparison.

"You shouldn't be here. This floor is off limits."

All she could do was swiftly nod in agreement. He didn't have to tell her twice. She was going to need a new plan, and the quicker she could return to Ferenc and Dormouse, the better.

The thought of knocking him out with a little electricity and stealing his keycard did cross her mind, but she shoved it down as an option for later. She didn't need to be in more trouble than she already was.

She slid out before the door even fully opened without casting him a second glance and made her way into the lobby and out the front door, focused on the car she'd borrowed from Ferenc.

What a fiasco.

Olivia's heart hammered against her chest in frustration at the whole situation, while embarrassment tightened its grip on her stomach as she tried to fathom why it had been so hard to stick to the script they'd gone over a few dozen times. It wasn't because she doubted Ferenc's thoroughness. With his overly analytical mind, he thought up whatever situation she hadn't—and then some—and they'd put it to the test from multiple angles.

"So stupid . . ." she muttered to herself. "You should've swiped his key."

When Olivia pulled into the driveway, she was calmer, but not by much. Ferenc opened the front door as she exited his car, and she tossed him the keys when he approached, Dormouse close behind him.

"How'd it go?" he asked.

"You mean besides totally blanking on everything we went over?" Ferenc shut his eyes in defeat, and Dormouse dropped her gaze to the ground. "I'd say that I never want to set foot in there again, but something's fishy."

"Fishy how?" he asked, opening his eyes again.

"Like one elevator with keycard access to only the top floor and a third basement."

Ferenc raised a brow. "The one on the left?"

Olivia nodded. "I *accidentally* found myself down there and was promptly told it was off limits. What are they hiding?"

"Who knows." He shrugged, then added, "Dormouse and I were going to grab some food. Want to join us? We can discuss on the way to the diner."

Olivia's stomach rumbled, and she smiled. "Sure. I'm starving."

177

Ferenc and Dormouse started walking, and Olivia followed along next to them.

"How did you accidentally find yourself down there?" he asked.

"I was investigating it when the guy in the basement was coming up." Ferenc nodded in understanding as he lit a cigarette. "Nobody knows who Duane Cordell is either."

"Hm." Ferenc took a drag, his eyes narrowing in thought as he walked. "Then why did he have their card?"

"Maybe what Amy said was true; maybe he really was just a client."

"There's no way—"

"Ferenc!"

Dormouse's gasp and tiny squeak caught both of their attention, and when Olivia followed where the tiny girl pointed, she swiftly bristled, on the defensive. There, ahead by the main road, was a figure in a silver filigree mask.

"There's another one," Ferenc muttered, and Olivia followed his gaze to the right, where one approached from the neighboring street nearby.

Olivia cussed her displeasure before hooking her arm around Dormouse's. "Keep walking," she instructed, and Dormouse heeded.

"When I give the signal, you both run." Ferenc flicked his unfinished cigarette to the side.

"What about you?" Dormouse asked, a tremble in her voice.

"He'll be fine," Olivia replied. "He's buying us some time. Where are we going to go?" she then asked Ferenc.

"Dormouse knows the streets, so follow her. And keep her safe. Ready? One . . . two—"

"Wait, no!" Dormouse squeaked.

"*Go!*"

At Ferenc's signal, Olivia pulled Dormouse and ran.

CHAPTER 31
Ferenc

Ferenc knew they'd go for Dormouse if they split up. They were adamant about taking her, and he had no idea why, but sending Olivia with her was his best option. She had better control over her abilities than he did, so Dormouse would be safer.

And while they were busy dealing with Olivia, they'd never see him coming. His pulse sped up, his heart pounding as heat flushed through his body, and a rumble in the sky echoed his rage.

His abilities had been lackluster at best while training, but now, he was beyond angry. He wouldn't allow them to take Dormouse. Not with a car, not with those beasts . . . not if he could help it.

As Olivia and Dormouse bolted ahead, he thrust his arm out at the approaching person on the right, shooting an air gust so strong it knocked the individual onto its back.

The second figure ahead rushed to cut off Olivia and Dormouse, summoning two creatures with a wave of its hand, but Ferenc was ready. He shoved both hands forward, and a blast of air shot forth. The resulting shock wave of pure force sent debris exploding everywhere. His heart skipped a beat when Dormouse screamed, but as the dust settled, he barely made out a clear shield around both women as they continued to run, more than likely cast by Olivia.

Thunder crackled overhead. The sky rapidly filled with clouds so black, it cast the city in a darkness akin to night. He couldn't risk innocent people being involved and getting hurt, nor could he risk regular people seeing them use their abilities. If it was dark, the less likely they were to see. And if it rained, the less likely people would be out and about. He glanced upward as the heavens suddenly poured down like a waterfall before racing to catch up to Dormouse and Olivia.

The unfortunate part of the deluge was the roar it produced. Ferenc couldn't hear them running up ahead, splashing in the sudden puddles. He couldn't hear the traffic as cars whooshed by. They could've gone in any direction—they even could've been caught, for all he knew.

"Dormouse!" he bellowed, but even to him, his voice sounded distant and drowned out. He skidded to a halt at the intersection, soaked from head to toe as he searched through the torrent and darkness for any sign of where the two could've gone.

A distant scream came from his right, and his already-racing heart pounded even faster in fear that it might be Dormouse, but he couldn't be sure. He went to move in that direction when something hit him in the back of the leg, and his kneecap hit the flooded pavement.

He didn't even have time to cry out when something struck him on the side of the head, knocking him over with a large splash. Dread filled him to the core as something shoved his face into the puddle.

He tried fending off whatever it was, but something gripped his left arm while pinning his right arm next to his face. There could've been one single beast atop of him. Or one person. Or maybe even two or three of them; he couldn't tell as he wrestled to break free, to use his abilities, to breathe . . .

He was going to drown.

His fingers flexed in his panic, and the puddle spread out from a shock wave just long enough for him to gulp down some much-needed air. The earth beneath him vibrated, and whatever was on top of him wasn't any longer.

Scrambling to his knees, he gasped for breath, coughing from the inhaled water. Three masked people lay on their backs around him, but before he could react, pops of gunfire sounded straight ahead.

Ferenc covered his head defensively with his arms as he flinched, unable to see what was going on, but the familiar scream was so close. He jumped to his feet and limped as fast as he could to rescue her.

"Dormouse!"

Lightning flashed through the sky, illuminating everything just long enough for him to spot Olivia out of the corner of his eye, surrounded by masked figures and monsters alike, and Dormouse only a few paces ahead, trying to make herself as small as possible. A large and deafening explosion occurred after a swift flash—Olivia had dealt with her immediate aggressors, but there were suddenly so many more, as if they'd been hiding this whole time in some sort of intricate trap.

Olivia yelled something, but with his ears ringing, he couldn't distinguish what she was saying. And whatever it was would have to wait as he spotted a pair of glowing eyes approaching a helpless Dormouse.

His stomach dropped when another pair of eyes appeared, and a third and fourth.

"Dormouse!"

He sprinted as fast as his agonizing knee would allow him, fueled by pure panic and dread. He needed to get her as far away from everything as possible. And the only way to swiftly escape their current situation was to do what Olivia had done when they'd quite literally first run into each other: lightning travel.

Skidding to a halt before Dormouse, he dropped to the ground—the pain from his already-injured knee so intense his stomach lurched—and yanked her against him while raising an arm to the sky as the beasts leaped. Somewhere, someone shrieked his name. He couldn't tell if it was Olivia or Dormouse, but it was the last thing he heard as lightning engulfed him.

It was over in the blink of an eye—or multiple blinks, as the flash had been intense. The disorientation was immediate, and he thought himself permanently blinded. He couldn't tell where he'd ended up, whether he'd brought the creatures along with him, or if he'd successfully rescued Dormouse or not.

When she fell limp in his arms, Ferenc's heart leaped in his throat as a sudden heaviness overcame him. Though his partial blindness faded, the putrid, burning stench and radiating heat hit his senses first.

In a panic, he laid her in the sand beneath the pouring rain, his hands trembling from dread as he tried to find a pulse at the side of her neck. He couldn't tell if he was doing it properly or not due to his own heart's jackhammering, but he couldn't feel anything at her artery.

"Dormouse!" he whimpered.

As a pilot, he had classroom training about medical emergencies. Performing CPR was one thing, but with her heart stopped, he needed a defibrillator. And there were none along the beach coast.

"Damn it, Dormouse, don't do this to me!" he said, gently cupping her cheeks.

His attention paused on his own hands. He didn't need a defibrillator—he could *be* one.

He brought his hands together, swiftly rubbing them until tiny sparks emitted from between his palms. A small snap sounded upon contact, despite the continuous downpour, as he brought his hands down to her chest. He shot a short burst to stimulate her heart, then checked for a pulse, unsure if it was enough. There was still nothing.

"Come on!"

Cautious not to release too much, given the rain acting as a conductor, he tried again. Sparks scattered around them, and she gasped before going into a coughing fit.

"Dormouse! Oh, God, Dormouse . . ."

He scooped her into his arms and cradled her, allowing her to breathe without swallowing too much rain. Her eyes briefly fluttered open before they shut once more and the coughing ceased.

Ferenc's heart skipped a beat. "Don't you *dare* leave me!"

He checked for a pulse and found one, albeit faint. She hadn't given up on him. With her body in his arms, he got to his feet, his legs like gelatin and his knee screaming rather loudly in protest.

A crack of thunder startled him, and Olivia crumbled in the sand, holding her bloody shoulder.

"I need to get you both to a hospital—"

"Don't!" Olivia warned with a wince. "I'll be fine, but they'll find her there. Is she still breathing?"

"Somewhat. Her heart stopped, but I—"

"Her imperviousness wasn't up," she replied, cutting in again. "But she's breathing, and that's all that matters right now." Olivia got to her feet, stumbling forward. "They're looking for her. She'll only be safe with you. Take her to your place, and stay there until I come back."

He didn't have time to take her home; he needed to get her to a hospital as soon as possible. "She's dying, Olivia!"

"Then start healing her until I get there!" she snapped. "She's in good hands. But right now, you need to go. They're coming, and I can only hold them off for so long."

"But what about you?"

"*Go!*"

She darted past him, sending a large sonic boom out toward what he assumed were more of the masked individuals and strange creatures. He wasn't going to stay around to find out. Not with Dormouse unconscious and exposed.

Ferenc ran, cradling Dormouse like his life depended on it—and it did. But between his injured knee, his exhaustion, and the rain soaking them both to the bone, he struggled. Thankful for the proximity of his house to the beach, he arrived moments before his body gave in, and he sank to the floor in the dark hallway, Dormouse still in his arms.

His entire body ached; he wasn't sure which part screamed in agony the loudest. He wanted to lie there longer—maybe even forever—but he really needed to tend to Dormouse first and foremost. With one final heave, he got back to his feet, his entire body trembling, and carried her to the spare bedroom, where he set her on the flowery comforter of the full bed.

He pressed his trembling lips together, then scrubbed a hand over his face. His fingers pulled in, pinching the bridge of his nose, and he shut his eyes. He'd failed her. He'd promised he'd never hurt her, and yet he had—albeit accidentally. He hadn't known it would hurt her. All he'd wanted was to get away, to protect her.

But he couldn't dwell on that; she needed to be healed. His eyes snapped open, and he reached down to touch her when frantic pounding occurred from the front door. He jumped, startled, and his heart raced. Olivia said she'd be back, but the masked individuals could've also found them.

"Ferenc!"

Olivia's voice was muffled but unmistakable, so he rushed as fast as his aching body would allow him and opened the door.

In a flurry, she burst inside, slamming the door shut behind herself and slumping against it.

"Did they follow you?" he asked.

"I don't think so, but I couldn't be too careful—*ow!*" Her last utterance came out as a partial whine.

183

He didn't have the strength to be useful. He had no control, and he couldn't even protect those that mattered to him. But he reached out to Olivia in case she collapsed. "How can I help?"

"I'm fine," she dismissed. "Let's help Dormouse first."

Ferenc motioned with his head. "In the spare room."

Olivia pushed off the door, leaving a streak of blood behind her. His brows drew together as he followed her with his eyes, unable to will his feet to move until she called out from the spare room.

"Let's get her dry," she suggested.

With that, his feet unglued from their spot, and he hastened to the linen closet, where he grabbed some towels. He lightly tossed them on the foot of the bed in passing, as he made his way to the laundry room and grabbed a shirt from one of the hangers.

Olivia had peeled off Dormouse's clothes in no time, and Ferenc stood against the doorframe, staring down the dark hall as he waited.

"Here," she said, handing him the sopping clothes.

He didn't have the energy to wash them. In fact, he wasn't sure how much longer he could go without passing out from exhaustion himself. And so, he left them in a heap in the utility sink before returning to the spare room, where Olivia was using both a soft healing wind and electrical stimulation on Dormouse.

"What now?" he asked, when she was done.

"We keep doing that, twenty minutes to an hour, up to four times a day," she replied, focusing her healing now on her own bloodied shoulder. "Other than that, I don't know. There's something going on, and I don't know what it is. I feel like my answers will be in that basement."

"If Richard's firm is involved, then they have access to where I live. They could be busting through the front door any minute."

"All the more reason for me to go back to investigate right now."

They didn't have a plan, and the mission was practically suicide. If the firm was really involved, Olivia could be marching to her death. But they had no other choice. They *were* coming for Dormouse; it was only a matter of when.

Ferenc hated it. He should be the one investigating, but Olivia knew how to handle herself way better than he did. She also wouldn't risk alerting Richard—or even Amy—if they were still on premises. With a solemn nod, he finally replied.

"Go see what you can find out. Just . . . be careful."

CHAPTER 32
Ferenc

Ferenc awoke in a panic, sitting upright in the small folding chair next to the bed. He'd fallen asleep again, but that seemed to be what happened each time he did a healing session on Dormouse: he used up all his energy to the point of exhaustion.

Ferenc groaned from the sudden dizziness and black spots in his vision, remaining as still as he could until it passed. With a yawn, he glanced at Max's form at the foot of the bed through the dim blue twilight of the sky. He couldn't check his phone—he'd fried it when he summoned the lightning—so the best he could guess was that it was early.

His gaze traveled up the covers to Dormouse's face as he stretched his sore muscles and released a shuddering breath.

"I'm sorry," he whispered as he leaned back in. "I'm sorry, I'm sorry, I'm sorry." He trailed his fingers through her black hair. "I didn't know it was going to hurt you; I just wanted to get you to safety."

For someone who was supposed to be a guardian—or so Olivia claimed—he was the worst in existence. He was pretty sure guardians didn't kill their wards, accidental or otherwise. Thank goodness for electrical stimulation . . .

He got to his feet and stretched some more, ruffling Max's fur as he yawned before leaving the room in search of Olivia. His knee felt better—he'd used electrical stimulation on himself in between Dormouse's healing sessions—but he could definitely use Olivia's expert touch. He found the couch as he peeked into the living room, but she wasn't there. The loveseat and his recliner were as empty as the couch, just as they'd been all night. His heart skipped a beat; she was nowhere to be found.

Ferenc made his way up the stairs and peeked into his bedroom just in case, before crossing the kitchen to the sliding door. There was still no sign of her. He rubbed at the sudden tightness in his chest. He'd sent her to her death. All she'd wanted were answers . . .

God, he needed a cigarette so bad, but he refused to go outside. Who knew where those masked figures were lurking. He never smoked in the house, but the temptation was growing stronger with each passing moment.

With one final scan around his backyard in the dying twilight, he returned to Dormouse. Keeping himself occupied with healing her would keep his mind off his craving.

In the spare bedroom, he pulled back the comforter to her waist before rubbing his hands together, his eyes on her unconscious form. Olivia always wiggled her fingers whenever she activated the ability, but that didn't work for him. Thankfully, he'd found another way. The friction caused by rubbing his hands together produced static, so he'd used that as his anchor to trigger the power.

But it didn't seem to be working on Dormouse. Maybe he was doing it all wrong. Olivia wasn't around to correct him, and it wasn't exactly like he could fully research this kind of stuff. All he had was newly gained knowledge on defibrillators, pacemakers, and transcutaneous electrical nerve stimulation. Everything else was made up on the spot, and he hated it.

Sparks formed between his hands, and he lightly touched her chest with his fingertips, the sparks coursing just below the surface of her skin as he splayed his fingers until the palm of his hand rested over her heart. He took a few deep breaths before shutting his eyes and concentrating on the healing current.

He tried to stay focused and keep all roaming thoughts at bay, but just like when he watched Olivia summon the lightning, the traumatizing flashbacks flooded his brain. The entire event replayed in his mind: the walk to the diner, summoning the rain, almost drowning, invoking the lightning, her falling limp in his arms . . .

Ferenc flinched at the intensity of the flashback before internally scolding himself. He needed to focus, but no sooner did he anchor his attention back in place, his mind flooded with memories once more.

His heart raced and his breathing hitched, each exhale nothing but shuddered breaths as he slowly pulled his hand away. He drew the comforter back up over her as a wave of exhaustion washed over him, and he shut his heavy eyelids.

He might've fallen asleep, or he might not have; he couldn't be sure. All he knew was that Dormouse began coughing, which startled him and sent uncomfortable shivers throughout his exhausted body. But he jumped up nonetheless, knocking over his chair, when he saw her eyes open wide in fear.

"Dormouse!"

She was *awake*. But she jerked back, whimpering between coughs as she rapidly looked all around herself in both fear and confusion.

"I'm sorry," he whispered. His legs gave out, and he fell to his knees. "I'm so sorry . . ."

A sob escaped her, and his heart grew heavy with grief and regret, but when she flung herself off the bed, wrapping her trembling arms around his neck, his heart wept right along with her.

He'd failed her. He'd broken his promise; he'd not only hurt her, but he'd accidentally killed her. Yet there she was, safe in his arms, still somehow trusting him, and a part of him couldn't help but feel it was a tiny sign of forgiveness.

When her crying had died down to hiccups, he cupped her face, wiping her tear-stained cheeks with his thumbs.

"How do you feel?"

"I don't know," she whispered.

He parted his lips to rephrase his question but paused when Max jumped off the bed and sat in the doorway expectantly, whining and excitedly wagging her tail.

Ferenc's heart skipped a beat. Someone—or something—was in his house. He shifted to protect Dormouse when a hand reached for Max, but Olivia's voice came across as she petted the dog's head.

"Hey, Max!" Olivia leaned against the doorframe. Aside from dark circles under her eyes, there wasn't a scratch on her, not a platinum-blonde strand out of place. "I hate to break up what you two have got going on, but I have something to show you."

"Olivia!" he said with a gasp, clutching his chest, where his heart was doing somersaults in his ribcage. "Jesus Chr—I thought you were—"

187

"Dead," she finished for him, motioning with her head for him to follow her as she stepped away. "Yeah, I've heard that one before."

He turned back to Dormouse, who looked down at the floor as she hugged herself. He cupped her cheek again, and she leaned into his touch before her eyes rose to meet his.

"Go," she said. "I'm not going anywhere."

He studied her for a moment before getting to his feet. Max, content, padded to Dormouse's side and sat next to her, as protective as ever.

He followed Olivia into the living room. "What the hell happened?"

"There was extra security, so it took me a while to get back in, but . . . look what I found."

His blood ran cold when she handed him a silver filigree mask. "Where did you find that?"

"There's a door in that basement. It's unlike anything I've ever seen before. It's not solid at all. And that mask was sitting on the table next to it. There's a staircase that leads up behind it, but—"

"Olivia," he suddenly said, his tone grave.

He'd had moments of distrust in her in the past, back when she was more of a stranger than anything. But with the mask in her hands, for a split second, he wondered if she really might've been working for the masked people all along. His mind couldn't wrap around how she got in and out unnoticed, how she returned without a scratch. But at the same time, he needed to know if all of this was real. His fierce irritation with Richard compelled him to want to confront him on all these *coincidences*, but he'd be in a lot of trouble if Olivia was lying.

"I need you to be truthful, because this . . ." Ferenc took the mask, wiggling it in his hand to show her. "This is serious, and I'm about to go off on my ex's lawyer."

"I've never lied to you."

She replied so quietly, he almost missed the tremble in her voice, but he caught the now-familiar impulsiveness loud and clear, that irritation that often flared when she tried not to appear weak. She was insulted by his words, and the truth then became crystal clear.

"I know."

His reply matched her silent tone, but it carried the massive weight of his regret and remorse at having suspected her even for a second. Then, a sudden rush of adrenaline and rage coursed through him, and he headed for the front door.

"Where are you going?" Olivia asked.

"Take care of Dormouse," he instructed.

"Wait! You need a plan!"

"My plan is to get answers." He swung the front door open.

"Then take this!"

She flicked something toward his face, and he swiftly snatched it with one hand: a key card.

CHAPTER 33
Ferenc

Y ou can't go in there—" the receptionist warned.

"Like hell I can't," Ferenc snarled, seething.

When he'd stormed into the firm demanding to speak to Richard, he hadn't considered that it was still early, and Richard probably wasn't in yet. Usually, he would've gone over every possible scenario and gone in with a plan, but he was too exhausted, too enraged to think straight.

He stood in front of Richard's double doors. They were locked, of course, but there was a keypad lock like the ones by the receptionist, and a card slot. The best part was that it was all electronic.

Perfect.

He rubbed his hands together before banging them into the double doors, releasing a current strong enough to not only scramble and disengage the locking mechanism, but also cause the lights to flicker dangerously on edge of blowing out. The receptionist gasped as the doors flung open and slammed into the walls when they could open no farther.

The office was empty, as he'd been told, but he didn't care. He stepped inside.

"Sir," the secretary tried again, "I'm calling the police."

Ferenc whirled around, narrowing his eyes at her—Edith, if he recalled correctly. "You go do that, then." He swung an arm out, and a strong gust slammed the doors shut in her face.

It was no surprise that Richard had lied to him about not being involved. But that dishonesty mixed with all the other unethical, slimy things that made up Richard's being transformed his irritation into pure, venomous anger. He was so outraged, he didn't care what anyone did. Yet common sense came down on him like an anvil, and he scanned the room, at a loss. If lawyers or courageous civilians weren't busting down the doors to get him out, then the police surely would. And then what?

Hands on his hips, he hissed his displeasure before his gaze settled on the phone on Richard's desk. He marched over to it and it took a few tries to figure out how to dial out, but he managed.

"Honey?" came a woman's voice on the other end.

Ferenc frowned. She sounded millions of miles away. But he didn't have much time, so he cut to the chase. "Where's your boyfriend, Amy?"

"Ferenc? What the *hell*?"

"Where is he?" he bellowed, as if it would help her hear him more clearly over the technical issues that made it seem like they were on the other side of the world from one another.

"You seriously need mental help." She huffed. "I'm calling the cops."

"Don't bother," he snapped back. "They're already on their way."

He slammed the receiver back onto the device. He knew she wouldn't have been any help and wondered why he even bothered trying.

Sirens approached; his time was running out. He should've made a plan with Olivia. He shouldn't have burst into the firm out of pure anger, no matter how desperate he was to protect Dormouse. Now he'd get arrested, and the masked figures and monsters would continue freely chasing her.

The only option he had left before getting caught was to rummage through Richard's office for a lead. Maybe he'd be able to tell Olivia what he'd learned when she visited him in prison. *If* she visited him in prison.

He quickly scanned the spine of every binder on the shelves, but other than business jargon, there was nothing immediately telling. There was more of the same inside the drawers and cabinets, which meant Ferenc had nothing: no lead, no proof, and nothing stopping him from getting arrested as the police pounded on the double doors.

Edith's muffled voice on the other side informed the cops that Richard wasn't answering his cell. But that wouldn't help him.

He reached for the closet in one last ditch effort to escape. Maybe he could hide until they left. No, that was a ridiculous option. But as he closed the closet door, something caught his eye: a hatch on the floor.

It was a very odd thing to have on the top floor of a building. He pulled the black handle. It wasn't locked. Ferenc raised a brow at the confined spiraling cement stairs he found beneath, wondering why Richard had a hidden staircase. It was far from an emergency exit and wasn't up to code, but Ferenc swiftly shut the closet door behind him and descended into the darkness, closing the hatch as he went.

He tried to make as little noise as possible—both with his footsteps and breathing—but he couldn't see a thing. The last thing he needed was to trip and alert everyone on every single floor that he was there. Too bad he'd fried his phone—he could've used the flashlight.

A thud came from above, and he paused, looking straight up, but nothing else happened. And while he focused on the hatch however high up, he suddenly became hyperaware of the echo the noise had produced. Apparently, his abilities included echolocation.

He rolled his eyes at the ridiculousness of it all, but he needed out, and there was no other way. With a faint
wave of his hand, he shot a tiny gust downward, and bit his tongue to prevent himself from gasping out loud. Not only could he hear the whoosh hitting each step as it continued down, but it painted a pretty vivid picture in his mind.

It wasn't too long ago that he wouldn't have wanted to give in to Olivia's theory of being connected to elementals. But there was no logical explanation for knowing how to do the things he did without her help, and especially how easily it suddenly came to him in the heat of the moment, or how he even did any of it, period.

But now he knew better. He'd have to mull over the how later, however, as he was out of time. And so, he continued down the spiraling staircase with the help of his newly acquired echolocation skill.

Eventually, a faint light grew brighter until Ferenc could finally discern the bottom of the seemingly never-ending staircase. Once he touched the concrete of the ground, he peeked around the corner.

There, before him, was a swirl of black and gray—a portal, just as Olivia had described it to him. Now that he thought about it, she'd mentioned a staircase too, but he'd cut her off in his rage.

For a basement, it was pretty empty, but also unnecessarily huge for a law firm—regardless of size. Cautiously, he approached the portal. He couldn't be sure Richard was on the other side, and if he stepped through, there was no promise he'd ever be able to come back.

He couldn't just sit back and wait. If not for himself, then he had to do this for Dormouse. With a deep inhale, he raised his hand, his fingers inches away from touching the dark swirls when he stopped himself.

No, he couldn't do it without knowing. His analytical mind wouldn't allow it. It could hurt him or even kill him, and he'd be truly useless to protect Dormouse.

He glanced about for something to shove into the portal first, but other than a white folding table and an accompanying folding chair, there was nothing.

Ferenc grabbed the chair and slowly pushed it halfway through the spiraling gateway with little to no resistance. When he pulled the chair back out, it was intact. His eyes shifted back and forth between the chair and the portal. He fully tossed the chair inside and waited. He didn't hear it land, and it didn't pass through to the other side of the basement.

He had to do it. His heart raced as he stepped through.

Dusty gray rocks lay scattered everywhere, and he practically tripped over the chair on the ground before him. Ferenc looked up to inspect his surroundings first, and his jaw dropped as he audibly gasped.

Planet Earth in the starry black sky was the last thing he ever thought he'd see coming out the other side.

Awe instantly shifted to panic as he gripped his throat with both hands. He was going to suffocate and die in the vacuum of space. Advancing over the threshold before further investigating had been such a careless mistake, and he rebuked himself for it when his thoughts shifted to never seeing Dormouse again.

But his self-criticism was short-lived as the fact he was still breathing—in *space*—halted all other cerebrations in his mind. It was impossible; he was creating his own oxygen. Or maybe there was a breathable atmosphere on the moon that all astronauts and scientists had somehow missed.

He took long and slow inhales, testing the burned charcoal-scented air as he waited for his racing heart to relax back into a comfortable canter. Alert and attentive, Ferenc scanned the area, then squinted at something near the portal. Ferenc approached but did not go through again. Instead, he tentatively reached out beside the swirls until the palm of his hand rested against something solid and clear: a dome. He followed the faint clouded view up and around until he faced the pathway before him, flanked on each side by columns akin to marble, toward a large temple not too far away.

"Hello?" he tried, but no answer returned to him. He wasn't sure anyone could hear him or if his voice even traveled on the moon just because he could somehow breathe.

He slowly followed the path, the crunch of lunar rocks and minerals foreign beneath his feet. But the inconceivability of air and sound in space was nothing compared to the likelihood of extraterrestrials. None of the space explorers had ever mentioned anything about intelligent life on the moon, let alone buildings, yet there was an erected temple before him.

Ferenc followed the dusty path until he was close enough to spot a tiny silhouette sitting on the topmost smooth step leading to the enormous archway entrance. He squinted as he approached, homing in on its features, then froze in place.

"*Amy*?!"

With the sense of paralysis gone as quickly as it came, he dashed over to her. She stood, her lips downturned and her stare distant.

"What the hell are you doing here?" he asked. "How is this even possible?"

"I'm sorry, Ferenc . . ."

He slowed down at her words and stopped at the bottom of the steps, looking up at her, confused. "What's wrong?"

She slowly descended to meet him, tears filling her eyes. "I didn't mean for this to happen."

"Didn't mean for *what* to happen?"

Despite how malicious and mean she'd become, despite his anger against her new beau, he still loved her. Even if that love had slowly shifted—with each new argument, each new lie—like threads snapping against his taut heartstrings. It became more and more difficult to rekindle that original sensation, but it didn't prevent him from being concerned. His brows drew together.

"Are you hurt?" he then asked. "How did you get here?"

"This is as far as you'll go."

His heart sank as her foot settled past the final step, inches in front of him, but he stood his ground, despite the sense of impending doom hardening in the pit of his stomach. "Amy, what have you done?"

She winced. "I can't let you hurt Richard."

"I just want to talk to him."

"He said you'll hurt him, so I'm here to stop you."

She winced again, harder this time, and his firm stance softened some from her involuntary grimace. Something was clearly wrong with her.

"We need to get you back home," he started, reaching for her hand. He needed to get her off the moon and back on Earth.

"I'm sorry, Ferenc," she said with a whimper as she recoiled from his touch.

Before he could react, she lurched back and screamed as her body shifted, bones protruding and cracking sickeningly as she grew taller and darker until she became one of the creatures he'd been fending off from Dormouse.

He took a few quick steps back, eyes wide. "Amy!"

With a deep, guttural growl, she lunged at him.

He swiftly side-stepped and shot out a strong gust of air, which slowed her next leap. He didn't want to hurt her, especially if she was still somewhere inside the beast she'd become. "Amy, stop!"

The beast pounced forward in one amazing bound, knocking Ferenc onto his back. It opened its maw wide with a deafening howl, then lashed out at his face with massive, sharp claws.

195

CHAPTER 34
Olivia

A low, dangerous growl seemed to come from everywhere, yet nowhere all at once. Olivia's eyes shot open, despite the exceedingly bright sunlight, as a bark forcefully pulled her from her exhausted slumber.

She'd fallen asleep in Ferenc's recliner after Dormouse convinced her she'd rather not rest in bed all day. Olivia had given in with a promise to rest on the couch instead.

She fixed her sleepy gaze on the source of the growl, which came from Max—she stood protectively in front of the loveseat, guarding Dormouse, baring her teeth at something Olivia couldn't quite see yet.

A soft swoosh, like a vacuum, surrounded them, and she squinted at the large windows to see if one was open and catching the wind. As the sound increased, a dark spot formed in the middle of the room, hovering and swirling, slowly growing in size.

Her heart skipped a beat, and in an instant, Olivia jumped from the recliner, protectively standing in front of both Dormouse and Max. She'd seen something like this before: the portal inside the firm's basement.

"Go to the bedroom and shut the door," she instructed.

Dormouse shot up and scampered away, followed by Max.

A figure stepped through in a long white robe that shimmered almost as bright as the gold filigree mask upon its face. Olivia slowly backed away, never taking her eyes off the intruder, until she was defending the hall that led to Dormouse.

"Stay where you are," she warned, glaring daggers as the figure took a step forward.

"Hand over the elemental, and nobody gets hurt." His gravelly voice was slightly muffled behind the mask.

"Yeah, that's not gonna happen," Olivia replied.

"Such a pity."

The vortex vanished behind him, and he raised his hands. Two creatures formed from what could only be explained as liquid shadows, melding and molding until they towered over the man before hunching over to look her in the eyes.

This was not good. As big as Ferenc's house was, there wasn't room to fight. She really didn't want to risk destroying his house, but some things were far more important, like making sure the air elemental didn't end up kidnapped by the masked man and whatever the hell those beasts were.

They approached menacingly, their backs curled akin to something used to walking on all fours instead. Olivia stood her ground, flicking a sharp gust of wind toward the closest monster. But as she did so, the second creature lurched forward, snatching her by the throat as her feet lifted from the floor.

Eyes wide, she gripped the beast's arm, digging her nails into the bark-like texture of its skin to get it to let go. Her legs kicked about wildly, but it was no use: she couldn't get the thing to let go of her.

Olivia couldn't breathe, and soon, she'd lose consciousness. She'd just have to use her abilities inside the house and apologize to Ferenc later. She focused on her gasping breaths, gusts of air sprouting about sporadically throughout the living room, but it wasn't enough to fully grab their attention.

Her focus intensified, and she imagined her struggling breaths as smooth as a single breeze. She concentrated on all that energy, then released it, knocking everyone but the monster holding her onto their backs.

She shot out an arc of cutting air with both hands, and the creature dropped her as it lost its entire arm. It howled in pain as Olivia landed back on her feet with a thud.

There was no guarantee that if she took out the masked man, the beasts would follow, but Olivia wasn't taking any chances. She used a gust to push off, launching herself at him, knocking the mask right off his face as they both hit the ground.

He glared in irritation with russet-colored eyes before smirking. The way the smile crept to the corner of his lips made her skin crawl, and before she could react further, his arm shot forward.

A spiraling flame hit her dead on.

Olivia shrieked in surprise. The blazing heat scorched her skin, and she quickly extinguished it with a strong gust, but her skin continued to sizzle. She inhaled deeply to heal herself, but a giant clawed hand grabbed her by the throat once more, blocking her airway. She struggled to break free as a screech came from down the hall, reverberating like nothing Olivia had ever felt before.

"Go *away!*"

The air accentuated the voice in every pitch and tone imaginable, causing all windows, bulbs, and any other fragile items to shatter. The pain against her eardrums was pure torture as it continued on, coursing through her entire body, and she cried out in agony as she covered her ears. The monsters mixed their own tormented howls to the cacophony, releasing Olivia.

When everything stopped, the loud ringing in Olivia's ears was almost as deafening as the scream had been. She pulled her trembling hands away from her ears and found them coated in blood. She then whipped around to face the source.

Dormouse stood, petrified, in front of the bedroom door like a deer caught in headlights. Olivia didn't know what to do or say. Dormouse had saved her life, had used her elemental skills, had stood up to a threat . . . but before she could react, Dormouse squeaked and retreated back into the safety of the bedroom, slamming the door shut behind her.

"Kill her and bring me the elemental!" the man bellowed, enraged.

Olivia's stomach dropped as she turned back around. Powers newly awakened or not, she wished Dormouse hadn't chosen to be brave and reveal her location *now*, of all times.

She couldn't let them take Dormouse. There was no way she'd fail to protect the air elemental, no way she'd fail to follow the air guardian's orders.

She connected her hands and swiftly pulled them apart, manipulating the air to dissipate from around the man entirely until it was gone. His mouth fell open, and he grabbed his throat. She was asphyxiating him and wouldn't let go.

There was a glint in his eyes she almost missed. Unfortunately, she spotted it too late. As she cast a quick glance over her shoulder, something sharp punctured through her, and she gasped in both surprise and pain. It was so intense, she couldn't tell where it originated from, and she struggled to stay conscious as she crumpled on the floor.

Her own heartbeat accompanied the ringing in her ears. She followed the man's footsteps as the creatures dissipated into nothingness, and she passed out before he opened the spare bedroom door.

CHAPTER 35
Ferenc

"Amy, stop! I won't fight you!"

There was a drastic difference in strength between Amy and whatever creature Amy had become. She was stronger, faster, and *angrier* than he'd ever known her to be. But Ferenc refused to fight her.

He'd never been on the defensive so much—even while training with Olivia—and his exhaustion with trying to overpower Amy's attacks and keep her at bay weighed heavier with each gust thrown at her. There had to be a way to change her back, and he was pretty sure the answer was Richard.

He'd never liked her lawyer—even less so when he found out Richard and Amy were dating. Getting married, even. His heartbreak had intensified then. But when all the coincidences involving the masked people after Dormouse began centering around the law firm, his dislike had increased.

Maybe Richard was an elemental or was being controlled by one. He couldn't see any other explanation behind Amy's change—both physical and emotional. And as much as her emotional change unsettled him, her current physical form concerned him the most.

She lunged at him, and Ferenc swung his arm out, sending another large gust toward her, which carried her leaping form back a safe enough distance.

His shoulders ached as if he'd been exercising strenuously, and it took everything he had to not drop his arms limply at his sides. He couldn't keep up the momentum. He couldn't keep defending all day—or whatever measure of time it was on the moon. The stalemate dance they performed couldn't last forever, and at the rate they were going, he'd be the unfortunate one to fall first.

"Amy, please . . ."

She leaped again, and as Ferenc pushed her back, his stomach dropped when a familiar voice screamed: "*Let me go!*"

"Dormouse?" He spun around, trying to pinpoint exactly where her screams were coming from. "Dormouse!"

He turned back to the temple with that familiar sensation of overwhelming dread building, only to be knocked and pinned to the ground by the monstrosity that was Amy. Before he could react, she stabbed her needle-sharp claws straight through his shoulders.

His vision filled with spots as the searing pain enveloped him, and it took him a moment to realize the anguished cry ringing in his ears was his own.

The hairs on the back of his neck bristled from the delight in Amy's howl when she looked back down at him. With a dangerous growl, she parted her maw, her teeth as sharp as the claws currently pierced through him. Ferenc raised his hands as best he could to stop her from biting down on him, from snapping his neck.

With his injuries, exhaustion, and her new form, she overpowered him. His arms trembled violently as he held her at bay by the snout with what remained of his might. It couldn't end like this. He wanted her back to her beautiful self, even if she hated his guts.

Dormouse's screams grew more frantic, and Ferenc's heart sank in fear and panic. He had to get to Dormouse but also dreaded finding out what had happened to Olivia.

"Please, I—"

His arms gave out, and suddenly his hands were the only things between Amy's jaw and his throat. Her acrid breath sent uncomfortable shivers across his skin, and when Dormouse shrieked again, he felt a sudden shift inside himself.

Dread and panic no longer weighed him down. Instead, a rage brewed within so intensely, blasts of wind picked up the moon's dust, billowing and blowing it in a cyclonic motion around them.

With each of Dormouse's tormented screams, his fury intensified, and the squalls picked up. Amy needed to change back, and he'd be the one to do it.

"That's *enough!*" he bellowed.

The winds churned so quickly that they started pulling Amy off from him. It was distracting enough that she stopped trying to snap his neck in two, and Ferenc couldn't help but gasp in relief as his trembling hands could finally rest. But he was far from done with her.

Amy continued to float up through the whirlwind; the only things keeping her low to the ground were her claws through Ferenc's shoulders. She gripped him tighter, and he cried out as the searing agony amplified, but he wouldn't give up.

The vortex continued, intensifying in strength, and Ferenc waved his weakened hands as best he could, sending gust after gust into her face, making it difficult for her to breathe.

Amy swiftly shook her head in irritation, then opened her maw wide, chomping at each blast. Finally, she yanked her claws from Ferenc's shoulders to swat at him but was pulled up into the cyclone before she could touch him.

His vision darkened from the throbbing in his shoulders, but he couldn't succumb quite yet. Concentrating on the twister, it closed up, encapsulating Amy inside a sphere of wind, which glowed a bright white.

Amy's howls mixed in with Dormouse's screams, but Ferenc just focused on manifesting the end result: purifying the air until it purged whatever had physically changed her. When Amy's howling ceased, Ferenc exhaled, and the sphere shattered, sending the glowing dust floating to the ground, healing his wounds as it touched him.

There, in the air, was the curly-haired woman he'd grown to love. She floated down just as delicately as the dust, and Ferenc got to his feet, catching her in his arms. He pulled her down to the ground as he checked for a pulse, and relief washed over him when he found one.

Her eyes fluttered open, and he gave her an insipid, near-apologetic smile. "Hey," he greeted.

"Don't you dare kill him, Ferenc Janos," she said, her voice hoarse.

"Amy—" he started. What little smile he held faded instantly.

"He said you were going to kill him. Don't touch him, Ferenc. Leave him alone—why can't you accept that I don't love you anymore and leave us alone?"

His eyes narrowed for a split second before his brows drew in and his chest tightened with pity at her delirium. After everything that happened, she was still loyal to Richard. She still loved him. And in a sense, he'd been doing the same with her all along.

He released her after making sure she was comfortable, then got to his feet, his attention on the temple's entrance. His hands formed into fists when he realized he couldn't hear Dormouse anymore.

"I make no promises," he said to Amy as he strode forward, Amy's weak pleas behind him.

He'd failed to keep Dormouse safe. And if she was dead, well . . . he wouldn't be held responsible for his next actions.

Inside the temple, his eyes immediately fell on glowing wisps of cloud at the center of a large dome on the platform in the middle of the inner chamber. Fronds of static arced outward to the dome like a giant plasma globe. And there, standing in front of it all, was a man Ferenc recognized all too well.

"Richard!" he roared.

"Mister Janos," Richard greeted in turn. "Welcome to the moon. I'm a little disappointed you made it this far, but no matter. I have what I want."

Ferenc's nostrils flared as he stared him down. "Where's Dormouse?"

"You'll have to speak up, I'm afraid your charge did a little damage to my hearing." Richard brought his hands up to his blood-stained ears and checked them for fluids, and a fraction of Ferenc's rage broke away, transforming into smug pride. By the looks of it, Dormouse had put up a decent fight. Richard then pointed his thumb over the shoulder toward the dome behind him. "But I suspect you're inquiring about her?"

Ferenc furrowed his brows in confusion at the wisps of cloud and electric sparks. Dormouse wasn't inside. But the strands shifted, and a pair of familiar dark-blue eyes peered out at him.

His breath hitched, and he shuffled back a step in surprise at whatever Richard had done to her, a sudden coldness hitting him to the core.

"This is your elemental, Mister Janos. Based on your reaction, you're not fully awakened yet, are you? How intriguing . . . and how unfortunate for you."

Richard spread his arms wide, and when his hands closed into fists, Dormouse screamed in pain. The fronds grew bright, all arcing in one spot on the dome, and a thin vapor emerged, enveloping Richard in a warm glow.

Whatever Dormouse had become, she was in massive pain, even if she didn't look corporeal. And really, that was all that mattered to him. With an enraged growl, he thrusted forward, his hand forming into a fist to strike Richard square in the jaw. No amount of wind magic was ever going to be as satisfying as beating him to a bloody pulp with his bare hands.

Richard launched a sonic wave before Ferenc could get anywhere near him, sending him flying into one of the decorative pillars by the door. Ferenc dropped to the ground, gasping for breath as the wind was literally knocked out of him.

"The air elemental's power is quite strong, isn't it?" Richard said as he approached. "That's why the elementals are venerated, Mister Janos. They're elemental deities. And now, that raw power is mine."

Richard hurled a blast of air out, and Ferenc knocked some of it away with a strong gust, but the blast continued, striking Ferenc straight on, sending him back into the pillar. An audible crack came from either his spine or the marble-like material. He didn't doubt the possibility of it being both.

Still weakened from his battle with Amy, the chance of winning against Richard alone diminished by the second. He needed Olivia's help, but he'd left her to protect Dormouse—who was currently immaterial inside the dome.

Ferenc struggled to his feet. "Where's Olivia?"

"The blonde? She was in my way, so I dealt with her."

His head spun, and a rather large lump formed in his throat as he fell back to his knees. She was the strongest of them all. She couldn't be dead. He needed her.

His mind reeled back to the time they'd protected Dormouse in the parking lot. She'd thrown blow after blow out at the masked figures, and she'd made every attack up the whole time. Every move was anyone's guess if it would succeed or not, but she'd done it anyway. For Dormouse.

Gritting his teeth, Ferenc got back to his feet, his legs trembling beneath himself. *Two can play that game*, Olivia had once said, before launching a taste of the figure's own medicine back at them.

If Richard wanted to play dirty, then Ferenc would have to somehow beat him at his own game. That would require being on the defensive again, but if it meant there could be the slightest window for an opportunity to win, he needed to do it. For Dormouse.

And for Olivia.

With a deep breath, he flung a blast right back at Richard, who threw up a shield. When the debris settled, the dangerous grin on Richard's lips unnerved Ferenc to the core. And before he could do much else, Richard shot a flaming gale at him.

Ferenc hastened to form a barrier between himself and the on-coming attack. While he'd saved himself from the fire, he'd been shoved right back into the pillar, which crumbled from the force, burying him beneath the rubble.

CHAPTER 36
Richard

After all this time planning and scheming, despite the constant setbacks, not only was Richard finally one step closer to his goal, but he was actually *winning*.

The essence and power of the fire and air elementals—the phoenix and the sylph—were all his, and soon, he'd get it from the other elementals too.

Ferenc didn't move from beneath the pillar's rubble, and Richard's entire being swelled with satisfaction. He'd successfully caught the guardian off guard, and nothing tasted sweeter than that irony. Even the few grunts and groans that occurred soon afterward couldn't bring him down from his new high.

Ferenc crawled out from the debris, stumbling as he got to his feet, and Richard grinned as excitement bubbled through him over the endless possibilities of what kind of torture he could enact next.

"Glad to see you're still alive, Mister Janos. I was a bit disappointed, thinking it was that easy to fell a guardian . . ."

"I don't understand." Ferenc struggled to stand upright. "How is any of this even possible? A temple on the moon, being able to breathe here, you using fire . . . Are you an elemental?"

"Oh, no. Not an elemental," he said bitterly. His people weren't granted the luxury of having one among them; they were only the middle ground, thanks to the keeper of the realms. "And not everything needs to make sense. You've been living here so long, Guardian, you've become as close-minded, yet strangely open in all the wrong senses, as the humans are."

"What do you mean?" Ferenc asked.

Richard chuckled to himself. Closed-minded and *dense*. "Humans don't believe in magic, such as that which is currently protecting the lunar kingdom from prying eyes, yet they believe in the supernatural, like ghosts and the spirits of the dead. They don't believe intelligent life exists outside the solar system, yet they themselves evolved to create anything from single cells to clones inside of labs. And humans don't believe that other worlds or realms exist, but they go to war over whether their made-up, divine idols really created life on Gaea—or Earth—as we know it."

Ferenc shook his head. "You keep saying 'human' like you aren't one of them, standing here in front of me, made of flesh and blood."

"Not all beings of *flesh and blood* are human, Mister Janos."

He was done with the conversation. He had better things to do, like finding the other elementals. Their little chit-chat was wasting his time, and Richard was ready to end it.

He raised his hands, and flames erupted from the debris at Ferenc's feet. Ferenc swiftly extinguished it with a strong gust, but Richard continued his offensive strike, sending a spiral of wind and fire in his direction. Ferenc threw up an air shield and braced for impact as the attack crashed into the defensive wall, and everything dissipated.

The corner of Richard's mouth twitched upward. If that was the extent of the guardian's dormant abilities, then this would be an easy win.

"So, what are you, then?" Ferenc asked, remaining in a defensive position.

It was such a shortsighted question, coming from the guardian of the elemental of air. But he'd cater to the fact that the guardian wasn't fully awakened yet. "I'm but a humble priest, loyal to the lunar kingdom," he replied, spreading his arms for Ferenc to get a better look at him in all his glory. When Ferenc scoffed, Richard continued. "I'm the temple's high priest, actually, but that doesn't change my priorities."

"Yeah?" Ferenc said, narrowing his eyes. "And what priorities are those? Taking over the world?"

Richard tsk-tsked. "Your mindset is much too small-scale, Guardian. I'm after the bigger picture: I want to take over all the realms."

"Why?"

207

"Are you genuinely curious, or are you goading me into a villainous monologue?" he asked with a smirk.

"Listen, we both know I'm not winning this fight," Ferenc admitted. "So the least you could do is answer all my questions before I die."

"Nice try, but I'm the one who became the lawyer here, remember? I know better than to incriminate myself."

The smug smile on Richard's lips slowly vanished as his reason, his why, appeared at the front of his mind. All that rage he'd kept inside for years resurfaced, propelling the satisfaction of this very moment by leaps and bounds.

He'd show them he wasn't weak and pathetic. He'd prove his worth to Keris, the keeper of the realms, by taking all the elementals' powers and ruling all the realms, earning her respect . . .

And her love.

"Then at least release Amy from your spell," Ferenc ordered.

"Oh, there is no spell there. Those are her true feelings, magnified."

"Well, un-magnify them!" he replied with a snarl, but Richard only laughed.

"They're magnified by the moon, like the tide."

Being from the moon, that amplified and charismatic sway had its benefits on the humans of Gaea, and he wasn't afraid to use it to his advantage. He loved how easily Amy had become his puppet because of it, even going so far as to sabotage Ferenc by shutting off his phone the day before one of their court sessions.

But Richard needed to get back to business, and the guardian needed to die.

He raised a hand, and dozens of billowing shadows rose from the ground, filling the entire temple—wispy, then solid, becoming gnarled beasts. Molded on the dark side of the moon from the sheer intensity and raw power of both need and desire, the well from which he drew his army of dark lunanites was as finite as humans were desperate—and he currently had a bottomless supply.

"My lunanites will see to your demise, Mister Janos. I regret not being able to do it myself, but I have other elementals to find."

He waved without turning back and made his way down the hall as the army advanced on Ferenc, claws and fangs bared.

CHAPTER 37
Ferenc

This was it. This was his end. Ferenc would never find out the rest of Olivia's mission. He'd never play fetch with Max ever again. And his heart ached stronger than his sore and exhausted muscles at the realization that he'd never again cook breakfast for Dormouse.

He never even knew her real name.

The scene instantly turned chaotic as mayhem descended upon him. He used everything he knew—and *didn't* know—making up so much of it as he went, but wave after wave of lunanites advanced on him, and he was dangerously close to drowning.

There were so many of them. Ferenc didn't even know how he was still fighting, how he was still alive. He didn't know how many he'd defeated, or if they even stayed down. Maybe when he destroyed one, two more spawned.

And as limitless as the depths of his rage were, his exhaustion had capped out long ago, his body running solely on the dutiful fumes of protection and liberation.

His body gave out, and he stumbled to the ground, his muscles refusing to cooperate any longer. He braced for impact—defeat, death—when a deafening explosion cracked through the temple, and a bolt of lightning struck the floor inches from his knee. The impact from the sonic boom fully sliced through a wide range of enemies while easily knocking the rest over like dominoes.

"Need a hand?"

Ferenc never thought he'd hear Olivia's voice again. It hadn't dawned on him that he'd considered the assertive and impulsive woman as a trusted friend until he'd believed her gone forever. But there she was, alive, and a sudden lightness spread through him, alleviating the weight of battle and failure. A friendly hand reached out in offering, and though Ferenc's muscles strongly protested, he gripped it tight as if their lives depended on it—and they kind of did.

The healing buzz of her touch coursed through his muscles, giving him just enough energy to silence the exhaustion for at least a few more minutes.

His heart skipped a beat when he got a good look at her as she knelt next to him, wrapping his arm around her shoulders. Battered, maybe even bruised, Olivia used her own weight to help him to his feet.

"It's not as bad as it looks," she reassured him with a playful quirk of her lips. "Besides, you look like crap too."

"This superhero business is pretty rough," he quipped back with shaky laughter as he tested whether his legs could withstand his weight on their own. He then surveyed the lunanites as they got to their feet, growling and snarling. "Can you deal with the rest?" he asked her. "I have a lawyer to pummel."

"Oh, no. I'm not letting you have all that fun," she replied.

"Fine. But I get first dibs."

Ferenc shot out a shock wave toward the newly oncoming creatures, and Olivia struck down a few with some sharp gales. He slogged forward as fast as his wobbly legs would allow, sending beasts flying if they got too close, until he reached the dome in the center of the room.

Dormouse's wispy form watched him from inside, sadness and regret painted in her eyes. Ferenc carefully studied the rounded vault. He cautiously tested the waters before finally placing his palms against the smooth surface.

Nothing happened. His touch didn't even trigger the fronds.

On the other side, Dormouse imitated his movement with a silky, strand-like hand of her own. The sudden lump in his throat became difficult to swallow with the dome between them, preventing him from holding her, shielding her, comforting her . . .

The pressure building in his chest from remorse was near overwhelming, crushing him beneath its weight.

The berating thoughts weren't any better. He should've thought his actions through. The number of poor decisions he'd made within the last few days were so very unlike him, and now Dormouse and Olivia were paying the price.

Ferenc swallowed hard, lifting his hand to trace the outline of her sheen face into the dome with his fingertips. He'd own up to wrongdoings and find a way to repay Dormouse for failing her. And that started with Richard's end.

"I'll be back for you. I promise."

The single, stormy tear that fell from her cheek nearly slayed him on the spot.

"What are you doing?" Olivia asked as she approached at a jog. "If I get to him first, I'm not sharing!" She slowed her pace, her own curious gaze darting over the dome before she stopped a few lunanites in their tracks with a forceful blast. "What's this?"

He pulled away. "I don't know, but whatever it is, it's absorbing Dormouse's power."

Olivia did a double take before approaching. "Oh my God . . ."

He needed to find Richard. "Come on," he said as he lightly tugged Olivia by the sleeve, but he was met with resistance.

"I'm so sorry."

The words were so quiet and unfamiliar that he swore Dormouse had spoken them. So when Olivia dropped her chin, face curtained by tangled hair, and clenched her hands into trembling fists, he realized it'd come from her instead.

"Hey . . ." he tried softly.

"I failed." Her eyes snapped up, tears threatening to fall. "They overpowered me, and I couldn't keep her safe—"

He released her sleeve to aim razor-sharp gusts out at the first new wave of creatures that leaped past the door frame leading down the hall, then fixed his gaze on Olivia once more. She was so passionate and protective. He admired her inner strength and drive, even when she forcefully hid her disappointment. But there she was, on the verge of breaking down. And he couldn't afford that. Not just because they were still under attack, but because *he* was trying his damnedest to keep it together. The whole undertaking would be for naught—and they'd most certainly be dead—if he followed suit.

"Olivia, listen to me." His own voice quivered, threatening to break. "I need you."

His eyes still locked on hers, Ferenc pushed the new wave of beasts away with a gale before throwing up a wind barrier at the door frame to keep the lunanites from interrupting the rest of his speech. Even on the moon, Olivia's eyes were vivid green, the same as the first time he'd seen them thousands of miles in the sky.

"This is not on you, it's on me. I'm the one who failed *you*. You're strong, you're smart, you came all this way and risked everything on me, only for me to turn around and do . . . this." He gestured at everything, which resulted in a faint crack of a smile in the corner of Olivia's lips. "You don't deserve how obstinate I've been, and I promise I'll grovel for forgiveness if—*when*—we get back home." At that, she smiled more fully, and he finished, "But now's not the time for that. Right now, I need you. Dormouse needs you. So let's do this."

She sniffled, and her posture straightened once more before both of their attention was drawn toward the sound of slow, sardonic clapping.

"What an inspirational speech," Richard said from behind the transparent barrier. "Even I'm fired up! I'm impressed to see you survived, blondie. You put up an impressive fight, despite my victory."

"I'd say you need to fire your minions for not finishing the job, but they won't have a master left once I'm through with you," she spat. Ferenc held her back by her shoulders to keep her from making good on her word just yet.

Richard's cackle echoed through the temple, growing louder as the snarls and growls from the lunanites behind him faded as they disappeared, melting into the marble floor. The hair on the back of Ferenc's neck stood on end. He could only imagine what kind of unwelcome surprise Richard was planning, and his fears came to life as the beasts molded and formed all around them, as if they hadn't even been on the other side of the barrier just moments prior.

"I applaud your tenacity, Mister Janos, but it ends here."

"You coward!" Olivia snarled.

"You're in my world," Richard replied. "Don't forget I have control here."

Olivia growled. "Go," she said to Ferenc, launching a blast at a few of the oncoming lunanites. "I've got this."

He was so grateful for her. She had no idea how much he appreciated everything she'd done—hunting him down, showing him what she knew despite his suspicions and misgivings, giving him time, persisting, training him, and most importantly, getting back up when she was supposed to be dead.

He hated to leave her facing off against the army alone, but it was their only window of opportunity to get to Richard and end it all. He extended his fist to her.

"Be safe."

"You too," she replied, bumping her fist against his.

Ferenc then lunged, using a whirlwind to speed himself forward as he dissipated the barrier between himself and Richard.

"Don't you dare die on me!" she added over the ruckus. "I fully expect that apology session you owe me to be well worth my while after this!"

He didn't reply—just like with Amy's plea, he made no promises.

CHAPTER 38
Ferenc

Olivia's invaluable help in the thick of battle allowed Ferenc to focus on being what she'd told him he was all along: Dormouse's guardian. It was high time for him to take on the mantle—to earn that title, despite failing numerous times before. And he'd be lying to himself if he didn't admit that just the thought of beating the lawyer to a bloody pulp was immensely satisfying.

Richard dodged him with ease and flung a few blazing bombs that exploded on contact as Ferenc knocked them away with gusts. No sooner had he knocked the last one away, the ceiling rained down fire from a summoned flaming storm. Ferenc created an air barrier above his head, only to get hit by a wind blast straight on, sending him flying into the wall on the opposite end of the room.

He gasped for the air that'd been knocked out of him. His mind reeled, surprised that Richard, a priest from an invisible kingdom on the moon, was so *good* at fighting.

"Give it up, Guardian. You can't beat me," Richard called as he crossed the temple battlefield, the lunanites parting like the Red Sea all around him. "Not only do I have dark lunar power and the energy from both the air and fire elementals, but you can't even remember how to access your true powers."

"Fire elemental?" Olivia shoved a couple creatures back with a burst of wind in the middle of the chamber. "He has the fire elemental too?"

Ferenc couldn't answer her. He didn't recall seeing any fire elementals around—whatever those looked like. He hadn't even initially realized the wispy clouds inside the dome were Dormouse.

However, he'd never made it past the inner chamber. There could've been so much more to the massive temple.

Then there was also the matter of the *true powers* Richard spoke of. Ferenc couldn't remember being a guardian—much to Olivia's dismay. Remembering might give him access to something bigger than he was capable of, and that was probably what Richard meant when he'd said Ferenc wasn't fully awakened yet.

"Ferenc, we have to find the fire elemental!" Olivia called between grunts from her ongoing battle. "What if they have the answers I need?"

It was worth a shot. He really didn't know how else to help Olivia in that department. He'd tried everything. Hopefully the fire elemental knew what was going on.

He hoped the fire elemental was still alive.

A sudden flaming gust hit him while he was down, scorching his skin and singeing the tips of his hair, and he gritted his teeth to prevent from crying out. Clumsily scrambling to his feet, he countered with a series of air spheres. As much as his skin burned, he favored any chance to inflict damage rather than heal himself. The quicker he could take Richard down, the better.

A particularly evil grin formed on Richard's lips before a wall of flames exploded from the ground, surrounding the two of them.

"It's just you and me now," Richard said.

He was trapped. He couldn't run or dodge. His only options were defending and attacking, and at that realization, a brilliant idea formed at the forefront of his mind.

"Perfect," Ferenc replied.

He'd tried recreating the lunanites once before, and while he'd failed in that aspect, what came of it were those insect-like pixie things. Surely, they'd want to protect their elemental again . . .

With his arms thrust forward, he focused on everything Olivia had taught him about manifestation and the science behind it all. He hoped it would work.

No, he *needed* it to work.

But no matter how much he tuned in to his body, the sensations, the science . . . nothing happened. He concentrated so hard that his hands trembled, his jaw clenching so tightly that he thought his teeth would shatter in his mouth like glass.

But all that resulted from his effort was a cackle from Richard.

Exhaustion washed over him, as well as a pulsing in his head so deep and painful, black spots danced in his vision. Ferenc fell to one knee.

"Good effort," Richard mocked. "Now it's my turn."

A blazing whirlwind surrounded him, the base of the funnel quickly constricting, and the fire and the heat rapidly approaching. Caught in the center, Ferenc was still in a daze. He couldn't summon them. Maybe it was an Earth-only ability. Maybe he hadn't even been the one to summon them at all.

A flame licked at Ferenc's arm, and he recoiled, clutching the burn as it forcefully pulled him from his thoughts. He jumped to his feet, a low growl escaping him, and his knuckles whitened as his hands formed into fists. There was one more thing he could try, one more thing he actually knew how to do. He'd done it before, he was determined to do it again, and that required him to get close for proper execution.

His fingers flexed, cutting the oxygen from the air, snuffing the flames from the fiery tornado. He then slashed his arms at the whirlwind, breaking it. His eyes narrowed in determination, and he raced headlong at Richard, pulling the air, causing the wall of flames to dance wildly, licking at the priest's white robe. It distracted him long enough for Ferenc to grab his arm with both hands.

Richard turned back to face Ferenc. "Breaking my arm won't help you," he stated.

"Maybe not, but *this* might."

A large lightning bolt engulfed them both, and Richard cried out in pain and shock.

With everything Olivia had taught him, the student became the master . . . somewhat. He'd summoned lightning with every intention of it killing Richard just as it had killed Dormouse, but on the moon—inside a temple—the lightning acted differently. It exploded with a deafening crack, never taking them anywhere.

Richard collapsed in a coughing fit, his body smoldering. He was still alive.

With a growl of irritation, he stood menacingly over Richard. "Where is the fire elemental?" Richard gave a painful chuckle between coughing fits. "Answer me!" Ferenc bellowed, clasping Richard by the collar and shaking him.

But Richard did not reply. He simply raised a hand and weakly swatted at Ferenc's face until he connected his palm to Ferenc's cheek.

Ferenc felt the heat but failed to react in time as flames engulfed the side of his face. He cried out and released Richard, pulling away and grabbing his cheek. It burned. His singed hair reeked more than anything he'd ever smelled, and the pain was so intense, it was all he could think of. He cooled it off by chilling the air around him, but the side of his face still cooked.

That was it. He'd had enough. "You need to tell me where the fire elemental is, or so help me—"

But the only word that played on Richard's charred tongue was a name.

"Keris . . ."

The smoke that emanated from Richard intensified, and his body went up in eerily dark flames.

"No!" Ferenc cried out, falling to his knees and scampering toward Richard's burning body. He extinguished the flames with a heavy gust of wind. "Where is the fire elemental?"

But it was too late; Richard dissipated into the same shadowy substance the lunanites were made from.

"Ferenc!"

His heart skipped a beat as Olivia called to him, thinking she was in trouble. He shot his attention back to find her speeding toward him in a twister.

"They all just vanished!"

He nodded, glancing down to where the body had once been. The way he'd just vanished into thin air . . . Ferenc doubted Richard had died.

"I told you to leave me a piece of—oh my God, Ferenc, your face!" she gasped, landing directly in front of him.

She dropped to her knees and reached for his scorched face, but he swatted her hand away. He didn't have time for this. He had to turn off the device and rescue Dormouse before it took too much of her energy and did the unthinkable.

"Find the fire elemental," he ordered. "And be careful—I don't know if Richard is dead or not."

Olivia's brows drew together in concern as he stood and stumbled some, but she nodded. "On it."

217

Without a second glance, he trudged over to the dome as fast as his exhausted body would allow him.

He searched for a way to stop the device, but he was so exhausted, he couldn't quite figure it out. His eyes fell to Dormouse's before he pressed his palms against the glass.

"Watch yourself," he warned.

He'd accidentally shattered his sliding door when he'd punched it, but he remembered the faint vibrations before it'd happened. All he needed to do was replicate it. And he was confident enough—desperate enough— to do it again. His hands trembled from the effort, but so did the dome. And with a strange undulation on the smooth, solid surface, the glass cracked before shattering.

Dormouse's wispy body fluttered to the floor like a leaf, but he rushed forward and caught her in his arms. It was a strange sensation—she was both solid and airy at the same time.

"Dormouse!" His voice was practically in his throat as he lowered himself to the ground, setting her into his lap.

A choked sob escaped her before she cried like a howling wind as he held her close. Slowly, her body transformed back and she became flesh and bone once more, but the wave of relief he felt had washed over him long before.

She was alive.

CHAPTER 39
Ferenc

"There's nobody here."

Ferenc looked up at Olivia from his spot on the ground. He hadn't moved since catching Dormouse—his muscles downright refused. He'd tried to heal himself, even just a little bit, but his mind was going a million miles a minute, unable to become still for even a second, despite his exhaustion.

Dormouse flinched at Olivia's voice, and he gave her a soft squeeze to let her know he was there for her, that he'd protect her until his very last breath. He hadn't let go of her, even when she'd stopped crying, but she hadn't willingly moved either. They'd sat in silence while Olivia searched the temple for the fire elemental, their energy melding together, the rhythm of their heartbeats syncing until it beat as one. Elemental and guardian.

Olivia kneeled in front of them, gently reaching out for his scorched face, and leaned in close. He winced despite the softness of her touch, but his hiss of pain soon faded as the burning alleviated with her cool healing breath.

She pulled away, gasping for air. "I'm sorry. I'm too exhausted to do much more—"

"I know." The waves of his own fatigue lapped at him threateningly. "I appreciate the effort; you didn't have to. Thank you."

A weak smile appeared on her lips, faltering from both her exhaustion and regret as her attention dropped to Dormouse. "I'm so glad you're still with us." Her words trembled, and her gaze fell to the floor as tears brimmed, but she swallowed it down. He could tell

219

she was beating herself up on the inside, filled with regret and remorse over letting Dormouse get taken.

With shuddered breaths, Olivia stood back up and headed for the hall.

"Where are you going?" Ferenc asked.

"To find the fire elemental."

"You just said there's nobody here."

She turned back around, and about four different emotions flashed across her features one after another, settling on a pained expression. "I have to look again. I can't just—I need answers," she said, her hands falling helplessly limp at her sides.

"Come back with us. Eat. Sleep. We can formulate a plan better once—"

"I can't," she interrupted. "With Richard gone, I don't know how long the portal will remain open, and aside from traveling in a spaceship, I'm not sure how else to get here. If the fire elemental is here, I *have* to find them."

"What if the elemental isn't here?" he asked.

"I still have to try."

As Dormouse's guardian, it was his obligation to take her somewhere safe, somewhere away from the moon. But he wasn't Olivia's guardian. He wasn't even sure what her title was compared to him, but as a functioning adult, he couldn't *make* her do anything.

She'd allowed him to run off and seek answers from Richard without a plan, and the least he could do was give her the same permission. She was under no obligation to follow, especially as she'd always been the one with the most mastery over her abilities. But she was right about the portal—it could close before she had a chance to return to Earth and trap her here without his help. Richard may even still be alive, licking his wounds and gathering strength for another strike.

A few what-ifs buzzed through his mind, but he silenced every one of them as best he could. He just needed to trust her. She'd managed to get this far mostly on her own, and she could *definitely* handle herself.

"All right," he agreed. "Make sure you check any and every flame you come across." He glanced to Dormouse in his arms, remembering how he'd thought her nothing but clouds at first. If the fire elemental was anything like Dormouse's elemental form, then flames would be his best guess. "And just be careful. You'll know where to find us."

Olivia nodded with a deep inhale and exhale before continuing on her mission.

"I apologize in advance for your house!" she called out over her shoulder, and Ferenc's stomach dropped.

"What's that supposed to mean?" he asked, but Olivia had vanished down a corridor.

"It's . . . mostly the windows," Dormouse squeaked, bringing her fingernails to her mouth to chew on as she always did when nervous.

Her actions alone gave no comfort. "*Mostly*?"

"And the lightbulbs. And picture frames and vases . . ." she replied, shrinking deeper into him with each additional item she listed.

He groaned as he hung his head low. When Dormouse's thick brows bunched together in concern, he gave her a reassuring smile and placed a kiss atop her head, and her body instantly relaxed once more.

With her still cradled in his arms, Ferenc got to his feet. He struggled as his muscles still weren't impressed with him, but he'd rested enough to get through one final push. His feet dragged across the marble floor with each step as he shuffled out of the temple and down the stairs one at a time. But he slowed to a stop, setting Dormouse down on the final step and raising his index finger for her to give him a moment.

He gently approached Amy, who was in the same place he'd left her, and offered his hand. "Come home with us."

She shook her head, her mess of curls violently dancing over her shoulders, before scowling up at him. "I'll never forgive you," she spat.

Her bitter tone hit him as venomously as ever, but he remained where he was, his hand still extended in offering. "I saved your life," he pointed out, and when she said nothing, his hand fell limp while the other traveled to his frayed and coarse hair, where he attempted to comb through the crisp strands with his fingers. "Christ, he turned you into a *monster*, Amy! I'm not sure what made that worth dying for, but—"

"I was trying to protect him from you!" she cried. "You killed him, didn't you? *Didn't you?*"

221

He was at a loss for words. Still not completely convinced she wasn't under a spell, there still was no easy way to persuade her he'd done it for the greater good—that the realms, real or not, depended on it.

She'd never have any of it.

He turned away from her with surprising ease, as if the last thread from his heartstring had snapped, sundering that invisible bond tethering him to her. "Goodbye, Amy."

Someone else needed him; someone he'd silently pledged allegiance to in both this life and one he didn't quite fully know about. He scooped Dormouse back into his arms and shuffled down the path toward the portal in silence.

***

Ferenc looked out the newly installed sliding door, where Dormouse played fetch with Max in the yard. He smiled softly as he dried his hands from having done the dishes.

It'd been a week since their misadventure on the moon, and he still, at times, tried to analyze what'd happened, what hadn't gone well, and how things could've gone smoother with a plan.

A knock at the front door pulled his attention away from the back yard activity, and as he descended the stairs, the front door opened.

"Olivia!"

He froze at the bottom of the stairs before rushing toward her, pulling her into a hug before she could even finish shutting the door.

"I've missed you too!" she said with a giggle.

He'd never been so grateful to have somebody walk through his door, as proven by the hug that lasted longer than necessary. When he finally pulled away, he kept his hands on her shoulders as he looked her over. There wasn't a scratch, cut, or bruise on her—she'd obviously healed herself, as he'd done for himself. But it'd been a week. He was surprised she'd lasted so long in the temple . . . if she'd even been there the whole time.

Before his mind went into overdrive, he shoved his thoughts aside and asked the most important question: "Are you okay?"

She smiled, resting a hand atop of his and giving it a light squeeze. "I'm fine."

"Come on in. Are you hungry? Can I get you a coffee?"

"No thanks." She followed him up the stairs and into the kitchen.

"Let me just tell Alexis you're safe—"

"Alexis?" she asked. "Oh, we're on a first-name basis now?" She wiggled her eyebrows suggestively.

He cast her a look before opening the sliding door. It was nothing like that. Dormouse had finally opened up to him, and then some. From telling him about being homeless, her general distrust in men, and even her name, she'd come a long way and was finally comfortable enough to be vulnerable right back. Dormouse looked straight at him from the yard, and he motioned with his head for her to come inside.

Max didn't need convincing; she rushed up the stairs straight into the kitchen, where she excitedly jumped up on Olivia, violently wagging her tail in her excitement.

"Hi Max!" Olivia cooed as she dropped to her knees and hugged the dog.

"What's up?" Dormouse asked as she slipped inside, then paused as she looked at the commotion. "Olivia!"

"Hey!" Olivia smiled from the floor while trying to keep Max under control.

"What—how are you?" Dormouse asked, blinking in surprise. "Did you find the fire elemental?"

Olivia got back up and dropped into one of the chairs with a sigh. "No."

Ferenc pinched his lips together in frustration for her as he leaned against the kitchen counter. All of that for nothing. She was still no closer to finding her answers.

"I'm sorry," Dormouse said, barely above a whisper, as she slid into the farthest chair.

"I searched every inch of that temple multiple times. I even went to the palace."

"What palace?" Ferenc asked.

"The Lunar Palace, home to the lunar prince," she said in a fancy, exaggerated tone, before it fell normal again. "Apparently, there's a kingdom up there hidden behind holograms, but the prince wasn't home."

Richard had briefly mentioned the lunar kingdom. Ferenc hadn't put any more thought into the lawyer's—or priest's—words because in his anger, he couldn't focus on trying to decipher what was real. He'd been standing on the *moon*, for crying out loud. Still, it seemed Richard had spoken true, and Ferenc needed to silence the part of himself that wanted to research it. He knew he wouldn't find anything.

"In fact, other than a skeleton crew, the kingdom was strangely deserted. They were skeptical and afraid of me when I came knocking, which, I can't say I blame them, but they weren't very helpful, so I left."

"So you're just gonna accept that as an answer and move on?" he asked.

A smirk played at the corner of her lips. "I thought you knew me better than that."

He met her playfulness head-on. "Oh, I do, and that's what I was afraid of." He then crossed his arms over his chest. "So, what's your plan?"

Olivia's gaze dropped briefly before looking back at Ferenc. "I came here to prove I wasn't dead, for one, but also to ask if you remember anything about being guardians and elementals. Especially you," she added, turning to Dormouse, who shrunk farther into her seat. "You did some pretty powerful stuff when I was in a tight spot trying to protect you."

Dormouse predictably brought her fingers to her mouth, and she flicked her gaze up at him before dropping it to the floor. It'd taken her a while before she'd talked about what had happened when she'd been taken. He'd heard her having vivid nightmares in the middle of the night, and they unfortunately didn't cease after she got it off her chest.

"I saw you as the air elemental. So unless that awoke something within you that can help me . . ." At this, Dormouse shook her head. "I'm going to keep looking for the other guardians and elementals."

Ferenc studied Olivia in silence. He didn't want her to have to search for them alone. She'd done it once already. But as much as he wished he could help, unlike her, he couldn't drop everything. Sure, he was a freelance pilot and could work on his own terms, but he wouldn't burden friends with watching Max for an indefinite amount of time, and he had no idea if Amy would still drag him to court for ridiculous reasons now that Richard was *maybe* out of the picture. If she'd even made it back through the portal.

Dormouse was still traumatized by everything, so he couldn't forcefully drag her along, but he couldn't just leave her either. Not as her guardian. Not with the possibility of Richard still being alive.

"Can you feel the others?" he asked Olivia.

"I don't know. But what else can I do except try?"

He'd had a feeling she'd say that. With a silent sigh, he uncrossed his arms and reached for his wallet, pulling out a business card and handing it to her. "Keep in touch whenever you're near a phone. Or if you need help. You know where we are, and you know how to reach us. So just . . . be careful."

Olivia took the card, sliding it in a small pocket in the waistband of her leggings, before getting to her feet. She turned back to Dormouse, her brows drawn together in a pained expression.

"I'm sorry I failed to keep you safe."

Dormouse paused in her fingernail chewing long enough to flick her eyes from Olivia to Ferenc and back. She then lowered her hand, wringing them together in her lap.

"You did what you could. We both did. They were just . . ." She trailed off.

Ferenc stepped over to her, resting his hand comfortingly on her shoulder while he spoke to Olivia. "Don't apologize. We weren't prepared. It's in the past."

He wouldn't risk it happening again. Without knowing if Richard was still alive or not, he wasn't taking any chances. He'd continued to train, ready to protect Dormouse, whatever the cost.

He gave Olivia a comforting smile. "Go. Find your elementals and guardians, then come back and tell us what you've learned."

Olivia's features softened, and she eventually nodded. She reached down, petting Max, as Dormouse got to her feet.

"Good luck," Dormouse said, surprising both Ferenc and Olivia as she pulled her into a hug. Ferenc smiled softly as Olivia squeezed her tight before letting go.

"Make sure you call," Ferenc ordered as he hugged her in turn. "Stay safe."

"I will. Thank you." She pulled away. "I, uh, spoke with Amy along the way . . ."

His heart skipped a beat, and he slowly shut his eyes, recalling their last moments before he'd walked away from her on the moon. "What did she say?"

S.W. Raine

"Nothing of importance, but . . . she might hate you just a *teensy* bit less now."

Ferenc's eyes shot open to see the unease in her face. "How reassuring," he said with a slight chuckle.

With a wave over her shoulder, she descended the stairs.

"Don't get run over by any more jets!" he called after her, resulting in a giggle from both Dormouse and her before she disappeared out the front door. A faint smile found its way to his lips, and he slowly shook his head at the memory before heading out onto the deck for a cigarette.

His mind wandered, and he allowed himself to get lost in his memories. At first, they were about Olivia and everything they'd been through—from hitting her with his jet, to her showing off her abilities, to working together to protect Dormouse. From there, his thoughts shifted fully to Dormouse.

He wanted her to go back to as normal of a life as she could. She'd never shown interest in being an elemental. But despite the traumatic events that had forced her into physically becoming one, she was still willing to accompany him when he trained.

He had a feeling, deep down, that none of this was over. Richard had mentioned Ferenc wasn't yet fully awakened, and he now believed it, based on the small fraction of what he was capable of compared to what Richard was able to wield. He'd used a mixture of dark moon abilities as well as stolen air and fire powers. He'd seen the air elemental firsthand with Dormouse but couldn't figure out where Richard had hidden the fire elemental—Keris, maybe.

A hand rested on his, pulling him from his thoughts.

"Are you okay?" she asked, ever so quietly.

He looked down at Dormouse—his little protected air elemental—and gave her a gentle smile and nod. "I will be." He pulled his hand away and wrapped his arm around her shoulders instead. "Let's go for a walk. I could really go for some cheesecake.

226

SIGN UP FOR S.W. RAINE'S AUTHOR NEWSLETTER

Be the first to learn about S.W. Raine's new releases and receive exclusive content!

http://swraine.com

ALSO BY S.W. RAINE

Raine is Canadian, born and raised, and constantly moved in between Ontario and Quebec with her military family. She moved to Michigan, USA, in 2004, where she currently still resides with her husband and son.

She has always had a vivid imagination and loved reading and writing from a very young age. Her new adult steampunk debut published in 2020. She took courses in Children's Literature through ICL in Illinois and has participated in NaNoWriMo for over a decade.

Connect with S.W. Raine
Website: http://swraine.com
Facebook: @swraine
Instagram: @s.w.raine
Twitter: @SWRaine1